SINNERS PLUNGED BENEATH THAT FLOOD

By G.D. BROWN

First Edition

ISBN: 979-8-9851070-2-9

Leftoverbooks.net

Cover and Interior Design:

Patrick Trotti, LEFTOVER Books

Praise for *Sinners Plunged Beneath That Flood*

"*Sinners Plunged Beneath That Flood* stands as a monumental achievement. . . . [G.D. Brown] has created a world from scratch and populated it with a large cast of characters who pulsate with desire and fear and dark energy. It's a story with not only a thrilling plot but also a wrenching moral lesson, which it conveys by suggesting that Jim and his henchmen embody an evil that's ineradicable yet must be fought. The prose is excellent throughout: limpid and direct."

-John McManus, recipient of the Whiting Award and the Literature Award from the American Academy of Arts and Letters, author of *Bitter Milk*, *Born On A Train*, *Stop Breakin Down*, and *Fox Tooth Heart*

"*Sinners Plunged Beneath That Flood* is a bleak, soulful look at the ravages of the burgeoning meth trade in rural Oklahoma circa 1998. . . . [It is] finely told, with a deep rhythm of inevitability and autumnal regret . . . a satisfying, if sorrowful eulogy to the human heart behind the meth epidemic in middle America. . . . [Brown's] work here shows a thoughtful new voice from a section of the country too often ignored."

-Sherri L. Smith, award-winning author of *Sparrow*, *Flygirl*, *Orleans*, *Pasadena*, and *The Blossom and the Firefly*

There is a fountain filled with blood/Drawn from Immanuel's veins/And sinners, plunged beneath that flood/Lose all their guilty stains

-William Cowper, "There Is a Fountain"

Chapter 1

The fall of Jenn's senior year of high school, she learned that a person could be missing without having been gone 48 hours, among other things. The leaves were brown and crunchy then, shriveled letters from the summer sun to warn of the coming cold. They covered up the dead grass in between the Mayes County tree lines. Hardly anyone so far from Tulsa found a reason to stuff the leaves in plastic bags or make them into garden mulch. Clean lawns didn't do much for the people of Branch Creek. Few others ventured far enough off the Oklahoma State Highway 20 to take notice of the landscaping there. So, the leaves piled up without resistance. A news reporter said the fire that gutted Ava Springtree's double-wide was likely caused by all those leaves. The fire marshal said a spark from some bad wiring had sent them to burning. Those burning leaves, the flaming devil hands, slapped against the vinyl siding for hours and melted anything of value inside, Ava's father too, in the middle of the night.

No one called for help until the trailer was just a black-ringed skeleton with glowing eyes under columns of smoke. It was bonfire season, so there was not much to say about a little smoke here and there. The trailer was just far enough off the highway to disappear altogether to the passing motorist, which gave Ava and her dad some privacy, kept strangers out of their business. The talking head on Jenn's television screen said Ava wasn't home when it happened, the fire, but Jenn didn't know where else she could have been. Most everything in Branch Creek and the surrounding county closed down at 9:00 p.m. sharp, and Ava wasn't too interested in doing much of anything in Branch Creek.

The day after the fire, two deputies from the Mayes County Sheriff's Office laughed together as they walked into Branch Creek High School in their thick khaki shirts and with their patches and their guns. Ava hadn't shown up to class. The deputies came to ask Jenn and Scribbles if either of them knew where she went.

"Jennifer Armstrong, Matthew Hartford," a teacher in wire glasses read their names off a Post-It note, "can you step outside and talk to these gentlemen?"

***

Scribbles's real name was Matthew, but Jenn had started calling him Scribbles in the sixth grade, when she'd caught him drawing a penis in his notebook during music class.

"I saw your drawing back there," she'd told him afterward.

"Those were just scribbles."

"You're just scribbles."

Scribbles's cartoon penis, its erect ovals and prickly lines, had made Jenn feel foolish. She had not before realized that the member depicted in her well-worn textbook diagram from science class was an actual human body part possessed by real people, people she saw every day in class and at the convenience store. The penis in the textbook had felt to her like an ill-kept secret. She was certain the other kids in her sixth grade class had seen it too. They had not, however, referenced the diagram in front of her, and its placement near the back of the book promised weeks-long units on cellular respiration and the classification of organisms before she'd have to view the penis in the presence of anyone else. Jenn's father had run off to Mexico before she was born, and her mother never brought around any other men or dirty videos, nothing with a penis, real or recorded on magnetic tape. The only human penises she'd ever seen were the fleshy knobs on cherubs in old paintings. So, she'd been intrigued by Scribbles's drawing, though she knew better than to mention it to anyone.

Two weeks before she came across the drawing, she'd had her first period. She was eleven-and-a-half years old. She had been crying when she brought out a pair of bloody underwear in her hands like an offering to her mother, who had just come in from work at the dollar store. Her mother had sighed and explained, over the top of a cigarette and while holding the textbook, what all that bleeding was about. Jenn had asked about the textbook's penis diagram too, but her mother, like any good member of the Assembly of God Church, told her to wait another year or so before she again brought up that mystery organ filled with Latin words and its miraculous tadpoles. The night after she saw Scribbles's drawing, though, Jenn took her education into her own hands and spent a considerable amount of time poring over the book by flashlight. She felt then like a detective, a regular Nancy Drew. In the dark, she'd resolved to ask Scribbles to show her the drawing again the following day for further inspection, but when the sunlight returned, the question seemed impossible to speak out loud.

By the time the two were in high school, Jenn found it hard to link Scribbles to the curiosity she'd felt years before. She wasn't sure that Scribbles could possess any sex organ whatsoever, not even the member used in the unromantic coitus-making from the old science textbook. He smelled like a grass stain. He didn't comb his hair, and it fell on his shoulders in greasy tangles. Jenn ate lunch with him nearly every school day, barring illness, and they spent most of their afternoons together at Scribbles's splintered two-by-four rent house, where he lived alone after his father moved further west to work the oil line and his mother went back to her own parents in Arkansas to recover from her husband's leaving. Because Scribbles was eighteen when his folks split, they told him that he could pretty much do whatever he wanted. He stayed in the Branch Creek house by himself and slept next to a box fan on the bedroom floor. The landlord never seemed to mind. A faux leather couch filled the living room. Jenn and Ava had helped Scribbles push it to the house one summer afternoon after he'd found it peeling away in a ditch across the railroad tracks. He didn't own any other furniture. His dad sent him $400 a month to use on rent and food, and that was about all he ever had, rent and food and a couple outfits that he wore until they were oily and shining. Jenn once opened his bedroom door and learned that he slept on a sleeping bag, but she never told that to Ava, because she knew Ava would tease him.

Jenn liked that Scribbles showed no interest in sports or in the Future Farmers of America, though she figured she still would have gotten along with him if he had shown a prize hog and been captain of the football team, just so long as he never asked questions about her dad or mentioned the mole on her cheek. When they were alone, he talked just enough to keep her from feeling lonely. He often spent the afternoons looking out the window from atop the arm of the couch and picking at the dead skin around his fingernails. When Ava came over, she and Jenn talked about magazines they'd seen at the counter of Murphy's Grocery Store or about whatever had happened beneath the stands at the previous week's football game. Scribbles spoke even less when Ava was over. Jenn once admitted to him that she wasn't too enthusiastic about magazines either, but he just shrugged. Ava never seemed to notice when she monopolized a conversation, so the magazine talk kept on through junior year. All three of the teens enjoyed the free beer that Ava brought from her dad's trailer on weekends. Jenn thought the beer alone was probably worth every magazine and dead skin flake in the world.

★★★

The day the deputies came, Jenn spent the slow ride to school imagining Ava asleep on a forgotten family member's couch or in a makeshift tent at the lake. When the teacher called on her to talk to the deputies, she told herself that they'd only showed up because Ava's daddy was dead, because he couldn't tell the proper authorities that they had nothing to worry about. When Jenn prayed about it, God didn't tell her otherwise.

The chubby deputy talked to Jenn in the vice principal's office, used words that she understood by themselves but that she could not string together into anything coherent. Her mind moved past the words to images, to the reporter standing outside the place where Ava had once lived, that reporter going on and on with the newsroom formalities of the situation. Jenn wondered whether Ava was aware of the fact that her father, her own flesh and blood, had become charred bones and ashes. Perhaps the slight man who had only spoken in coughs and who had never gone to church or Friday night football games had scared Ava too. Who would attend the funeral of that sort of man? Jenn pictured Ava sitting alone with her dark clothes in a funeral home pew. Then she really missed her friend.

The deputy asked Jenn when she had last seen Ava, and Jenn told him that she had seen her at school the previous Friday. She had sat in the cafeteria with Ava and Scribbles, filled her plastic tray with French fries, and joked about which cities the three of them would move to when they were older. Ava was supposed to meet the others at the pizza restaurant across the street from the bank on Saturday, but she never showed up for some reason or another, and Jenn told the deputy that too.

"And you didn't find that strange?" the deputy asked. "You didn't think to give someone a call?"

"I don't ever call Ava. She never answers the phone. Her daddy always does, or did, and he doesn't, or, I guess, didn't, like it when she hung out with us."

"Why is that?"

"He didn't like it when she hung out with anyone."

The deputy wrote something down before he continued. His hand moved like he was signing someone to damnation.

"Still, you could have contacted someone about it when she didn't show up," he said.

"I thought she was busy. She does this sort of thing. Don't people have to be gone 48 hours before they're missing?"

"That's just on TV."

Jenn blushed.

"I guess I watch too much TV, then," she said.

Scribbles was gone talking to the deputies for at least twice as long as Jenn was, best she could figure. She stood outside the high school office and watched him through the door's narrow window instead of going back to class. Scribbles sat on a bench where sick kids usually waited for their parents to come pick them up. One of the deputies was leaning over him, and she heard a voice rising and falling. She wanted to press her ear to the door, to know with certainty that the deputy was reassuring Scribbles and talking about how everything was going to be alright. Then the door opened. Scribbles had tears in his eyes.

Jenn had never seen him cry before, although he had seen her cry plenty, he and Ava both, when a classmate had dealt out hurtful words about Jenn's twice-worn outfits and when her mother had been handing out unfair punishments over her messy room or lackluster grades. Scribbles, on the other hand, was always dry eyes and a half-smile, no matter what anyone said to him or the letters on his report cards. It made sense to Jenn, the way he cried when the dam finally broke. His face was covered with enough tears to make up for the whole of adolescence. The saltwater drops ran down onto the long sleeve t-shirt he was wearing, and she felt them on her skin when she hugged him in the hallway. Scribbles sniffed, and the mucus worked its way through the cavities in his head. Jenn held her breath the best she could until they parted, until someone told them to get back to class.

That afternoon, they walked together around the playground behind the elementary school. The PTA had paid somebody to paint the jungle gym green during the summer. It had been red before, but most of the paint had worn off and exposed the metal skeleton of the jungle gym, the swings, and the rest of it. Now, it was all green and born again. Only the slide, an orange plastic chute that had been bleached by the sun and that would charge kids full of static electricity and have them shocking one another, remained as it had been when Jenn and Ava played on it. Now, Scribbles kicked foot-fulls of pea gravel out of the beds around the equipment. Every few steps, he took off his shoes, fat sneakers he'd bought from a catalog, and dumped bits of gravel back onto the earth, his modest offering to the newly-painted playground.

"You don't really think she's at her aunt's house or something, do you?" Scribbles asked.

"I don't know."

Jenn sat on a swing with her chin in her hands. She rocked back and forth on the balls of her feet.

"I mean, she's never done anything like that," Scribbles said.

"It wouldn't be much of a stretch, though."

"Jenn," Scribbles said, his voice flat and fluttering like a one-winged butterfly, "they don't think she's with her family."

He stopped kicking the pea gravel and sat down on the swing next to Jenn.

"I doubt they know more than we do," Jenn said.

"I bet they do."

"Why?"

"I just know it," Scribbles said. The torn seam at the end of his jeans leg dragged across the rocks as he swayed over them. "Do you think she could have been the one to do it?"

"To do what?"

"They asked me if she'd ever said anything about her dad, and that just rubbed me the wrong way, I guess."

New tears broke free of Scribbles's eyes, enough tears to suffice for the rest of his friendship with Jenn. His shaky voice became a moaning, a ghost calling for the living to remember the dead. He put his head down by his knees. Leaves blew across the playground.

"Scribbles, kid, listen to me, Ava didn't burn her house down. There's no way. She's probably up to no good, but she's not breaking the law."

"She breaks the law all the time," Scribbles said.

"She drinks beer and steals lighters from gas stations. She doesn't burn down buildings, not with her dad inside."

"We don't know that. She's always been, you know, to herself, or whatever, and her dad was a creep. What if he was hurting her?"

"She didn't do it. They said on the news that it was a bad wire. They can't just lie on TV like that."

Scribbles sat up straight and wiped his face on his shoulder. Gray snot streaked across his shirt.

"You really think everything's gonna be okay?" he asked.

"I don't see why not."

Scribbles laughed behind his wet eyes.

"You're ridiculous," he said. "Our friend is like, out on her own and going through who knows what after her dad burned to death in their house, and you're acting like it's just another day at school."

"It may end up being just another day at school."

"That doesn't seem right."

Jenn spit onto the grass that surrounded the gravel bed.

"Whatever you say," she said. "Either way, you don't have any proof that things won't go on as normal. As far as we know, she'll still stop by your place before dinner."

The chains that held the swings whined from the welded metal loops that joined them with the swing set piping. Jenn and Scribbles moved past one another without speaking. The whining sound seemed to cover the playground. Then Jenn kicked up her feet and pushed herself high into the air. Her stomach leapt as she came back down toward the earth and then swung up again. Scribbles only watched and dug holes in the gravel.

Chapter 2

Ava wasn't the first person to vanish from Mayes County that year. In the spring, a nurse named Cindy Rawlings was last seen showing off a picture of her kids in a windowless bar a few miles outside Branch Creek. The picture showed two girls bent over their landlord's yucca plant in a rock garden, a towheaded girl smiling with half her mouth and a little brunette with scrunched-closed eyes and missing teeth. Cindy put the picture back into her purse and went home early the night she disappeared, according to the bartender, a thin thirty-something with acne scars. He said she had been tired and short on cash, but because she was a regular and he had known her since junior high, he would have covered the cost of her drinks if she hadn't vanished.

He said he saw Cindy's car in the parking lot when he drove by the next morning, so he telephoned her house to see if she needed a ride to come pick it up. One of the little girls from the picture answered the phone. She asked if her mommy was coming home soon. It wasn't long before deputies from the sheriff's office showed up to the bar. They found the picture of Cindy's kids in a drainage ditch. They looked it over and told the bartender he could keep it. Cindy's face was on the evening news, and that's the last anyone saw of her. The bartender kept the picture of her kids in the center console of his car.

***

A month later, there was another disappearance, and Angie Wilkerson sat on her couch in Branch Creek with her own photograph, a blurry man in a cowboy hat, the product of Bill Pickett and Jesse Stahl, of John Hayes and Crawford Goldsby, of those thousands of Black men who moved west and made waves and lost their spots in the fantasies of little white country boys to the likes of Wild Bill Hickock and Jesse James. Angie was studying the picture and calling local news stations while her husband played solitaire on the computer. She was telling the news outlets to look into what had happened to her brother, to Paul Washington, the cowboy. She said he hadn't called for his usual Sunday chat for two weeks in a row. She said he was missing from the hollowed out school bus he lived in by the creek.

"You need to put his picture on TV like you did for that white lady," Angie said. "You need to get him found."

Three of the four news stations out of Tulsa all but hung up on her. They offered useless words like "thank you" and closed their ears with telephonic clicks. When Angie called the fourth station, the young man who answered the phone took down her information and asked if she'd filed a police report. She said that the representatives of the Mayes County Sheriff's Office had listened to her about as well as the other news stations, that it was a God-given miracle the deputies had let her say anything at all. They hadn't given her a report to fill out. She said she couldn't remember committing any crimes, but she had good reason to keep small and quiet where the law was concerned. She said that invisibility had been better than the alternative for people like her in that part of the world since at least 1921 and maybe as far back as 1492.

The young man on the phone told Angie that he would pass her information along to the producers at the station, and then he wished her luck. He made no mention of calling back or sending for a picture of Paul. Still, Angie told her husband that he'd better answer the phone if it rang. In the end, though, the phone stayed silent in its cradle. Angie's brother did not appear on the evening news.

***

In the middle of June, two teen boys also vanished from the area, but somebody found them. Jonathan Ingalls and Chris Turney didn't come home from Mayes County's Second Annual Green Country Fest. The outdoor concert and craft festival took place on an empty plot cleared of fescue grass between Pryor, which was the county seat, and Branch Creek.

It spanned an entire weekend and brought people from places like Oklahoma City and Little Rock, Arkansas. Rain fell all through the first day of the festival, and all the attendees, or nearly all of them, retreated to a tent village erected at the edge of the field to wait for drier weather. The road between the concert grounds and the highway became covered in rainwater, and the half-drunk deputies acting as security said it would be best if no one left until things cleared up. Late the next day, the sun came out again, and the music resumed. The deputies soon said the road was clear enough for drivers.

Two days after the end of the festival, Chris's mother called the Mayes County Sheriff's office to say that her son hadn't come home. She was apparently under the influence of television, which claimed that the relatives of the missing had to wait so long to file a report. The sheriff's office sent out what they called a task force, six deputies with dogs and flashlights and loaded rifles, who searched the area around the festival grounds for more than three hours. One of the deputies said he found the back of a pickup truck sticking out of a nearby creek. The front of the truck was smashed into the sandstone that made up the edge of the creek bed. The water line had been well above the top of the cab during the storm, and leaves and bits of moss clung to the wreckage. The boys were still buckled in. The funeral service was at the high school, and two hundred people showed up to pay their respects. The highlights were on TV.

***

All this happened, as most things happen, under someone's jurisdiction, which meant that people had somebody to blame when they felt uncomfortable or when they were short on words at the dinner table. Sheriff Douglas J. Taylor of the Mayes County Sheriff's Office, however, was the kind of local fixture who became difficult to invoke during suppertime gossip, the kind of middle-aged smile who reminded the old folks of Mayberry and that other Sheriff Taylor and a world without computers, who took the time to tell the young folks they'd better stay in school when he saw them at the grocery store. He'd been sheriff long enough that no one knew anymore whether he was genuinely friendly or simply practiced in what it meant to appear official. They voted him in four times, at any rate, and nothing much had happened in Mayes County for the better part of fifteen years.

Sheriff Taylor had done the best he could to keep the local media out of his jurisdiction since he was first elected in the eighties, but it was largely thanks to the local media that he had been able to first win the hearts of the county's cattle farmers and lake people, both those who lived on Lake Hudson and those who worked for the dam authority making hydroelectric power there. Sheriff Taylor had been Deputy Taylor back when he'd first appeared on nearly every television between Stillwater and Joplin, back in 1981. He'd happened upon a robbery at a convenience store outside Locust Grove and arrested John and Bailey Dunham after a brief standoff involving a hostage. The couple eventually confessed to more than a dozen robberies throughout northeastern Oklahoma. The hostage, a gummy old woman who worked at the convenience store, later wrote the sheriff to tell him that her granddaughter would have named her baby Taylor in his honor if it hadn't been stillborn. Three years after the arrest, the residents of Mayes County remembered the handsome man from their TV screens and made Sheriff Taylor the first Republican to hold the office since before the Great Depression.

The sheriff's wife, Barbara, was the daughter of a half-Native mother and a blue-collar Democrat father who'd spent his days growing soybeans before the state bought up half his land to build one of the three reservoirs in the county. Barbara liked to tease Sheriff Taylor about his "iron curtain," and she told him more than once that the only reason he kept the cameras out of Mayes County was to keep some young hotshot from being elected the first Democrat sheriff there in more than a decade. Sheriff Taylor didn't laugh at these jokes. He didn't explain to Barbara why he didn't like having the media around, either. She probably knew, though. She always seemed to know.

That is not to say that Sheriff Taylor could not articulate his reasons for keeping the reporters out of his hair. They had made him nervous for as long as he could remember.

It was a wonder he had been able to look so good during the 1981 interview that followed the robbery arrest. He blamed those natural enhancers, adrenaline and other chemicals, for his balanced words behind the microphones. During his first campaign for sheriff's office, the hero deputy had been sweating and shaking at the mere click and flash of a camera. In the years that followed, Sheriff Taylor's nervousness grew to contempt as he found that news broadcasts gave regular people the idea that they could do his job. When reporters stopped by, it meant that armchair lawmen would be calling his office to say this or that could be somehow done better, when, of course, the suggestions would result in the complete bungling of whatever it was they were calling about.

The nature of the recent disappearances made it especially hard for the sheriff to welcome the media into Mayes County. He wanted what was best for the county, and he knew that depended on his continued tenure as sheriff, at least until he could retire. He didn't believe that he had done anything criminal in his handling of the disappearances. The victims, though Sheriff Taylor did not want to call them that, had been addicts, and the county was actually cleaner without them. Surely even the armchair lawmen would have to agree. Though the days of mob evictions were no more, they were not long gone from rural Oklahoma, and as far as Sheriff Taylor knew, these missing folks had just been run out of town. If that were the case, he couldn't even say for sure who had actually made them leave, which rung from the ladder of local power had become a pitchfork. The sheriff knew who it was at the top of the ladder, though. A good sheriff should know who's behind everything that happens in his jurisdiction. Sheriff Taylor still believed himself to be a good sheriff.

So, when the August sun decided to burn its hottest, when it left the creek nearly dry and the rest of the county brown and thirsty, Sheriff Taylor called for all four of the Tulsa news stations, any local newspaper interested in a good story, and other journalists from as far as Fayetteville to the brick building on Pryor's First Street that housed the sheriff's office. He had his deputies fill the foyer with chairs and set up a podium at one end of the room. Two dozen reporters, writers, and photographers showed up by 2:00 p.m., and the sheriff found his chance to discuss the disappearances on his own terms, to keep out in front of the troublemakers.

The air was thick and moist with summertime bodies when he stood up to speak to the reporters. The open space above them wriggled in the heat. The sheriff wiped the top of his head, the hole where his hair used to be. Already, sweat formed on his back, and he hoped that it wouldn't work its way over to his belly. He read from a sheet of paper on the podium.

"I don't think our old air-conditioner is able to keep up with all of y'all," he began. "I'll try to make this quick, so we can go cool off somewhere."

A collective chuckle gave way to a drooping room.

"Around 08:00 Monday," the sheriff continued, "we received a call about a missing woman, identified as forty-six-year-old Lori Cummings, who disappeared from her home near Highway 82 and East 490 Road outside Salina. During the investigation into Ms. Cummings disappearance, we determined that she was likely forced to leave her home against her will. We are investigating the disappearance as a possible kidnapping."

Sheriff Taylor was sure to say that his office hadn't determined any suspects, that they were just as in the dark as anybody else. He gave a description, a verbal portrait of Lori's body, though it could have been one of many bodies, the way he described her, reduced to a list of physical features. He told the reporters there would be a picture of Lori waiting for them on the way out. He said that anyone who knew anything about her should give investigators a call. He knew there wouldn't be any useful calls. The sweat continued to build up on his back, on his head, and he hoped that no one noticed.

"Does anyone have any questions?" he asked.

Raised hands filled the room. Sheriff Taylor wiped his head again. More sweat had pooled there than he'd expected, and he wondered if time or circumstance had caused his increased nervousness. He called on a young, dark-haired woman with a notepad.

"Do you think this case could be connected to other recent disappearances in the area?" she asked.

"I assume you are referring to the boys that went missing in June," the sheriff said. "Unless Ms. Cummings drove into floodwaters from a storm so isolated that no one else knew about it, I'd say there is little chance of there being any connection between these cases."

"What about the nurse who disappeared from that bar near Branch Creek?" the woman asked again.

"We don't believe there was any criminal element in her disappearance," Sheriff Taylor said.

"She just left without a trace?"

"We believe her leaving was deliberate. Next question."

The sheriff pointed to a close-shaven man with sunglasses that peeked out of his shirt pocket, hoping the man would ask about protocol or the air conditioning.

"I've heard reports of another missing man from earlier this year," the close-shaven reporter said. "Can you verify that this is true? What does your office plan to do about the increase in missing people throughout the county?"

The reporter had not asked about protocol or the air conditioning.

"We don't have any reports of an additional missing man," Sheriff Taylor said. "We are investigating the disappearance of one person, Ms. Cummings, which is why I invited you all here today. There is not, to my knowledge, any cause for alarm over disappearances in Mayes County."

"Then where are these people going?" the man asked.

Sheriff Taylor's face was flushed. The heat in his blood worked its way close to his skin and turned him red. He tried not to think about the sweat. He tried to think about his wife.

"These things happen," he said. He would not tell the reporters that the missing people had been run out of the county. He would not even consider that what had happened to them was somehow worse than that. "I've seen folks get involved in the wrong crowd and leave town for this reason or that. My office only becomes involved if we believe a crime has been committed. We do believe that Ms. Cummings's disappearance may have a criminal element to it, but we do not think that there are any other disappearances within our jurisdiction that warrant concern at this time. I'm going to be frank here, but our corner of the earth ain't what it was twenty years ago. We all, for the most part, try to get along with our safe and quiet lives, but it's nearly the end of the century, and we'd be fools to forget that troublemakers do exist."

The popping sounds of unvoiced murmurs moved about the room. The sheriff's eyes jumped from one uneasy reporter to the next. Their heads were nearly in their laps over his words. He took a breath and tried to clarify.

"What I'm saying here is that this conference concerns a single incident that I believe should be put out there for the public," he said. "There is nothing more."

The reporters scribbled in their notepads again. Sweat ran down onto Sheriff Taylor's forehead. He glanced at the window and wondered if he should burst through it and leave the press conference behind him, if his legs could carry him far enough away to justify his leaving, if there was enough money in his retirement fund to last him until he died. He called on another reporter who had his hand in the air.

"Are you saying that there's gangs and drug dealers in Mayes County?" the reporter asked.

The sheriff scowled. He did not want to answer that question. He hated the way that the reporter had taken it upon himself to bring that question into the world. These were among the things that Sheriff Taylor wouldn't say out loud.

"No," he said, "but it would be childish to assume that drugs aren't here the same way they're anywhere else. I think sometimes people involved in that sort of world have reasons to leave. Their neighbors don't want them around the kids, maybe, or their supply dries up, thanks to the work of people like me. Maybe they run out of money. I'm sure we can come up with a dozen different reasons. Now, if you think I'm telling you to worry about safety in my county, then you missed the entire point of what I just said. I'll reiterate: a woman disappeared here, and we're investigating that. That's all we've got going on right now."

The man who'd asked the question nodded. Others asked for more details about the missing woman, but Sheriff Taylor didn't have anything else to tell them. He assured himself that they probably just liked to hear themselves talk.

He tried to keep them happy, to give them the memorable lines that made for good television. The clock above the podium showed 2:17 p.m. He spoke again, ignoring the few hands still raised across the room.

"That's all the information we will be releasing at this time," he said. "If it's fine with you all, I'm going to go cool off. I suggest you do likewise."

The reporters picked up pictures of Lori Cummings from a deputy at the back of the room and left. Sheriff Taylor went to find a sink where he could splash some water on his face. In the public bathroom, water mixed with his sweat and ran down the creases in his jawline. It made him shine in the mirror. He wiped himself off with a paper towel and stared into the sink. His face was reflected in the faucet, long and knobby. The sheriff in the sink was distorted and unfamiliar. Sheriff Taylor wondered if the mirrored image was the same man as the hero deputy at the convenience store seventeen years before. He considered heading home early, considered asking Barbara whether she still saw that deputy beneath all his sweat, but he already knew how she would respond.

Suddenly, the sound of humming made its way from the bathroom stall, the rising and falling of worship hymns. Boot toes poked out from beneath the stall door. Sheriff Taylor continued to sweat as he approached the boots and the unseen man above them, the man who only met with him when there was bad news to share, the man at the top of the Mayes County meth ladder, Jim.

Chapter 3

Sheriff Taylor first met Jim at the Assembly of God church in Branch Creek shortly after he was elected to his third term. It was winter then, and the daytime rain had turned to sleet and left white pellets sprinkled all over the crunchy grass and the roadways. It was a fairly important happening back in those days, the sleet. The sheriff's office was charged with keeping the county's drivers from running off the road or into one another. Sheriff Taylor was watching a weather forecast in his office and worrying that some station or other would call and ask him about how he was keeping the county safe. He planned to talk about "coordinated efforts" and the ways in which his deputies would apply their "top-notch" knowledge about the county's many roads to closely monitor the conditions in problem areas. In other words, he planned to say a whole lot of words that were nothing more than a whole lot of words. Then, pleased with his performance, he'd go home to Barbara and the warmth she kept hidden for him in her chest.

As the night wore on, his eyes hardly left the television screen. His head became foggy. Someone brought him coffee. When a call finally came through, Donna said it was from a deacon in Branch Creek. The caller, Jim, had something to say about a rash of crimes across the county and insisted on talking to the sheriff directly. Sheriff Taylor hadn't heard about any crimes, but he felt it would be irresponsible to ignore the possibility. He was tired of worrying about the forecasters that talked about the ice that piled up in the counties south of Tulsa. So, he loaded up into his pickup and drove through the sleet to Branch Creek.

The door outside the peeling church building was locked when Sheriff Taylor arrived. He waited out in the cold for some time before he decided to get back to the office and listen for the ringing phone. Then the door creaked and opened before him. A man, Jim, peered through the open door from the dark church hallway inside.

"Sheriff," Jim said in a feeble, disarming tone, a tone that the sheriff couldn't remember him ever using again, "please come in."

Sheriff Taylor wondered at first if Jim was a drunk who'd broken into the old church and found the phone to call his office out of boredom or out of loneliness. Jim was a tall man that bent slightly at the waist. He had the sort of hair that turned white quickly only because it had been so close to white when it was blond. He was older than the sheriff, but it was hard to tell just how much older he was. He was thin the way drunks were thin, but so were plenty of other folks.

Still, Sheriff Taylor followed him inside and sat down next to him on a pew in the sanctuary. The building was all cracked walls and mildew stains, and it was apparent that it had not been well cared for. Someone certainly could have made their way inside without stirring up a noticeable mess. Stains from road salt and muddy boots already covered the faded carpet. Though it was warmer inside the church than it had been outside, Sheriff Taylor thought the house of God should have been cozier. The air was stale and seemed to lap at his skin.

"Do you ever have dreams, Sheriff?" Jim asked. His voice was hushed and creeping like a vine.

The question puzzled the sheriff.

"Just about everyone dreams," he said, "best I can figure."

Later, Sheriff Taylor decided that he had lied in saying that. He learned what it was to live without dreams and to fill the void with the sort of boulder-pushing that kept him occupied, kept him from wandering.

"No," Jim said, "not just earthly dreams. I'm talking about scripture here, Acts 2:17, visions and dreams from the Almighty above."

"I don't know if I follow," the sheriff said.

Jim put his hand on the sheriff's shoulder and pressed his fingers into his flesh like he was feeling around for something inside of him. His eyes were too lit up and living to be the eyes of a drunk man. There seemed to be something deep inside of him that caused splendor to spill out of him like quicksilver, but Sheriff Taylor assumed that it was just the reflection of the church's flickering lights.

"Last week," Jim said, standing to pace the sanctuary, "I had a series of dreams, and let me tell you, they really bewildered me. I knew they were special, but I couldn't put my finger on what it was I was supposed to go and learn from them."

Sheriff Taylor's mind wandered to his wife as Jim kept on about dreams. He saw a composite of her across their sliver of shared time. She was at once the girl he'd first kissed in the back of his Chevy under the little spotlight stars and the woman who still held his hand on the porch swing. Even the thought of her was more important than whatever it was deacon was saying. He wondered how long it would be before Jim told him about the crimes.

"First," Jim said, "I dreamt I had Biblical knowledge of a dog that I'd kept when I was a boy, probably twelve or so, poor as the very dirt I slept on."

Sheriff Taylor stood to leave the sick bastard alone in the dirty sanctuary with his talk of dreams and of animal sex, but the deacon put up a finger to stop him and carried on with his story. The older man's words were made up of syrup and rubber cement then. His stiff finger plucked at unseen strings. Sheriff Taylor sat back down in another pew, suddenly unable to leave even a sentence unattended and wandering in the church.

"You grow up poor, Sheriff?" Jim asked. "I can't imagine you did, not real poor. I was working when I was five years old, helped haul feed all the way down from the granary in Independence, Kansas. It was different then, kids would go out and do that sort of thing, at least the real poor ones."

Sheriff Taylor felt his body become rigid and wary as if it knew something he didn't about the strange deacon. He was looking around the room more than he was at Jim. He had not grown up poor, but his father had. He'd heard stories about walking the streets and looking for aluminum, about loading cattle for a couple brothers who lived outside town for a hot lunch and a handful of change.

"But that's not the point," Jim continued. "The dog—well, have you ever dreamed of carnal relations with an animal?"

The sheriff was standing again, hardly able to believe that the old man had called an officer of the law to talk about his bestial fantasies.

"I realize it's detestable," Jim persisted, "vile, the worst dream I'd ever had up to that point, an honest to God nightmare, but not impossible to imagine. I had loved that dog as a kid, not the same as I'd 'loved' it in my dream, but with that warm fondness any country boy has for his dog."

"You have thirty seconds to get to the point and tell me whatever it is you called about," Sheriff Taylor said. He felt like a cop in a movie, talking like that.

Jim continued speaking as if he hadn't heard the sheriff. His face was lit up like someone followed it with a spotlight. No, it was as if his face *was* the light, not an object affected by it.

"It was bad enough I thought God would come do away with me that very night," he said. "I got sick all over the floor beside the bed."

Sheriff Taylor didn't understand what the dream had to do with crime, but it was only right that a man, much less a deacon, should be physically ill after dreaming about that sort of thing.

"I felt the stink from my own guts calling out to me from that floor," Jim was saying, "and wouldn't you know it, I couldn't find it in me to move. I just had to leave it there. I had no control over my own body. I don't know how long it took for me to drift off again."

Even though Sheriff Taylor was himself sickened by what Jim was saying, the deacon spoke with such authority that the sheriff trusted Jim to lead him somewhere. He carried his words like he knew how to use them and avoided merely tossing them about with his tongue.

"After I'd gone back to sleep," Jim continued, "I had another dream. This time, I was sick, worse than I'd been after the dream about the dog, and a witch in black robe fed me a strange soup from a cauldron. It was about like Halloween, and I knew that I had done evil by drinking the witch's brew, but I couldn't help but continue, as it made me feel like I'd begun to regain my strength."

Sheriff Taylor felt his pocket for a notepad.

"Are you saying the crime you'd mentioned over the phone happened on Halloween?" he asked.

"All sorts of wickedness happens that night. I need you to listen to what I'm telling you. You would highly regret ignoring this Gospel tale looking for unimportant details."

The sheriff wrote "Halloween" in his notebook. Jim kept talking.

"I wondered what it was that man could drink to bring himself to health in such sickness," he said. "I wanted to take the brew from the witch and offer it up to God so it could be cleansed and poured out for the nations. I wanted to share it with every person I'd ever met. I felt it was mine to give. But I woke up again, and, again, I threw up at the side of the bed."

His voice began to rise and take on the form of a sermon, the kind of speech that demanded something from its listener. The sheriff watched with his arms crossed over his chest. He noticed that Jim had teeth that were whiter and straighter than most folks in the area. Those teeth bothered him, though he wasn't sure why. In fact, the whole ordeal made him squirm, but, nonetheless, he was expectant. Reason escaped him in the knots of the deacon's now-roaring speech.

"And then brother, I tell you what, in the blink of an eye, I was here," Jim said, gesturing to the room around him, "in this very sanctuary, and I was unable to speak a lick of sense. I was laying here in the aisle. I was praying in unknown tongues. Then the door behind me opened, and that dog from the first dream came and licked my hand." He paused, and Sheriff Taylor realized he was holding his breath. "Do you know what I did to that dog?"

The sheriff didn't have the words to respond. He was afraid the deacon would talk about having sex with the dog again, in the very church, no less.

"I took the old bitch, and I broke her cursed neck for the sins of the first dream," Jim said. He'd taken to full-on yelling. His voice filled the room and seemed to pound against the sheriff's ears. "I left her body at the altar, and then I wept, and biblical manna came down on top of me. I ate it, Sheriff."

Jim lost his odd charm when he yelled. He was no longer as feeble as he'd acted at the door. He didn't likely have any information about area crimes, and he had suckered Sheriff Taylor into leaving his warm office and hearing out his perversions. Still, the sheriff sat and listened. He did not want to return without something new to talk about.

"That manna tasted just like the old witch's brew," Jim said. "I could see then the heavenly crown that the Father had stored up for me. It was as if I, like the great Apostle Paul, had been told to 'go forth and eat.' I could give the manna to everybody. I knew I'd never be poor again."

Jim slowed his pulpit theatrics and leaned over into the sheriff's face. Sheriff Taylor could feel the heat rising off his skin.

"Do you know what those dreams mean, Sheriff?" Jim asked, quiet then, nearly whispering. His breath stank, but the sheriff kept from drawing away from him. At last, maybe there was something to be said. Jim was pacing again.

"I'm a brand new man," he said. "The dogs of this land will eat from my hands, and I'll bring them to their knees in sacrifice. I'm gonna be the new judge here, and I'm gonna be a righteous and holy judge. I'm gonna share my manna with anyone who will partake in it. I'm gonna right things in this county and reap the blessings that God has for me, and ain't no one gonna stop me from it."

"I think you'll probably have to go to law school before you become any sort of judge," Sheriff Taylor said, half-laughing.

He put his notebook back into his pocket. Jim continued to glow from around his face as if he still held onto mountaintop glory a month after seeing the rear end of deity. Sheriff Taylor thought about Barbara again, about the way she was likely sitting in the quiet of the otherwise empty house, about the way she was probably looking out the window and missing him something awful. He wanted to go home. Perhaps the sleet would turn back into rain and cut him some slack.

"This here is no joking matter," Jim said. "If you want this manna, you're gonna have to head into the wilderness with me. I'm about to dive into the belly of the beast, but when I return, even a man like you is gonna fear me."

Sheriff Taylor didn't hear the last bit as a threat, but as a delusion. He had no idea what Jim was talking about.

"I assume this means you don't actually have information about any crimes in Mayes County," Sheriff Taylor said.

He started toward the door to the sanctuary again.

"I mean it, Sheriff," Jim said with wide pupils and a heightened voice that summoned an impression of forcefulness, that tiptoed to the edge of real harm. "When things start happening around here, I'll need you to stay on the side of goodness, on the side of Jesus Christ and his present-day apostles. You are going to hear more about me. I am going to change this place."

Sheriff Taylor waved Jim off like a religious fanatic as he walked out of the church and into the sleet that piled up on the road. Though he could have sworn he heard a chorus of voices singing hymns behind him, the night would be too long for the sheriff to worry much about it.

Sometime after midnight, Barbara asked him from the bedroom why he'd been out so late and whether or not the roads were bad. She didn't like to watch the news.

"Roads are slicker than snot," Sheriff Taylor said.

She came out in her robe, a bulky purple thing stained with bleach and old toothpaste. Her eyes were heavy, the lids drifting down over them every few seconds. Sheriff Taylor knew she'd been up waiting for him in that stinking robe, same as always. She said she couldn't sleep until he was there in bed with her, but he liked to tease her when she said that, to make her promise that she wasn't just a coffee addict filling her cup into the night.

"Any wrecks?" she asked.

"Nothing bad. Nobody's dead."

"Come on to bed then," she said. "You look like hell."

She was probably right. The sheriff hadn't seen a mirror in hours. He took his wife into his arms and kissed her softly. She unbuttoned the top of his uniform and pulled him close. The front of her robe parted and fell down around her.

He kissed her again. Her chest was warm against his bare skin. He wouldn't ever say so, but he only really felt safe when he was pressed up against her, and after the long night with the sleet and the deacon and the crumbling church dreams, it was time to be safe.

"I look like hell, huh?" he said.

★★★

For the first few weeks after the meeting, things went on as normal around Mayes County. Sheriff Taylor nearly forgot the dark rapture in Jim's voice and those perfect, smiling teeth. Then a little trouble started here and there. People robbed the dollar stores and the convenience stores for cash. They were caught with pills and no prescriptions. That didn't bother Sheriff Taylor much. It made things a bit more interesting in an otherwise slow-moving jurisdiction. No one got hurt. The whole thing was just broken glass and shotgun promises from the local business owners. The crimes were about wrinkled greenbacks and bitter pills, not power, not revenge, and, at first, they always ended with an arrest.

Eventually, though, the painkillers stopped filling the pockets of the local drifters, and all sorts of folks were turning up with methamphetamine. Deputies were bringing in farmhands with early mornings ahead of them and other members of the working society who needed tongues of fire to kick them into ecstasy. Before long, though, they were bringing in skinny people with jumpy eyes and scabbed arms nearly every night. When a woman in pajama pants kept going on about the "old preacher man" and the "demon dog eating out of his hand" as she was booked, Sheriff Taylor remembered the meeting with Jim in the crumbling church. Despite its incoherence, the woman's rambling offered a rare lead in the early investigation. None of the other robbery suspects or methamphetamine users seemed willing to admit anything about who it was that was selling to them. They appeared loyal, as if they felt safe under their dealer's toe. Still, Sheriff Taylor kept the meeting to himself, afraid that he was wrong about his conclusions, or maybe, afraid that someone smarter than him would think him a fool for not having drawn a conclusion sooner.

There were also the occasional gifts, some petty cash here and there, a wicker basket full of cellophane-wrapped perfumes for his wife in the bed of his pickup. A note had come with the perfume. "Because you love her, you'll leave me be, Sheriff," it said. The day he found the note and the perfumes, Sheriff Taylor sat alone in the truck with the note and traced over the words with his fingers until the sun went down and Donna came out to make sure he was OK. He told her that he was and nearly drove to Branch Creek right then to turn the son of a bitch inside out, procedures be damned.

A few days later, it rained, and he threw the perfume basket into a half-empty dumpster behind a McDonald's near the sheriff's office. The rain rattled the cellophane as it fell. The sheriff imagined a funeral march. The press would eat him alive if they ever found out about it. They would claim he hadn't brought down the drug-dealing deacon on account of *perfume*. In the days that followed, he looked both ways before opening envelopes, before starting up his truck. He tried to prod his deputies toward Branch Creek, but he was afraid that if he outright told them that he thought an old deacon there was behind all the meth they were finding, they'd either laugh at him or figure he was in on the whole operation. It wasn't long after that that the phone calls started.

Jim got into the habit of calling Sheriff Taylor the morning after just about every reported wrongdoing in the county to tell him what business wasn't worth getting involved with. The first time, Donna buzzed his office and told him there was a deacon from Branch Creek on the line. She seemed wholly uninterested, just smacked her chewing gum. Sheriff Taylor told her to transfer the call.

"Hello there, Sheriff," Jim said. "If you haven't heard yet, then I reckon you will soon hear about a home break-in by Branch Creek. I'm telling you now, it was only the work of some apostles out doing the Lord's work. I think it's best if your investigators find that also to be true."

"You're a fool, then," Sheriff Taylor laughed nervously. "I figure I should tell you that bribery is a crime in this county."

The sound of heavy breathing filled the receiver. Jim continued.

"I really do like what you and your wife have done with that house off the three mile road," he said. "That is your house, right? The one with the little garden and the new roof?"

Sheriff Taylor didn't respond. He'd never done much to hide where it was he lived, but he didn't think that it was public knowledge.

"Your wife's been home all morning," Jim said, "but I'm sure you know that. She spends quite a bit of time at home, doesn't seem to go out much."

Sheriff Taylor felt the edge of anger rise up out of his gut and into his head.

"What do you want?" he asked. "Why are you watching my house?"

"Well, I can't say I'm the one watching, Sheriff. It doesn't interest me too much, but it does interest others that would, well, how can I say this, would hate to have their routines interrupted. Dozens of folks, probably hundreds. I lose count."

Sheriff Taylor pounded his free hand on his desk.

"You stay away from my house," he said.

"I plan to. I never spend too much time that far out, myself. Got the church to attend to. Other folks, though, these other folks are wild with all their guns and their awful hunger and what not. The coming millennium's got us all a little antsy, and a woman planting petunias makes a fine target if there's any incentive."

"You said you were a man of God. . . ."

"According to the Book of Job, the Good Lord, Himself, spends some time with the devil every now and again."

Sheriff Taylor couldn't remember ever feeling so much panic. He had been able to work his way through life with one foot in front of the other, confident in spite of his humanness. He'd been elected that way. He'd been reelected that way too. In that moment, though, the lines running up and down his spine screamed and threatened to burst out of his skin and leave him dead on the floor. His stomach filled with acid. Sweat dripped down his forehead. He promised to ignore the break-in. Jim said he thought that was a pretty good idea.

The phone rang more and more as time went on. Sheriff Taylor learned to do what he was told and to curb his physiological response. He had no reason to believe that Jim wouldn't hire the area rabble, the farmers and convenience store clerks who had bought into the methamphetamine gospel, to keep a reticle on his wife. It wasn't long before Donna began to call Jim the sheriff's "spiritual advisor" when she transferred the calls to him, and though the sheriff hated that, he found it to be a fine cover for the deacon's frequent requests. He didn't think it was worth taking the risk of calling Jim on his bluff over the low-level break-ins and possession arrests.

As time went on, Jim sent his goon Carlson to join the force and twisted the sheriff's arm to make sure the tall man was made deputy. He promised fewer phone calls and less talk of guns and shooting and all the nasty business that came along with the deacon's venture. Everything had changed for the sheriff, and he wished it had been the sort of change that happened all at once. He realized after hiring Carlson that it was too big an issue to tackle without losing some skin himself, but he knew that it was only that way because he had refused to tackle any number of small issues in the months prior. Carlson told Jim about every happening in the sheriff's office. He told the sheriff that Jim knew people from as far as Missouri who would do whatever it took to see his will done. Carlson, himself, had come from Joplin.

A few months after that, folks started skipping town. Five years had passed since Sheriff Taylor first spoke to Jim. Now, he often found himself full of sweat and panic and words that were rehearsed in front of mirrors and behind closed doors. He wished he'd loved his wife enough to risk her once instead of keeping her in the hands of Jim's minions. He wished he wasn't running his own name into the ground and always blaming her very existence for it, at least to himself. He learned to be sad to keep from anger and exhaustion.

After the second or third disappearance, Sheriff Taylor began to spend his free time in Branch Creek whenever he could make an excuse to do so. He darkened the door of the church on the occasional Sunday to keep an eye on Jim without drawing suspicion from the average Mayes County resident. His efforts felt like sand in his fingers. Folks continued to stop showing up to the places where they were supposed to show up, and Jim continued to tell Sheriff Taylor what he was going to say to anyone who asked about it. Barbara put out a church shirt for him every Saturday night, but the sheriff refused to attend services regularly. Part of him wondered if Jim liked his casual visits to Branch Creek, if the meth-dealing deacon actually thought it nice to keep a close eye on him. He felt like a prisoner and had to discard the thought. There wasn't much use in making things worse than they already were.

***

"Sheriff," Jim said in the bathroom of the sheriff's office, "I don't particularly like all the drug talkin' you were doing in there with those reporters."

Sheriff Taylor did not want to speak to the old man. He would have rather held another press conference. These unwelcome conversations with Jim often ended in revelations, in the sharing of information that should pull sheriffs' hands from beneath their asses, in the knowledge of good and evil.

"I had to say something," Sheriff Taylor said. "I still have a job to do."

"Well," Jim said from the stall, sighing as he spoke, "I also have a job to do, and, frankly, if your job gets in the way of my job . . . well, neither of us really want to have to go through all that, I'm sure."

Jim clicked his boots against the wall. He spat. Sheriff Taylor saw the saliva bubbling on the tile floor. The first time he had met Jim, he had laughed at the old man. He had laughed back then. He remembered that. People had laughed along with him. The town hadn't yet grown crystalline. There'd been more clean heads than addicts, maybe too many drunks, but that was manageable.

"Of course, I understand you," the sheriff told Jim, "but I'm still the goddamn sheriff, and there has to be some sort of law and order here if I'm gonna keep on being the goddamn sheriff."

"I think your wife would appreciate it very much if you kept on being the sheriff, but, of course, if you do that, you'll need to be *my* sheriff."

Sheriff Taylor could hear his breaths moving out of his body and toward Jim. He thought about his wife, and he feared the space between them, or rather, feared the possibility that Jim could cut through that space and then make it impossible to close that again, could make good on his threats. He knew then he was no longer the same man who had stopped the convenience store robbery.

"You wouldn't find another person this side of Arkansas who'd let you run your operation the way I do," the sheriff said. He hoped Jim couldn't see him red and sweating in the gap of the stall door. He was shaking with either anger or fear. It was often impossible to tell the two apart.

A hand burst into the room. The sheriff blocked the door before the body behind it could follow. There was a shout outside. The hand slapped the bathroom wall.

"Jesus Christ," the hand's owner cried, "I've gotta piss."

Sheriff Taylor recognized the voice of one of his deputies. He pushed harder against the door, sure that he was more angry than afraid of being caught with Jim. The deputy's arm was trapped between the door and the jamb. The hand continued to writhe around like it was its own animal, like it was fighting for life.

"Shitter's stopped up," the sheriff said. He pulled the door back, and the hand exited the bathroom. The deputy complained about his arm as he went away. Sheriff Taylor was nearly panting. He was relieved that the deputy had left, but that relief faded away as Jim spoke again.

"It looks like you've got some things to attend to," the deacon said. "Now, if you'll excuse me, I'd like to wash my hands here in peace before I get on my way."

Sheriff Taylor left the bathroom. He heard the whooshing of running water as the door fell shut behind him. His office didn't release any new information about Lori Cummings for some time after that. Within a week, Mayes

County was free of reporters and photographers and crime scene tape, and that lasted for nearly two months. People could either forget what had happened or draw their own conclusions as to why it didn't affect them. They could watch their televisions at 6:00 p.m. with a sense of detachment that allowed them to feel comfortable and entertained. The space between the people of Mayes County was wide, and folks there could turn their heads away from anything they didn't want to see without worrying that anyone else would notice.

And then there was Ava.

Chapter 4

"Jenn, if I don't see your feet on the floor next time I come by, I'm getting the spray bottle."

Jenn pulled the comforter over her face. Her mother's steps shook their house as she moved from bedroom to bathroom and then back to the bedroom. The sun was up, but Jenn couldn't see it on account of a thick layer of clouds and a navy curtain that covered her room's only window. She sat up, tried to force her eyes open, adjusted to the burning fluorescent bulb that hung over her bed. Her mother stomped some more through the house. Jenn remembered that she hadn't heard from Ava in more than a week, that she would likely spend the afternoon alone or with her mother. Her stomach twisted in its tiny burrow. It reached deep into itself and tightened with the spasms of a drink-too-many alcoholic. The morning air ran its jagged fingernails down her back. Her musty skin shook, and she sneaked past her mother and into the bathroom. She locked the door behind her. She heard the honking spray bottle from down the hall, her mother laughing at the ongoing joke, the cold water she used an alarm clock.

In the bathroom, Jenn curled up the damp towel she and her mother used as a bathmat. The room filled with steam, and she draped another towel on top of herself to retain as much of the warmth as she could. She closed her eyes and felt the deep dark between sleep and wakefulness, the fuzzy place where Ava wasn't missing anymore, where Jenn could still hear the low voice Ava used with people that were older than her because she thought they would take her more seriously for it. The gap where her friend had been filled with a haze of half-thoughts. The thoughts became scenes that flashed and then disappeared. She saw the beginning of a memory from outside Ava's locker, a walk through a pasture they weren't supposed to be in, an empty bucket they'd tried to fill with fish from the creek when they were fourteen. The bathroom door shook and ended the scenes before they could take hold of Jenn.

"You about done in there?" her mother asked, pounding again on the door with her open hand so that it made a slapping sound. "I'm gonna skin you alive if we're late."

Jenn shot out from under the towel and into the shower. The haze became panic.

"I'm almost done," she said, tossing aside the shower curtain.

The water had become lukewarm. It ran down her skin and made goosebumps. The steam that had gathered on the mirror had started to clear. By the time she was done rinsing her body, the water had grown completely cold, and no warmth remained for her in the bathroom. She shivered and gasped her way through the lather of generic shampoo her mom had brought home from work. They were out of conditioner. The empty bottle only wheezed. When Jenn moved into her room to dress, she still had suds on her ears. Her mother continued to stomp about the house.

"We needed to be gone five minutes ago," she said.

Jenn emerged from her bedroom in a black and white dress that puffed out around her breasts and her wrists. Jenn wanted to feel strong in the dress, not unlike a pirate, but not in the Halloween sense, a real pirate who could kill anyone she pleased and who had enough wealth to keep the law at bay, a hard woman with a story, a woman used to people's leaving. Her mother apparently saw something else in the outfit.

"You look like a clown when you wear that," she said.

"It's a good thing we're headed to the circus then," Jenn muttered under her breath. The two women went out the door together, and Jenn wondered for the first time in years if she needed to lock it. She didn't even know where they kept the key.

***

Jenn's hair was still wet as she sat in the red Ford Explorer, the car her mother had bought with some money she'd won at the casino. She'd said it was a gift to herself and hadn't let anyone but Jenn inside it for almost six months. Now, cigarette burns poked holes in the loose fabric above their heads. The steering wheel was covered in tar and dried-up hairspray, the leftover bits of dirty hands.

Jenn yanked at a tangle in her hair and then wiped the moisture from her hands onto her skirt. She tried to stifle her shivering as cool air spilled from the vents. Empty seats at the school lunch table and burned-down trailers haunted her as she toyed with a string at the end of her sleeve. She had been able to fill her head with tasks and leave little room for thoughts of Ava when she was rushing to shower and dress for the day. Now, the image of her missing friend returned, and she felt guilty for having been able to avoid it.

Her mother slammed on the brakes. Jenn swung toward the windshield. She pulled her core tight and reached out to stop herself, but she continued forward until the seatbelt caught on to what was happening.

"Son of a bitch," Jenn's mother exhaled over the top of the steering wheel. "Goddamn cows are gonna make us late for church."

In front of the car, a red cow with a white splotch on its face defecated on the road. The waste fell hot onto the gravel. A black cow moved on into the ditch beside them. It mooed, but Jenn could hardly hear it. Her mother rolled down the window and made a noise like a moaning giant at the cows. She honked the horn in short beeps.

"Get on out of here," she shouted between her mooing sounds and her hand's pounces on the car horn.

Then the car worked its way down the street. Jenn's mother confessed aloud that she would have stopped to tell someone about the escaped cows if she'd had the time. The clock above the cassette player showed 10:14, and church didn't start until 10:30. Jenn wondered how long it could possibly take to tell someone that a pair of cows were out. Her mother continued speaking to no one in particular. Jenn was soon doubled over in the seat next to her, panicking as the seconds passed. Ava was missing, the First Assembly of God Church of Branch Creek was less than a mile away, and the town was quiet and praying. The town fell under the shadow of empty promises and smiles about new ranches and dollar stores, and her mom was talking about cows.

In the church parking lot, blue-haired women in flowing dresses stepped over shiny white rocks and up a short flight of stairs into a once-white building made gray by the Oklahoma wind and decades of rain. Jenn's mother walked proudly across the parking lot when they arrived, ready to show her face before the rest of the congregation as she had her entire adult life. Jenn sought hard spaces for her feet as she shuffled along. They let the wooden door fall audibly against the jamb when they entered the church.

"There is a fountain filled with blood drawn from Immanuel's veins," a balding man in a tie and church slacks sang to himself inside. His voice rounded the sanctuary and weighed on the shoulders of sinners with their feet on the outskirts of grace. His words were fiery, the edges of burning onion paper, and his teeth stood in their immaculate rows as he smiled at the women. He was alone near the otherwise empty entrance to the sanctuary.

"Well, won't you look at these young ladies," he said as they moved through the foyer. His white shirt was pressed, and the creases pulled away from his lumpy body. He bent slightly at the waist, not as an old man bends under the weight of his experiences, but as a salesman bends to comfort the buyer into a decades-old sedan. When he reached out to grab their hands, his eyes looked as if they were the paws of a cat digging to cover its shit in the litterbox. "Glad you could make it."

"Glad to be here, Brother Freemont," Jenn's mother said. She turned and nodded to her daughter, who gave the man the only half-smile she had.

Brother Freemont kissed her hand and pointed her into the sanctuary, where a few dozen parishioners sat upright in their Sunday best, their hair locked tight by sprays and grease and their shoes wiped clean from the last Sunday's wear. They wore wrinkles in their thick skin, which made Jenn feel out of place and vulnerable. Sure, these were the sorts of people who would talk to her mother for hours in the dollar store or say hello to Jenn at the park, the grandparents of classmates who went to other churches, churches with youth groups, and the sweet young couples with babies and children who had just recently been babies, but their collective seriousness made Jenn anxious. She could hardly muster the mask of sacred sternness required for a room with a name like "tabernacle."

She was pale and silent behind her mother, who said her "good morning" blessings to several other congregants on her way to her pew, old Janice Atkins, who only had one eye, and Tom and Ruth Waite, who had seven kids, four of which were adopted, and who never smiled or paid their babysitters. Jenn was too tired to listen in on the stale greetings. The church-goers seemed to give her side-eyed glances with their tongues in their cheeks, as if they knew something about her, something they'd be willing to say to anyone but her. At the back of the room, Brother Freemont wiped drooping hairs behind the tops of his ears and looked at the clock with a frown. It read 10:31.

"And sinners plunged beneath that flood lose all their guilty stains," he continued his song.

Pastor Masterson, a short, thin man who usually walked with a cane, hobbled under his own strength to the front of the church as he did every Sunday morning to prove the power of a God who offered nothing in the way of welfare, even for His elect. Brother Freemont closed the double doors at the back of the sanctuary, shutting the congregation in with the coming flood. He was still humming on his way to the front row, where he sat by himself. He said his wife had gone and gotten sick. She hadn't been to service in months. She hadn't talked much at church anyhow. Maybe she'd always been sick.

The congregation stood, and Jenn wondered whether any of them had also seen about Ava on the news, had read her daddy's obituary in the newspaper and cried, not because of the printed words about the stern, skinny man, but because they left an opening for future print about a teenage girl who was somebody's best friend. A woman pounded the piano and called out a page number from the hymnal. She wore a wrinkled church hat she had been able to afford before her husband got hurt and lost his job. Jenn's chest tightened, and she couldn't force any words of glory or forgiveness from her mouth. Instead, she looked over the top of her hymnal at a bald spot on the back of an old woman's head. The spot seemed to grow and then shrink in the tangle of silver hairs as the woman moved forward and backward with the hymns. If Ava had been there, she would have been sure to nudge Jenn so the two could laugh at the open patch of skin, but she had only attended church after sleepovers, when Jenn's mother had insisted they all go together before she took Ava home. The woman in front of Jenn moved again. The bald spot was hidden for a moment by her hair. The body of Christ had come together to forget the troubles of the earth, and Jenn was left alone to remember Ava.

Brother Freemont's singing made its way through the cord of voices. His voice was thick and round, his words like the ends of far-flung spears, as if he'd have the entire church bleeding on the floor in order to have his head higher than their heads. Jenn did her best to ignore him, and then the song ended. The bald patch appeared and disappeared again as the congregation moved to sit.

The pastor returned to the podium and called for the collecting of offerings, the passing of velvet bags with worn wooden handles. The song leader wagged her paws at the piano some more and sang praises. Jenn's mother handed the offering bag to Brother Freemont, who stood in the aisle with his hands crossed over his waist. He took the bag to the next row, at once seeming to make eye contact with the entire congregation and no one at all. The smell of the soap he'd used to shower the night before covered Jenn. The oil in his hair lingered at her nose. Then he was gone, raptured away to count the offering money. The woman at the piano stopped her song, and the pastor took center stage.

***

No one mentioned Ava during the call for prayer requests. Did anyone else notice? The pastor listed other requests, a home-bound parent, seasonal allergies, a broken arm or leg, and they rolled across the wrinkles in Jenn's brain as she tried to find words worth praying.

"Amen," the pastor said, calling for open eyes and the congregation's full attention. Jenn's sparse, silent words came back to her from the ceiling. She often wondered if she'd ever talked to God at all. She'd wondered that for years and spent many nights in her bed thinking her prayers and then whispering them where no one could hear her.

The sermon started with a joke, and half the congregation laughed. Brother Freemont came back into the sanctuary smiling his perfect smile. No one spoke as he marched across the room toward his pew. His boots caused the floor to creak beneath the sanctuary carpet. The stained glass at the front of the church lit up and went dark with the whims of the Good Lord.

Pastor Masterson didn't speak of grace. He spoke of a holiness that was earned and flaunted and feared, the kind of good old American godliness that moved beyond the text and past the church fathers through the veins of normal folks who knew when to talk and when to only say "yes sir" and move on with the whole thing. He didn't often speak of hellfire, but most of the congregants seemed to think that he meant to. The others probably couldn't hear much of what he was saying. Brother Freemont nodded as the old man spoke.

"These truly are the days of Elijah," the pastor said. "I expect you people are about tired of me saying that."

Jenn slouched and picked at the dirt that, despite her shower, remained beneath her fingernails. The pastor continued between whispers and shouts. At times he crouched on the floor near the pulpit and then jumped into the air as if his bad leg had been healed by his own profundity. Jenn didn't notice. She thought about eternity. Forever in any one place was hell, she thought, be it flaming lakes or streets of gold. She felt nauseated from time to time, and her spine shook hot at the base of her neck. She wondered if Ava had found eternity. Then she let the thought rush through her like a river she'd crossed on her own way toward forever. The pastor jumped again and shouted.

"I'm talking about the end of days, brothers and sisters," he said.

"Amen," said Brother Freemont. "Preach."

Sparse calls from the congregation pushed Pastor Masterson into the fire of his own words. He shouted and waved his arms. Jenn wanted to plug her ears, to have a private word with God.

"Where are the rest of you, church?" the pastor asked. "Do you hear what I'm saying? Jesus Christ is coming back for His people, and the way you're just sitting there, I'm worried that you aren't His people! Now, listen to me, we are on the edge of the end of days. This is vital information to me. What about the rest of you?"

The congregation erupted in a cheer, and Jenn felt the color leave her face. Though she had never fainted before, something deep inside of her told her that she would soon pass out. Her legs shook and then seemed to float away from her body and vanish into a Holy Spirit cloud. Brother Freemont stomped his feet up and down the aisle. The little hair he had left on his head trailed behind him like a banner.

"We are going to be gone in the blink of an eye, every single one of us who loves Jesus," he carried on. "Who's ready to see Jesus?"

The people of the church were upward palms and speaking in foreign tongues as the Spirit enabled them. Jenn stood up along with everybody else. Then dark splotches like sneaking demons filled her vision, and she was lying down between the pews. She could see their scratched oak and stains from worship tears. The old woman in front of her continued to sit. Others gathered around Jenn and thanked the Lord that He had slain her human strength by the power of His Holy Spirit. She shook for a moment on the floor, and the praises around her continued quietly. The pastor carried on with the wrath of a resounding trumpet, though, and the worship from throughout the room seemed to hold up the ceiling. A strange, bitter taste filled Jenn's mouth. She felt her stomach would burst and ran out of the sanctuary and into a bathroom around the corner. There, she could hear the pastor's words, but she could not tell what he was saying.

The stall door was crooked and could not be locked. The toilet bowl was stained brown where the water rose up and swallowed the things that human beings could no longer contain. Jenn sat on the toilet seat. It had no lid. She cried and thought of Ava, begged another ceiling for a moment with the Lord. Outside, the piano began to fill the space between Pastor Masterson's outbursts. His voice took the long route into a song filled with hills and valleys. Jenn could make out the explosions of hallelujahs meant for mountains like Sinai and Hernon, places where God showed up, places far away. She put her fingers deep into her ears and removed them again. The tiring sounds became the whooshing of an ocean she'd never seen.

Before long, the singing stopped, but the piano player's fingers continued to sneak across the keys. The pastor was speaking again, his words calm and broken up by Brother Freemont's audible approval. Jenn imagined the parting of his white teeth preparing the way of the Lord. Another cheer erupted from beyond the bathroom door, and a ceaseless murmur followed it. Jenn flushed the empty toilet.

Outside, her mother was leaning on the back of a pew, talking to another woman who was all white curls and floral perfume. Others talked over firm handshakes and soft hugs throughout the sanctuary. Rita Cavanaugh, the woman talking to Jenn's mother, had a purse strap dangling from both her bony hands as if the purse was all she had left in the world. Jenn tried to listen in on their conversation, but then her mother spotted her.

"There you are," Jenn's mother said. "The Spirit really moved after you left."

"I'm not feeling well, Mom."

The old woman next to her spoke.

"Jennifer, did you know that young lady who went missing after the fire last week?" she asked.

Jenn felt her face might boil off her head and become a puddle on the sanctuary carpet. Her hands began to sweat.

"She was a friend from school," Jenn said. Her voice cut from one syllable to the next and nearly stopped entirely before she could finish the sentence. She was surprised to find that other members of the congregation had known about Ava and still neglected to include her on the prayer list. It seemed that even the most banal trials and tribulations ended up on that list.

"Oh," the woman said, still clutching her purse by the strap, "I'm sorry, dear. I'm sure she'll turn up."

Jenn's mother patted her daughter on the back. Jenn sat down in one of the empty pews.

"I have to wonder what she was up to so late on a school night, though," the woman continued. "Nothing good ever happens that late. She should have been home."

Brother Freemont's singing floated through the church once again. He had his hand at the pastor's back and showed him out of the sanctuary with a refrain. Then he turned to Jenn. He kept singing as he approached her. His gaze started at her feet and stopped short of her eyes.

"How about our God?" he asked, his hand on Jenn's shoulders.

She looked up at him. Her tears dripped onto her dress. Her mother spoke.

"God is good!" she said.

"What's wrong with this young lady here?" Brother Freemont continued. "This is no time for tears."

"She knew that girl with the burned-down trailer," Rita said.

"Is this true?"

Jenn nodded.

"It is a shame they lost her," Brother Freemont said, "but all sin comes with a price. We must remember that, especially in these dark times."

"She's just a little girl," Rita said.

"That don't give her any exemption from the wages of sin."

"What's sin got to do with it?" Jenn asked. She tried to pull herself from Brother Freemont's hand, but it lingered on her shoulder, a stone that would crush her.

"I'm never one to gossip, of course, but her daddy's been a druggie his whole life," he said, looking at Jenn like a wealthy man without a coin to offer beggars. "I guess it was only a matter of time before he got himself killed." Then he sang again. "Sinners, turn, why will ye die?"

"The fire is what killed him, though," Jenn said, her voice rising past the hole in her chest.

"The Lord works in mysterious ways," Brother Freemont said quietly, as if only to her.

With that, he left the women to their conversation. Jenn hardly felt like listening to them. When her mother finally said that it was time for lunch, Rita hobbled away with her purse. The sanctuary was nearly empty. Brother Freemont's voice covered the chatting heads of the remaining worshippers. Jenn thought she saw him smile as he stood alone singing beneath the stained glass.

Chapter 5

The fire rose up out of its pit and licked holes in the night sky, illuminated the gray backs of trees. Those trees saw everything there was to see, but still they were silent, save when the wind tossed them back and forth, when they needed a good clearing. Near the fire, a soft blue light hung over a makeshift porch and a mobile home, a dirt-caked trailer with a bed inside of it. The porch light was caught up in the hungry mouth of the fire, and Charlotte hardly noticed it. She sat next to Will on a dried-out log there in the flickering light. Will fed the fire so that it appeared to burn without consuming. It never grew, but it never shrank much either. Each log could have been the one before it. As the night marched on, the stars overhead turned from piercings in the sides of clouds to honey sparkles in the milky sky.

Charlotte was smoking cigarettes and tossing the butts into the fire when she was done with them. Her skin hung from her cheeks. Her lips were crusty and gathered up in wrinkles. She had her hair in a ponytail. Will occasionally spat chewing tobacco onto the bare earth beside her, and it irritated her, though she didn't look up at him when he did it. She had once been among the court of the homecoming queen in Tyro, Kansas. She'd been royalty. She'd told her daddy back then that she was going to learn to paint like the people in her schoolbooks. Then her old man left town with a teller from the bank. He'd taken the family money too. Charlotte soon decided that dreaming wasn't much use for folks who worked at the pharmacy after school to help pay for TV dinners and costume jewelry, but still, she said she was going to learn to be a teacher at the Kansas State College of Pittsburg. Before long, she was living in Branch Creek instead.

Will was younger than Charlotte by more than a decade. He was probably in his thirties, but he'd never said a number, at least not in front of Charlotte, in the five years since she'd first met him at the front of her trailer, the front of Jim's trailer. He said he made good money selling stuff by the gram, but Charlotte couldn't tell that by the way he looked. Dirty blond hair poked out of the bottom of his cap and covered the chubby parts of his face, the hills that gave way to his chin and his nose. He could have been just about anybody who lived in a trailer behind the Mayes County tree line. When Charlotte sat by him and watched the fire, though, the mystery of the earth turned to smoke in the sky like magic. The crackle and hiss in front of her was about the best song she knew. It didn't matter who he was, as long as he wasn't Jim. Charlotte tapped her foot against the log.

"It's s'posed to get real cold tonight," Will said, breaking the spell.

"I'm not staying here," Charlotte said, though she knew she would stay if she needed to. She would do whatever it took to stay away from Jim. She would cut off her fingers to keep him from sliding a ring back onto them. She'd forget love, forget matrimony, forget the visions of aisles and white dresses and the high-dollar accouterments that separated official weddings from the common law trailer-sharing she'd known since she was twenty. She would let this man take her to bed if it meant that she could choose to leave it when she was done.

The burning wood popped at the bottom of the fire. Charlotte lit another cigarette. A breeze moved over them, and she felt it through her sweatshirt. A tiny forest had sprouted on Will's face in a way that made him look a little grimier than he really was. He ran his hands over the coarse hairs like he was proud of them, like a kid ready to ask his dad for his first razor.

"Want a beer?" he asked.

"I stopped drinking," Charlotte said, though she nearly shook with want. She hoped that Will would not offer again, that he would not offer anything else. Someone had said that it would get easier to stay clean at some point, but it had not gotten easier yet. The past few days had lingered over her for what felt like months. The effects of the comedown had given her plenty of time to worry as she sat with Will in his pickup just a few hours earlier. She had looked back more than once to see if Jim was following them, but he hadn't even been home when she'd left.

"Jim said that you'd gone cold turkey," Will said.

"I didn't know you two talked about me."

Charlotte wondered if Jim ever mentioned bruises or the red skin caused by the *thwack thwack* of his open palms.

"He talks about a whole lot sometimes," Will said.

"Watch what you say."

She thought about her son, something she didn't want to do.

"Jim nearly killed my boy for talking," she said. "The kid still don't come around because of it."

"I'd say your boy doesn't have the chance to go much of anywhere outside the pen," Will said.

Charlotte couldn't remember the last time she saw her son. It had been long before he went and got himself arrested. He'd said on the phone that he was in jail for the things he knew, not the things he did, but Charlotte couldn't figure out how the court could hold him responsible for just knowing things. Either way, she hadn't attended the trial. She'd stayed far away from the sort of information that could send a person to jail. She'd been high with Jim in their trailer instead, hot and skinny and unaware.

She pulled on her cigarette. The smoke from her mouth mingled with the smoke from the fire. If it hadn't been for Jim, her son would have been able to stay at home for as long as he wanted without the fear of God. Maybe he wouldn't have known so much. Then again, if it hadn't been for Jim, she wouldn't have birthed the boy to begin with. She heard the rustling of rabbits and squirrels in the woods behind her. She imagined their tiny feet and noses, the pure things in the dirty trees. She longed for the day when she could wander and scurry and do whatever she'd like, same as those critters and same as the folks who'd never run into people like Jim.

"The boy had a mouth on him," Will said, talking about her son again. "I'd bet he doesn't anymore."

"That's his business."

"It's the state of Kansas's business."

"Missouri," Charlotte said.

"That's right. The 'Show Me State.'" Will took a beer from a cardboard box at his feet and drank from it. When he was done, he made a noise like he'd really enjoyed it, an opened-mouth grunt from a television commercial. "I've got kin in Missouri, and I don't have to show them much of anything. They just believe what I say. I tell them I'm working for a mechanic here and that I've got a real, brick-and-mortar house, and they eat up every word."

Charlotte had a hard time picturing Will with a family. He could have simply appeared in the trailer behind them one day and it would have been all the same to her.

"You talk too much," she said.

"Not like your boy, though."

Charlotte forced a blank space in her mind where her son's face had been, where there had been an orange jumpsuit and a whole lot of hell. It was easy enough to do now. She'd done it for years. She held the cuffs of her sweatshirt and stretched out her arms. She felt like she could fly, like the shirt could turn to feathers. The bottom of the sweatshirt pulled up over her bellybutton. She showed off the white remains of stretched-out mother skin in the gap between the clothes. Charlotte knew Will didn't mind the marks on her body. He had similar skin around his thighs. Another beer or so, and the memory of her belly would likely disappear from his mind altogether like the start of a card trick he'd learned as a child but could never seem to recreate after he'd gone and grown up.

"You really think he'd kill somebody?" he asked.

"My boy?"

Will took another drink and looked plain stupid.

"No, Jim," he said, "the old, wrinkly ball sack you know quite biblically."

"No doubt in my mind," Charlotte said. She'd hardly considered the question. "He'd lock you up and tell you he'd cut your toes off just for reading the wrong books."

"I don't read books."

"Me neither. He thought I did, though."

When Charlotte looked at Will again, she saw the flickering of the fire in his eyes, not the fire itself, but a reflection, a falsification. He wanted to be angry, firm, the way Jim was angry and firm. He had never been the tough one before, not when he was over at Jim's trailer. He had done what he was told without question. He'd come up with jokes and made Charlotte laugh. He'd been wide-eyed when she caught him looking at her while Jim was in the other room.

"You think I could stomp his face into the ground if he tried any of that with you again?" Will asked. His words were filled with the foam and pop of beer spit.

Neither of them talked for a moment, and Charlotte could tell Will was thinking hard about his question. He'd wound himself tight. His forehead was all wrinkles. He hadn't told any jokes when she asked him to drive her away from Jim. He'd found a reason to be tough, to be serious.

"No," she said.

Will tossed his empty beer can into the fire. Then he stood up and picked up another log. He raised it over his head and then flung it onto the fire as if he had no other way to show his might. Embers rose from the ground into the sky before they disappeared. The fire looked about the same as it had when they'd first sat down. Charlotte watched it twist and turn into the night, and then she was tired. She lit another cigarette and wondered when she'd get to sleep next, when it was that she would dream.

"I should head into town," she said. She believed what she was saying, but she knew it wasn't likely that she would head into town that night.

"Stay here and stare at this fire with me 'til we get so tired we can't keep from sleeping," Will said.

Charlotte rolled her eyes.

"You talk too much," she said.

Will unbuttoned his work shirt. Charlotte stood up and felt her pockets for her car keys, for Jim's car keys. She nearly tripped as she stepped over the log and tried to walk away. Will laughed at her. Her pockets were empty except for a pack of cigarettes.

"It's like you forgot I drove you here," Will said.

The soreness in her shoulders worked its way down her back, a reminder that Will's trailer would be better than another night with Jim. She didn't want to think of how that sort of thing would end. She just wanted a ride out of Branch Creek. Will towered over her when he came near.

"Stay," he said.

"Jim will kill you," she told him.

"He won't know," he said, stepping closer. "You aren't with him."

"He says I'm his property."

"You ain't nobody's property."

"You just want me to be *your* property," Charlotte said.

She stood with her arms crossed. Her shoulders were at the edge of trembling. Will was so close to her that she could smell the tang of the beer on him. She wished that her leaving Jim hadn't come with so many promises to herself. She wished she could afford to have something to drink or something to shoot without the self-hate that came after. She remembered what it was like to forget. Then she remembered what it was like to recall things again after forgetting.

"He told me the truth about the Harris boy," she said.

Will laughed and opened another beer. Charlotte frowned.

"Hell, I could tell you what happened to him," Will said. "He owed Jim money and left town because he didn't want to pay it."

"He *couldn't* pay it," Charlotte said. She sat back down on the log and hammered her heel against it again. "Jim told him he had to get out of town, money or no money. He thought Randy Harris was baking in the double-wide he stayed in down by the creek. So, Jim beat Randy's head in with a pipe he kept on the back of the truck, stripped him down and threw his tiny pecker into the creek and came back to empty out the trailer. Jim told the Harrises he'd run Randy out of town for trying to steal from the church. No one ever missed him."

"Someone would have found the body," Will said. He pulled a can of snuff from his back pocket and fingered out a lip's worth. He packed the dip into his mouth.

"Apparently not," Charlotte said, still soured by the thought of Randy's blood staining the rocks down by the creek and the rain then washing it clean. She hadn't been with Jim when Randy died, but she'd seen blood before. She knew that the amount of blood in any given person would likely surprise them if they could see it all spilled out.

"Not every fire is a call for ghost stories," Will said.

Charlotte pulled the last cigarette out of her pack and threw the empty cardboard into the fire, along with the butts and the beer cans and the never-ending firewood. Jim had grown bigger than a man for most folks. He was shadow wrapped in flesh. Will didn't seem to understand that. He likely couldn't imagine all that blood inside Randy. Charlotte watched the fire burning in front of her. Her head swam along the tobacco buzz. She wanted more. She wanted to move past the words she'd said or to laugh like the story about Randy had been a joke. She reached deep inside her stomach for a "gotcha, you fuckin' moron," but it wasn't there. Jim was capable of acting as deputy, judge, and executioner, and it was his God-given right to do so. He kept the town high and floating along the way it was supposed to. Everybody knew that. He was the hands of God, and a God who wasn't feared was hardly any God at all.

"Come on, baby," Will said. He spat his chew back into a beer can. "Enough talk about Jim. Let's go inside and relax a while."

Charlotte snuffed out her last cigarette on the log. She wanted to get high.

"We'll relax for a whole eternity while our bodies rot back there in the trees," she said.

Will stood up and unzipped his pants. Charlotte stayed still on the log.

"You can go on inside or stay out here in the dark," Will said. "Either way, I'm gonna put this fire out."

"You are disgusting," Charlotte said.

She moved away, turned her back to the fire. Will pissed without responding. The urine washed over the flames and made bitter smoke that wafted through the clearing. Charlotte covered her nose with the collar of her sweatshirt. Remnants of sweat made her skin stiff and sticky near her underarms. It was getting late. The night's stars were middle-aged and set in their ways. The torrent of urine became an occasional spatter. Then it stopped entirely.

After Will finished, the fire's glow had all but disappeared, and the artificial light from up by the trailer asserted itself into the night for the worship of insects. The little critters obsessed over the halo and forgot about the broad space around them that had been sufficient for their forefathers. No one spoke for some time. Will took the case of beer up to the porch and set it down outside the trailer door. The cans rolled around and resettled there.

"You really aren't going to take me somewhere to stay tonight, are you?" Charlotte asked. She sighed and patted each of her pockets for her cigarettes out of habit. Then she sighed again when she remembered that she'd finished the pack. "Do you have a cigarette at least? I'll stay a little longer if you'll give me some cigarettes."

Will walked around the back of the trailer, where the truck was parked, and came back with a half-smoked pack of cigarettes. He tossed it to Charlotte. She pulled one out and offered the pack back to him.

"Keep 'em," he said.

She lit the cigarette, and it burned stronger than the barely-glowing fire, all covered in urine. She thought about the deadly trailer fire she'd heard about the week before. She wondered why the man who died hadn't just pissed on it before it got to him. Here, under the thick stars and the black-cloaked moon, man conquered fire despite all its flashy brilliance and orange translucent hurdles, but under the same sky, though maybe it had been cloudy that night, fire conquered man and left him a few sentences in the local newspaper, the same kind of paper that Will had used to start the pit fire before he pissed on it. Life moved around that way.

"Let's go inside," Will said. "We look like a couple of thieves standing out here in the dark."

He walked up the stairs to his makeshift porch and picked up the case of beer. Then he twisted the doorknob and pushed the door open with his hip. Charlotte finished her cigarette and stamped it out. It didn't seem right to throw it on the dying fire. She followed Will inside, where a kitchen was painted green by a fluorescent bulb. The sink was filled with dishes that were stained with cheese and the remnants of casseroles. Flies jumped off the dishes when she entered. They scouted her out before she could shoo them away. The trailer was smaller than Jim's trailer. It reminded her of the little place in the mobile home park where she'd grown up, where her mother had lived before she got sick. If there was a heaven, there were no trailers there.

Will sat down in a recliner in the adjacent room and turned on his television, flipped through a handful of channels. Then he turned it off again. The case of beer was at his feet.

"Ain't ever anything on worth watching," he said.

Charlotte sat on a brown cloth couch across from the recliner. She sank into the cushion and felt the springs beneath her. In the light, she could see that the cigarettes that Will had given her were crinkled and bent as if he'd kept them in his pants pocket. She pulled one out and let it dangle from her mouth. The paper was dry against her lips. She dug a lighter out of her pocket. Will pulled a beer from the case and flipped through a TV Guide.

"Could you do that outside?" he asked, nodding toward the cigarette. "It turns all my shit yellow, makes it stink in here."

He took off his hat and used the bill to scratch the top of his head. His hair was oily near the roots. Charlotte wondered when he'd showered last.

"Any other rules I should know?" she asked.

"Beware the Sasquatch."

"I'll do my best," Charlotte said. She stood up and paused, staring at the floor between them. The day weighed on the tops of her eyes. She ached for a place where she could sleep, where she could be alone in the dark. "Why do you want me around so bad?"

"I liked going to Jim's house when you were up there cooking or sitting there at the table while we ate. We talked a lot back then, even when Jim was right there with us. I was hoping that maybe we could do some more talking now that you've gone away from him, maybe do a little more than talk."

"Jim won't have his hired hands putting their grubby paws in the piggy bank," Charlotte said, her shoulder halfway out the door and into the wild night, "especially the piggy bank where he likes to put his dick. He's really gonna kill you for all this. You have to realize that."

Will's cheeks were red from the beer.

"And still you called me," he said.

Outside, Charlotte pulled the door closed harder than she'd meant to. It shook the trailer behind her. Will shuffled around inside, and the sound of his stirring made its way through the open windows. Charlotte smoked her cigarette and looked around the clearing, trying to ignore the noise. She was unable to see much beyond the end of the porch light. The remnants of the fire were doing their best to light the world back up again, but they were less than a glow at the bottom of the logs where Will's piss hadn't reached. The remnants waited there to die while Charlotte watched from behind a cigarette and wondered if she would still be up to see the sunrise. Then there was movement on the other side of trees.

The deep-throated cough of a machine sounded from the nearby county road. Charlotte let a puff of smoke out over her head, sure that the sound only meant that somebody was making their way home from the bar. Then the growling moved closer, and she saw the blinking eyes of headlights that wound their way through the trees. Her lips parted and hung half-open in the dark. The growl turned to a stutter. She saw the old pickup truck pull into the clearing. It bounced and whirled against the night as if it would fall to pieces when it slowed. The pickup did not belong to Jim, but there was a good chance that the driver did.

Charlotte put out her cigarette and squatted down at the far side of the trailer in the dark before the pickup could pull around to where she had been standing. The fire residue hardly glowed at all. The truck writhed along the mowed-down path that led up to the makeshift porch where the light was still hanging and shining with all its meager might. Charlotte resisted the urge to peek out from behind the trailer and look at the pickup when it stopped. The driver called out with the hoarse voice of somebody who was in need, of somebody who saw the short ends of a forked road. An aluminum door slammed back against the truck's frame before the engine could quiet. Footsteps clopped their way to the trailer. The steps did not sound like Jim's slow, spaced thumping. They were sprawling and disjointed feet that wandered. An unseen fist knocked.

"It ain't locked, dummy," Will laughed from inside.

The door opened, and the laughing stopped. The footsteps shuffled into the kitchen. The door clattered shut. Charlotte heard Will speak again as his voice found its way over the chirping frogs and insects. She could tell that he was putting on his serious face again, the face he'd worn when he wanted to feel like Jim.

"Well, shit, Tom," he said. "I told you to never just show up here without a warning. I said I wasn't gonna be available this week. What are you fuckin' doing here?"

"I'm sorry," the driver's voice croaked as if it had been pulled thin between two points. Charlotte was surprised that she didn't recognize its flimsy tearing. "I'm all out," the voice said, "and I wasn't about to bother Jim."

"But you'll bother me?" Will asked.

Both voices paused. Charlotte could hear her own breathing as if someone else were panting beside her. She wondered if her lungs were louder than they had been back in high school, before she'd started smoking. She was certain that if she held her breath, her chest would burst. She didn't dare imagine how she would have felt if Jim had been in the truck.

"I just need a little bit, buddy," Tom's croaking voice began again. "What can fifty bucks get me?"

"I'll sell you half a gram," Will said. Charlotte pictured him with a gun. Jim always kept a gun nearby when he was selling.

"Shit," Tom said, "I can almost get three-quarters for that."

"You're lucky I don't just kill you for coming into my home uninvited. Now, I'll sell you half a gram, you'll get the hell out, and I won't ever see you here again unless I've called or written to you otherwise. You hear me?"

Charlotte didn't hear a response, but she figured the man must have indicated that he understood what Will was saying, because she heard the sound of drawers opening and closing, the sound of Ziploc baggies. Then the wild footsteps of the disjointed man made their way out onto the porch again. The pickup door closed, and the engine started back up with its sputtering.

The man sped away the same way he had come. Charlotte watched the taillights quiver and then disappear into the trees. She sighed as the weight of her fear left her sore shoulders. In the west, a shooting star urged her to go somewhere, but she could not guess where. There was nothing beyond the trees on either side of the clearing, nowhere to sleep but a messy bed inside the trailer. The low sky was quiet in the space where the pickup had been. The trees were still and waiting for something to happen. Charlotte took out another cigarette and wanted a pick-me-up, one last fix or a convincing bout of romance. Either way, Will would likely have to do.

Chapter 6

Despite his best efforts, Sheriff Douglas Taylor again stood alone in front of reporters and their photographers. He passed a sheet of paper back and forth between his hands. The notes on it were sloppy, crooked architecture through pen ink curls. People had begun to show up outside the Mayes County Sheriff's Office before 8:00 a.m. They had heard that he was finally ready to go on record about the missing girl. They had pounded on the office doors. When Barbara called to ask what he wanted for lunch, she told the sheriff he'd have to tell those people something worth reporting or else they'd never let him leave.

"It doesn't matter either way," he said, and he wasn't sure if he'd meant the meal or the media.

Then Sheriff Taylor had another call, and he scribbled down his notes like a courtroom stenographer or an old king's scribe, a recorder of words that were not his own. When he had been first elected sheriff, he had felt confident in his words. He had stood out in front of the podium on election night and made jokes about the county commissioners and their wives. He had still been the hero deputy, but with a new title and a bright future. That night, he'd been defined by the things he would do in the unmarked days on his calendar. Now, he was reduced to reading Jim's lies, to hiding behind the podium and paper notes. Anything that was important to Sheriff Taylor had already happened, save the prospect of his retirement, his coming days of idleness that would free him from meth and crime and the thoughts of all those reporters with their station jackets and their deadlines.

He found his way into an unused interrogation room where deputies had pulled plastic chairs into rows for the news conference. A woman seemed out of place in the front row. Her face curled from around her stagnant eyes, pits that Sheriff Taylor feared falling into, black holes circled with the soil from freshly-broken cemetery lawns. He'd seen eyes like them before. They belonged to the sort of person who searched for something they knew they'd never find. She hardly seemed to breathe as she waited for the sheriff to speak. She was the type of woman worth being afraid of.

Sheriff Taylor tried his best to avoid her gaze when he stepped behind the podium, but she stared at him while the rest of the room shuffled about. Nearly everyone else was bent-over and working to get the best shot or sound bite. The woman didn't appear to have any way of taking notes or pictures. The weather had cooled since the last press conference, but still, the tiny room soaked up the heat from the curious bodies until no cool space remained. Sweat was already soaking through Sheriff Taylor's undershirt. He checked his watch. The room's shuffling died down to a murmur.

"Alright, people, it's time to get started," he said, his eyes crossing the paper in careful strides. "On Saturday before last at about 23:00 hours, a fire destroyed a mobile home off East 4150 Road near Branch Creek. Firefighters were able to knock it down within about half an hour, but the home was destroyed by the flames. The fire marshal determined that the accidental fire was caused by faulty wiring in the home."

The sheriff went on with his list of facts, the sterile points at the intersections of webs. There were names, though the reporters already knew them. A man was called Louis Springtree. Firefighters had found him all burned up in the fire. He had a teenage child, but they didn't find her at the scene. That was cause for an investigation. The Oklahoma Highway Patrol and the Branch Creek Police Department would help the Mayes County Sheriff's Office locate her. These were all simple facts. Everyone in that room knew these facts to some degree or another. They didn't need explaining. They were instead what would pass for explanations, rubber stamps on week-old rumors. The sheriff wanted to make everyone happy, or perhaps it was more that he wanted to keep everyone from becoming unhappy with him. The wrong person's unhappiness would interfere with his dignified departure or make it impossible to find peace in his retirement. It would dissolve the carrot that hung from the string before him.

"Now, the teen's disappearance, like the other factors in the sad but strange incident, does not appear to be suspicious at this time," he said. "Even still, we are continuing to search the area for the teen to ensure that she is safe."

He found the end of his list. There would be no more facts, no name or description for the missing girl. Despite the sweat that pooled elsewhere, the sheriff's palms were dry, and he hated the way they felt against his paper notes. He'd made it clear that she wasn't in danger, hadn't he? Was there any reason to ask more of him? The room was all nods and scratching pencil tips.

"Any questions?" Sheriff Taylor asked.

He heard the smacking noise of his tongue against his dry mouth as the question popped out of him. He waited in the air behind the final word. Then hands shot up across the room. The middle-aged woman in the front row sat and stared. She chewed on the inside of her lip and put her hand up with the others. Sheriff Taylor looked past her and chose a more familiar hand toward the back, one that belonged to the sports reporter from the Branch Creek Republican whom he'd golfed with more than once.

"Did you say that you had the girl's name?" the sports reporter asked.

The sheriff would have smiled if he didn't think the other reporters were looking for a hole in him. No one smiled when they talked about the hardships of children. He knew that, the reporters knew that, and the folks at home would surely know that too.

"No, Ron, I didn't say that we had a name," Sheriff Taylor said. "It doesn't appear necessary that I release that information at this time."

His mind felt like it was stuck on the flapping wings of bees or hummingbirds, the quick-moving flapping that jumped from place to place. He tried to focus. Hands stayed high above the heads of the curious. He imagined the lunch he'd have that afternoon with Barbara, reheated goulash and corn, almost always corn. He didn't think he'd ever grow tired of corn.

"You, on the left," he said, pointing to a man with a pen behind his ear and glasses pulled low on his nose.

"Do I have this right?" the man asked. He must have been new to the area. His voice sounded more like Connecticut pine than Oklahoma bluegrass. "You said a man died in the home, and a teenager, I'd assume a girl by the way you said 'she' earlier, is missing, but there isn't any reason for you to believe it's suspicious?"

"Yes sir," the sheriff said. He no longer had to remind himself not to smile.

"Does that strike you as strange?"

"Strange, sure, but not suspicious."

"I don't understand what you're saying. A child is missing, and you aren't worried?"

Sheriff Taylor folded his arms. He'd read the list. He'd given the facts. Now, this hotshot was gonna try to milk more out of him, to force him open.

"We don't have any reason to think she's really missing, necessarily," the sheriff said. "We just know she wasn't at home when the fire broke out."

"Don't you think the two incidents could be connected?" asked the reporter.

"I don't have any reason to at this point, but I haven't ruled it out either."

"And there's no chance of arson?"

"Not according to the fire marshal."

Sheriff Taylor wondered if the reporter had been at all briefed on the situation before his boss in Tulsa put him in a van and shipped him to the sheriff's office. Surely all this had been said by someone at the scene. He'd been assured that someone would have said all this at the scene.

"Do you have any leads as to where she may be?" the reporter persisted.

"I do not have any public leads as to where she may be," the sheriff said. He leaned against the podium, his face hot and his stomach growling. "Now, I permitted you a question, but we don't have time for a full-on interview. I've got lunch waiting on me, and I'm sure you'd like to eat a bite, yourself. So, I'm going to let you know that I'm not releasing anything else, answer a couple more questions, and then go on my way."

"Do you think you're taking this seriously enough?" a voice came from among the shifting bodies and their raised hands.

The sheriff sighed and hoped that no one had noticed. His breath seemed to force the thinking parts of his brain out of the top of his head. In the space where there was supposed to be thinking, there were sheets of fog and thunderbolts, an explosion that was out in the world before it was realized.

"I could easily just ignore that," he said, "seeing as you don't have the decency to wait your turn like everybody else here, but instead I'm gonna tell you that we are doing everything we can to make sure that this is handled properly. There's no need to get anyone worked up and scared about a situation when we don't know all the facts. Our investigation simply has not yielded any results that would lead us to believe that we should be alarmed. I'm not gonna say anymore about it. If you don't think we are handling this, or any other investigation, with enough tender love and care, then I'd highly encourage you to run for my office at the end of my term. In the meantime, we are doing what needs to be done as it needs to be done."

A groan moved through the room. It stifled the hacks of single-syllable laughter from people like Ron, the good ones. The sheriff's head slowed then. He caught his breath. The eerie woman in the front row continued to chew her lip. She still had a hand in the air. Her other arm was over her head, and she gripped the raised hand tightly like a high school student desperate for extra credit. Sheriff Taylor carefully worked his gaze away from her and called on someone else, a reporter whose hand was inadvertently in front of her cameraman's face and, at points, in front of his camera too.

"When can we expect another update?" she asked.

"That would depend on when we have new information," Sheriff Taylor said, happy to take the sort of question that naturally segued to his ending the conference. "If we find out that this girl is staying with a friend or a family member tonight, for instance, I will alert each and every one of you. If we don't learn anything new, then I don't think I'd call you back here to stand around and say the same things over and over. Does that make sense?"

The woman nodded, and Sheriff Taylor was relieved to see more than one reporter close their notebooks. He had made it through, and he hadn't said much more than he'd meant to say, than what was on Jim's list.

"Anyhow, I'm done here," he said. "I will see you people soon, I'm sure."

Sheriff Taylor left the room alone. He headed toward his office to grab his keys and slip out back to go see his wife, thinking again of corn and of goulash. Reporter voices turned to a storm that washed the walls of the sheriff's office behind him. He ignored the noise on his way out the back door and left the remnants of the news conference inside as the door fell to its resting place.

Outside, he saw the woman from the front row walking circles by herself in the parking lot. She wore her hands on her face like a mask except when she occasionally waved them around her head. The sheriff thought she might have been talking to herself. He looked down at his feet as he tried to pass the area where she was walking. She saw him, though. Her shoes clapped against the asphalt as she ran toward him.

"Sheriff," she said, "what the hell were you doing back there?"

He acted as if he didn't hear her, but soon she was standing beside him. She looked older up close than she had sitting in the news conference. Her lipstick stained the skin around the borders of her lips. The sheriff kept walking to the truck.

"My name is Gail Adams," the woman said. "I'm the aunt of the missing girl you were just talking about."

She had made him uncomfortable during the press conference, had caused him to lose track of his thoughts and to flirt with the idea of fear. Out in the parking lot, though, this woman, *Gail*, became a simple nuisance. She was a problem to be solved or ignored. If the sheriff acted quickly, he could keep from letting her deeper into his thoughts. He tried to dismiss the woman with his words before his mind would latch on to the possibilities of harm that she would bring to him and, in turn, to Mayes County.

"You can leave a report inside for the woman at the front desk with any information you may have about her whereabouts," Sheriff Taylor said, his finger pointing toward the building behind him, but he kept his thoughts on the kitchen table full of food back home, his wife in an apron. "We'll look into it immediately."

"Well shit, sheriff," Gail said. "I'm sure you know everything that I know, but I'm not sure why you didn't say anything about the gunshots back there. The media need to know about the gunshots."

"What did you say?"

The sheriff slowed for a moment. Then he remembered the list of facts, his loyalty to the facts, and started toward the truck again. Gail trotted up beside him. He kept his cards tight near his stomach, and he didn't look into her eyes. He wondered if she noticed that, his absent stare at the pickup truck.

"The gunshots that killed Ava's father," Gail said.

The sheriff spoke quietly. He let his words fall out of his face more than he spoke them.

"Gunshots didn't kill that man," he said. "He burned up in the fire. I just told you that."

"That's not true. You have no place to hurt this family more by telling no-good lies. Don't be part of no cover-up. Be the hero this girl needs."

The sheriff wished she hadn't used that word, hadn't said "hero." Other folks had already given him that word nearly twenty years before. Who was this woman to take it away and try to sell it back to him? He felt his heart racing and tried to drown it out with his voice.

"I don't have time for conspiracy theories," he said, shaking his head.

"Your own deputy told me."

The sheriff stopped walking. He hoped the woman couldn't see his jumping heart, the gnashing teeth he hid with wrinkled lips. If a deputy was leaking information to the public, it wouldn't be long before Jim found out.

"The one with the lisp," Gail said, "the belly, the dark hair, and the lisp."

"Ain't a deputy on my staff with a lisp," the sheriff said. He walked faster, pulling his body forward, away from the woman, saving the open hole in himself from her devilish eyes. No one at the sheriff's office had a lisp, but almost everyone had a belly and dark hair. "If you need any additional assistance, you can hike your little ass back to the front counter and fill out a report."

The sheriff reached his truck and grabbed the door handle. Gail was a few steps behind him. She stomped on the pavement. Her shoulders drooped forward, and her chin shook like she had trouble keeping her teeth together. Sheriff Taylor wondered if she'd been using. She stomped again and put her hands together as if praying to the sheriff, as if she had anything she could give him as an offering.

"That girl is missing, and you're out here covering up the truth," she said.

The storm in the sheriff's head fired off again.

"I'm doing my job the best I can," he said, "same as I have since I was first elected in '84."

"You ain't shit."

"I'm gonna pretend I didn't hear that," the sheriff grunted. He was only a quick motion from the safety of the pickup truck. "Are you from around here ma'am?"

"Rogers County."

"Well, you aren't in Rogers County right now. You're in my county, where I'm doing my very best to investigate the very situation you keep going on about. What did you say your name was?"

"Gail. Gail Adams."

The sheriff took note of the name and considered calling Rogers County for her records.

"Of course. So, Miss Gail Adams, do yourself a favor, go inside that office, talk to the lady behind the desk, fill out a report, and, for Christ's sake, have a good day."

He slammed the door to the pickup truck. Gail stood the same way she'd sat at the news conference, like she was holding within her body a fire or a flood that could kill the whole of creation, at least everything living in northeastern Oklahoma. The sheriff looked away from her as he backed out of the space. She was still standing there, staring at him as he turned out of the lot. She had found her way into his head. Though he couldn't see them, he knew her eyes were ready to swallow him, ready to shake the hell out of him.

★★★

The pickup wavered like the brown and yellow leaves that worked their ways off the trees and into the ditches on either side of the road, into the yards, over the grass. The sheriff put the confrontation in the parking lot out of his mind. He waved at the drivers that passed him, the president of the bank and an old boy he'd arrested two weekends in a row for pissing all over the side of the bank. They waved back and kept on. The town of Pryor faded away in blocks of vinyl siding and concrete and gave way to fields where poor farmers had bailed their hay during the summer months. Cows dotted the fields.

Barbara had parked in the garage, as she often did on days when she returned from neighborhood club meetings with some of the other women who lived between the edge of town and the county line. She was washing her hands when Sheriff Taylor came inside. She washed them often, but the sheriff didn't know why. He didn't figure she could dirty them much. Regardless, he felt safe when he saw the quiet concentration in her face, as he watched her scrub at her fingers in the sink.

"I'm home," he said.

The inside of the house smelled like dirty sheets and vegetables. Barbara had put his lunch on a paper plate and left the plate on the dining room table. He passed through the kitchen, past the tiny Massey Ferguson tractor on the top of the refrigerator and the pictures of other people's grandkids, and sat down to eat. The room was messy enough to feel like home and clean enough for company if Barbara lit a candle. She stood at the sink, wiping her hands on a towel. A stuffed cow smiled at him from the bar separating the kitchen from the rest of the house. Sheriff Taylor picked up his plate and began to eat without saying anything else. Barbara leaned against the bar and watched him.

"You're later than I expected," Barbara said, "but club ran late too, so it's probably for the best."

The club meetings often ran late. The older ladies got to telling stories and handing out leftovers as if the monthly meetings were the only opportunities left for them to use their Tupperware and their long-term memories. Sheriff Taylor didn't mind when Barbara was out. He could put something in the microwave every now and again if she wasn't home when he arrived for lunch. He was glad when she got dressed and left the house at all. It wasn't right for the sheriff's wife to be such a recluse.

Perhaps the couple's childlessness had kept Barbara content to spend her days at home. She never appeared to be trapped there like other women who spent their waking moments following behind soiled diapers and whatever it was that came after soiled diapers. Barbara's time in the house was truly her own, just so long as the sheriff had space to recover from keeping the whole of Mayes County in line. Barbara and the sheriff had not, in their 35 years of marriage, had any sort of dinner table discussion about eschewing gender roles or feminism. They'd just gone about their lives as probably any other barren couple would have. As he grew older, the sheriff hardly wanted much more than three square meals. He'd never minded soiled clothes or unvacuumed carpets, just so long as he couldn't feel dirt or cat litter particles through his socks.

"This angry aunt from out of town had me tied up after the reporters left," Sheriff Taylor said.

"There you go, chasing your wild women."

When he was at home, the sheriff could smile just as much as he liked, but he didn't smile.

"I wouldn't chase after this one," he said.

He grunted out a pauper's laugh, though he was still unsmiling. Barbara toyed with a strand of her hair like a girl. Her hair was once long and blonde, but now it was graying in streaks beneath coats of dye. It barely brushed her shoulders.

"What did this aunt want?" she asked. "Whose aunt was she?"

"She's related to that missing Branch Creek girl. We had the conference about her this morning, told everyone that we're looking for her, but we aren't too worried."

"Well, that's good." Barbara took a cloudy glass of water out of the refrigerator and drank from it. "Where do you think the girl is?"

The sheriff thought back to the list, relied on assumptions that came with reading it.

"Hell, I don't know," he said. "Maybe with a friend."

"You think so? Did she start the fire?"

Though even the simplest questions during the press conference had turned circles in the sheriff's gut, he did not mind his wife's prying. Barbara was tender when she spoke, was clever, wrapping her voice in velvet and silk.

"The fire marshal said it was electric, so we're going to say it was electric," he said.

"What do you think?"

"It doesn't matter what anyone thinks," the sheriff said, clearing his plate. "That guy's dead and gone. Seems to me he was a druggie, so we aren't missing out on a whole lot. The girl obviously doesn't care too much."

"You don't think she's in danger?"

At once, the sheriff felt the urge to keep his breathing steady, but the tricks from the news conference wouldn't work here. Barbara would notice if his heart started acting up again at the whims of his conscience. He took another bite to bide some time. He waited to speak again until after he swallowed.

"I don't have any reason to think that," he said.

He hated lying to his wife.

"Girls don't go missing around here too often, though," Barbara said. Her gaze fell to her own feet then, and the sheriff knew she'd caught him in his lie.

He wanted to believe his list of facts, to will himself ignorant for even a few seconds, but Barbara demanded more than handwritten bullet points on a sheet of printer paper. So, he said what he thought someone clever would have said.

"If she doesn't pop up in another day or two," he said, "I'll get worried. Six, seven days isn't enough time to get too wound up. I don't think she has other family here, so, other than the woman I talked to earlier, no one seems real worried about her. She's just a kid being a kid somewhere. She'll come around." He stood up, leaving the paper plate on the table. "I'd better get back."

Barbara circled the table to pick up the empty plate. She didn't look him in the eye. The sheriff's heartbeat became a shaking, the tiny tremors of aftershock.

"Well, I love you," Barbara said.

The sheriff kissed her on the cheek as he passed her. He tried to offer her a smile over his shoulder on his way out, but he could only muster a half-opened mouth. Barbara possessed a silent power that was able to send him to ribbons, and he couldn't imagine living without that. He thought it beautiful, the way other men probably didn't find their wives beautiful until they had gone away for some reason or another. She didn't even have to say it out loud, but he knew that she didn't believe half his bullshit. Still, she trusted him, at least, kept her suspicions to herself. That's why he loved her. He paused at the door and heard her drop his plate into the trash. The plastic liner swished, a reminder of the demure, shared existence he'd grown so fond of. Then he was out the door and in the truck. He felt the roar of the engine and imagined the house quiet again. It was safe there when things were quiet.

★★★

Sheriff Taylor didn't tell anyone that he returned from lunch. He sat in his office alone, digesting. The room was dark under the cover of closed blinds and clouds that ate up the sun and spat it back out again. He saw a jostled pile of papers on his desk, a mental ski slope that would have to wait for another day. Outside the office, the roar of the reporters had quieted down to the purr of a normal afternoon. The sheriff put his head in one hand and tapped a pen against his desk with the other. The phone rang. Its circular whirring drove him to answer.

"Are you going to tell those reporters about the gunshots?"

The woman's voice sounded like her mouth was still shaking. The sheriff felt his own face turn red.

"I don't know what you're talking about, Gail," he said.

"I'm going to the media."

Sheriff Taylor was careful to make sure his words fell in line before he spoke them. The blood moved through his arms in discernible hops.

"The media already knows everything they need to know," he said.

"They don't know about the gunshots. That man was murdered. His daughter probably too. They were my family. I ain't gonna sit back and let this go."

He wanted to laugh at the woman. His face was upturned and wide, incredulous, sweating. The warm and twisting air of panic, of survival, surrounded him. He wondered how hard he would have to slam the phone against the desk for it to break. Then he returned to the list, the points that kept him at arm's length from danger.

"You know that's not the case," he said. "I've released all the information we are releasing at this time. It's best you leave this be and stop bothering me so I can figure out where that girl is. You're slowing up the whole operation, here."

"I'm going to the media." Gail repeated.

The sheriff stood up behind his desk. His voice became a sharp whisper, a knife intended for a throat.

"Like hell you are," he said. "I've been here for fifteen years. They won't believe a damn thing you have to say."

The phone clicked, and the woman's wavering voice was gone. The pumping in Sheriff Taylor's chest gave way to indigestion. He turned on the overhead light and felt like he was somewhere entirely different from the place that the woman had called just moments before. The sweat was sticky on his face. He picked up his phone again and dialed the front desk.

"Donna," he said, "if anyone else calls about that missing girl, will you do me a favor and tell them I'm out investigating that very case and write down whatever it is they want to tell me? Also, do we have any Tums up there? Can you bring them to me? Thank you, hon."

Chapter 7

No one else was talking in the pizza shop. Half-eaten pies lay under heat lamps near a sign that read "dine-in only." Bits of salad, the iceberg lettuce, cherry tomatoes, croutons, cheese, and strips of raw onions, filled a salad bar. The shop offered French and ranch dressings in squeezable plastic bottles that were chilled in a tub of ice. Jenn and Scribbles were sitting across from each other in a red leather booth with a stack of plates between them. Pizza crusts covered the top plate, because Jenn had heard that she should be careful about eating them, for her health's sake. She sopped up the grease from an uneaten slice with a napkin.

"Sometimes, I think Ava's not coming back," she said. They talked like that in the days after their friend disappeared, occasionally breaking up their usual conversation about classmates and about trade school programs and about recent television reports of presidential blowjobs to remind one another of the empty space in the booth next to them. They didn't need to say anything at all, though. The spaces that Ava had filled were plenty loud in their missing her. She prodded them more in her absence than she had in her presence.

"The cops are gonna find her," Scribbles said, his words dense as he forced them around one of Jenn's leftover pizza crusts. "I saw them talking about it on TV."

Jenn wanted to believe him. She wanted to hear Ava's voice thick with profanity and bad ideas. She wanted to see her sitting on her knees in the booth and leaning on her elbows as she toddled along the line between speaking and yelling about something that would not at all matter in the next few minutes, some minutiae that called for loudness before it was forgotten.

"Since when are you the shining light here?" Jenn asked.

Scribbles finished chewing and went to the pizza bar to fill a new plate without answering. Shirley, the shop owner, a round woman in a tie-dye shirt, rested her elbows on the counter at the back of the room.

"You've got fifteen minutes before the buffet ends," she said, her throat filled with tar and phlegm. "Do you want me to bring out another pie?"

"Do you have pepperoni?" Scribbles asked.

"I can make one."

Scribbles returned to the table. Jenn wondered how he was able to continue through life and lunch buffet as if the world were just as full as it had been the week before, when Ava was still showing up for lunch and school and meetups at his house.

"She's gonna come back," he said as if reading her thoughts.

He began eating again. Jenn sat still with her half-eaten slice. Her hands pulled at a napkin in her lap as if they were separate from her, and she stared down at them to watch, a spectator of her own body. She could hear the ticking of the clock from the wall above the counter. A calendar with the high school football schedule was tacked up beneath the clock. Scribbles's shoulder was a thick fuzz in the foreground as her gaze found the calendar. Her brain could make nothing of it. To her wandering eyes, it was just a blob of white and red against the wall. The counter was also unformed and made up of shapes and colors, useless objects without assignments or associations. They wobbled from across the room as backdrop colors for the spot where Ava was supposed to be sitting. Jenn shook her head and could make out the calendar's form for a moment. She thought of the football games that Ava would miss, the empty bleacher space. Then the room went hazy again. Jenn spoke the automatic words of someone talking just to stay out of her head.

"How much of that are you gonna eat?" she asked.

"Until I'm full," Scribbles said.

The plate in front of him was already nearly empty. Jenn wanted to ask if he had eaten since she last saw him. Part of her wished he had left town with his parents, but that part of her melted away against the thought of the afternoons she would have had to spend by herself. The kid shouldn't have to live alone, though, she thought. Shirley came out with a pan of pepperoni pizza and put it on the buffet.

"Once that's gone, then that's it for today," Shirley said. The objects throughout the room returned to their solid forms at the sound of her voice. Her hair was half-standing around her head, sticky from her time in the kitchen.

Scribbles nodded. His mouth was full. Jenn offered up a quarter-smile. Ava would have tried to get Scribbles to wrap pizza in napkins and carry it out in his pockets to eat after school, and he would have filled up his baggy pockets until Shirley caught him and threatened again to ban him from the restaurant. Ava had a way of getting Scribbles to try anything that way, and she never got into any trouble over it. She was never the one left with pockets soaked in pizza grease.

Scribbles pushed his empty plate next to the stack.

"Jenn? Did you hear me?" he asked.

She realized that he was talking to her.

"Sorry," she said, "I was zoned out. What did you say?"

"I said that we should leave."

"She just brought that pizza out for you."

"I'm full. I can't help it."

Shirley was back behind the counter and looking out over the nearly-empty restaurant. Scribbles stood up and hurried to the entrance. Jenn followed behind him. Her tipping toes were delicate against the checkered tile floor. Before they could reach the door, though, Shirley called out.

"Aren't you gonna eat any of this?" she asked, gesturing toward the fresh pizza.

Jenn's stomach turned. She had hoped the woman wouldn't notice their leaving.

"I made it just for you," Shirley continued. "You said you wanted it."

"We've really gotta go," Jenn said, pushing Scribbles past the "dine-in only" sign at the end of the buffet and out the door. She felt as though she'd been caught stealing, but she wasn't sure what it was she had stolen. In fact, they hadn't even tried to take the extra pizza.

Outside, Scribbles seemed like he could have been anywhere but Branch Creek. He appeared to float in circles on the ground without noticing that the world was still spinning. Maybe he was thinking of how to spend the rest of the afternoon.

"Let's go back to my place," he said.

"Look at you, taking initiative."

"Well, Ava isn't here to make the plans."

Jenn couldn't bring herself to verbally acknowledge what Scribbles had said. Instead, her feet spoke for her with the sounds of rubber on pavement, scratches and stutters that found their way past her mouth's silence as they shuffled down the sidewalk toward Scribbles's house. They took the long way and walked along the railroad tracks past the old granary, the way they used to when they were waiting for Ava to pilfer beer from her dad. The autumn air felt nice against Jenn's skin, neither warm nor cold. She decided that if it hadn't been for the occasional chilly breeze, she would simply dissolve in the perfect temperatures, her essence bleeding through the pores in her skin and becoming lost in the open air.

They turned into Scribbles's neighborhood, the place where the houses slouched and couldn't close their window eyelids on account of scrap wood planks that were nailed across them. Scribbles's house was on the same block as an old church where the Black citizens of Branch Creek had gone to services in the sixties, before the white working poor sent them packing for Tulsa or Arkansas. By the time Jenn was born, the church building was folding over onto itself, the home of ghost stories and legends told by teenagers to their younger siblings. Someone had tried to burn it down once, and the shadow from the ancient fire grew out of the old building like a mouth that would, at some point, swallow up the whole town. At least, that's how Jenn saw it.

She waited in the empty street as Scribbles tossed old grocery store flyers from his mailbox into the ditch that ran along the front of his house. She watched him flip through a stack of weeks-old mail and then hold an envelope up over his head.

"I'll live for another month," he said.

"What?" Jenn asked.

"My dad sent the rent money. He was saying he didn't know if it'd still work out, but here it is!"

Scribbles slapped Jenn's shoulder with the envelope as they went inside and sat on the couch. They kicked their shoes off onto the floor. Jenn picked up an empty ramen noodle wrapper with her feet, brought it to her hands, and threw it at him. The breeze blew in through the open window, and Jenn didn't like the way it felt on her shoulders. She called herself a "summer girl." Soon, the world would cool and cool until she could no longer imagine how nice the weather had once been, and only then would it warm back up again. Scribbles tore open the envelope from his dad, and neither of them talked. Jenn wondered if Ava realized that her friends were here waiting for her, waiting to help her mourn her funeral-less daddy or laugh off the whole thing if that's what she wanted, waiting to have something new to talk about. Scribbles grunted out loud like something had crawled up his throat and needed a good reason to leave. He flipped the letter onto the floor and knocked over the box fan from beside the couch. Then he was on his feet.

"Son of a bitch," he said, his mouth turned down.

He kicked the wall beneath the window. When he pulled his bare foot back for a second kick, Jenn saw that he'd made a dent in the sheet rock. Her eyes became the searchlights of rescue crews. The dent grew as he kicked it again. Jenn was behind him before she understood what was happening. Her arms were around his waist. She was pulling him away from the wall. She fell back onto the floor, and he fell down with her. He was writhing around, trying to stand up again. Jenn was surprised at how much force had come from his frame, from a body that could have been formed from fiberglass and balls of cotton.

"Scribbles, Scribbles, Matthew, Jesus Christ, stop it," she panted.

Scribbles pushed her away and stood up. The letter from his dad was in his hand again.

"Can you believe this shit?" he asked. "Can you believe this fucking shit?"

He pushed the letter against Jenn's chest. She took it from him, and he yanked at the hair above his temples with both his hands. The words on the paper were handwritten in pencil, the writing utensil of choice for children and those unsure of what they wanted to say. Jenn took her time working through the slim cursive script as she read.

Hey Buddy,

I'm moving again! This gal I met wants me to come stay with her in Texas. I know that must sound like a sin to you, a good man like me sharing yard ends with Texans, but they say when you've found one good to you, do the work to keep her. I wish I had done that with your mama. There's plenty of oil work in Texas, and I'm sure with my experience I will be out in the field in no time, but I'm not going to be able to send you any cash for a little bit. You're a man now. I know you'll make me proud. You'll make enough money for the rent before you even know it. They gotta pay you more than five dollars an hour for any job these days. You'll have it easier than I ever did. I'll write to you again once I've settled down a little bit.

Love,

Your Dad

Jenn looked up from the letter at Scribbles. He was pacing the floor and muttering to himself. His face looked as if it had been sunburned.

"I'm sorry kid," Jenn said.

"I'm gonna be homeless."

"No you won't," Jenn said. She put her hand on his shoulder. His body was sharp and full of the leftover anger he hadn't spent on the wall.

"You don't know what you're talking about," he said. "I have to make money. I have to pay rent."

Jenn wanted to be the dam that kept him from pouring out all over the floor. The overflowing anger reminded her of the way he'd cried after the interview with the deputies. She wished it would only fall from his eyes and onto her shirt the way his scared tears had. She wanted to keep him from further violence.

"We can go apply for jobs," she said.

"Where? The dollar store? You expect me to spend all day ringing out potato chips?"

"What's wrong with the dollar store?" Jenn asked. She pulled her hand away from Scribbles. His angry words were like deep-digging shovels that only displaced and that could never refill the holes they made. "My mom works at the dollar store."

Scribbles began to kick at the wall again, but his breath fell behind his will. He folded into a seated position on the floor. He shook in spite of his dry eyes.

"We have to make it through this," Jenn said. "Think of Ava."

"Oh, come on. Do you really think we will ever see her again?"

"You said she was coming back. . . ."

"I'm nineteen years old. I don't know anything," Scribbles said. His face turned flat in front of Jenn, a two-dimensional face from TV. The room disappeared into the space between his eyelashes. He was a distant object, and then he was a god of anger. The room was silent before him, the breeze hesitant as he exhaled. "I'm gonna be homeless."

"I won't let that happen, kid."

Jenn sat down by Scribbles on the floor. He stopped trembling. She traced the alphabet on his back. His skin was hot to the touch, even through his t-shirt. He didn't seem to notice her hands.

"You can stay with me," she said. "We have a couch. I'll take care of you."

"I don't want that. I just want everything to stay the way it's been."

"Me too, Scribbles. Me too."

The two sat together on the floor, unmoving. The breeze occasionally reached back in through the window to cool their bodies. Scribbles sniffed and swallowed the thick, sticky swallow of seasonal allergies. His cheeks began to lighten again. Jenn stood up and looked out the window. She leaned her elbows on the sill and put her head in her hands.

"Promise me you won't go anywhere," she said. "I need to know that I won't be here by myself."

Scribbles stared at the floor.

"I don't think I'm in a position to make any promises," he said.

Jenn's stomach fell down to her ankles.

"Figures," she said.

★★★

The sky outside became gray as the day aged and prepared to die the only way that days know to die in Oklahoma, through violence, through brilliant red, orange, a fire that burned down the sky. Jenn saw birds disappear into that blood and fire sky and wondered if they knew what they were getting themselves into or if they ever knew when they weren't coming back. Scribbles put his shoes back on and told her that he was going on a walk. He said that he wanted to be alone, and that scared Jenn. She couldn't imagine why anyone would want to be alone.

"I won't even talk to you," she said. "I'll just be there with you in case you want to say anything."

"I want to be alone."

He left Jenn by herself in the house. When she tried to follow him, she couldn't see him on the street. He was out at the mercy of the world then, the quiet town and also the world. Jenn wandered the neighborhood and hoped it would swallow her up. She hoped that in the belly of the town she'd find Scribbles and maybe Ava too. The town was small, but it was hungry. It ate good people every chance it got.

The world turned purple as the sun disappeared. Jenn went back by Scribbles's house, but the lights were off. She decided to walk home alone and leave him in the belly of the beast. Her shoes crunched against bits of gravel and dirt at the side of the blacktop. She didn't know if the sound had always been there or if Ava or Scribbles had drowned it out before. The noise kept on as she sought out her home in the rows of houses that had at some point joined together under the name "Branch Creek." She feared the crunching noise would never leave, that Scribbles was just as gone as Ava, that neither of them would ever again cover up the sounds of her solitude.

If the town was hungry for her, though, it didn't show it with its early autumn buzz and its smoky cool air. The grass along the street was long and waving in the dark. Mowing season had ended, but that year the grass grew through most of October. Kids in windbreakers were still out putting pennies on the railroad tracks. Jenn tried to listen to the kids as she passed them, but their voices were lost in the dark. One day, a train would fall off those tracks on their account. Someone at school had said so. Jenn had never hung out at the train tracks when she was little. She hadn't done a lot of things.

When she got home, she searched for something she could put in the microwave and eat before her mom returned from work. She thought about clearing the table and trying her hand at her math homework while she ate, but she ultimately decided against it. She had little space left in her brain for quadratic equations or polynomials. Besides, she had long given up on impressive grades. Her B- average would be enough to get her into community college if she ever decided to darken the door of a classroom again after graduation.

Jenn's house was old, though she did not know how old. It groaned at the back of the wind and settled crankily into place again. The kitchen was half-painted, a project started and then forgotten under the weight of other projects. Yellow splotches mingled with red paint and held onto their half of the room the best they could. Jenn hardly noticed them anymore. She put a Hot Pocket into its cardboard sleeve and heated it up. The timer went off with it's long, tearful beeps. Jenn sat on the counter as she waited for the pastry to cool.

The phone rang and filled the otherwise empty house. Jenn hopped from the counter to answer it.

"Is Jennifer Armstrong available?"

The man spoke to her with an official confidence and a preacher's authority. Jenn tried to respond to him, but no words came. She only needed to utter three letters, a single syllable, but something about the tone of the man on the other end of the line left her voiceless and afraid. She recalled creeping piano notes and episodes of *Unsolved Mysteries.* Powerful voices never seemed good for teenage girls who were home alone.

"Hello?" the man said.

Jenn realized then that maybe a similar voice had called Ava before she'd disappeared, that the man on the phone could have information about Ava's whereabouts. She tried again to speak and found that she could push air up over her tongue and make a whispered sound. She did it again and again, and she moved her jaw and her tongue and felt the beginnings of words in her mouth. She willed herself to speak.

"Yes," she finally said, or she thought she said. She could not tell if her quiet utterance could be counted as speech or if the man could decipher what she was saying. She only heard the pink noise of empty space between phone-call voices.

"Hello?" the man said again.

She worked up the courage to say the word again, to tell the man that yes, Jennifer Armstrong was available and ready to talk, but then there was a clicking sound, and the man's voice was gone.

★★★

Jenn tried to eat her Hot Pocket quickly so that she would be ready to speak if the phone rang again. The still-hot pastry filling burned her mouth with the first bite. She spat it into the sink. Bits of ham and cheese stuck to the porcelain. She washed the food down and poured herself a glass of water. The remaining slab of Hot Pocket was steaming. She used her tongue to toy with the newly-dead skin at the roof of her mouth.

The phone rang. Jenn rushed toward it, but when she raised the handset to her ear, all she heard was the Gregorian utterance of the dial tone. She hung up and paced around the telephone hook, praying it would ring again. Her teeth clattered. After a few minutes, her stomach closed in on itself, and she threw the remnants of her food in the trash. She couldn't believe how careless she'd been. Her pacing increased. Her quick, shallow breaths felt like they would cause her head to float off her shoulders. Any phone call could have held the answer to her missing friend, and she'd been unable to speak into the phone.

Headlights bounced their way through the window. Jenn stopped pacing. An engine died outside. Soon, there were footsteps on her porch, and then a pause. Someone knocked on the door. The knocks were tight, purposeful knocks from a closed hand. They were focused, businesslike. They seemed to penetrate the door and thump against Jenn's chest. The hairs on her arms stood on end.

The knocking stopped. Jenn couldn't tell how long it had lasted. She took a single step toward the door. The muscles in her legs threatened to lock up and throw her to the floor. She took another step, and they were tighter still. She imagined the shadow of a man in the porch light, a tongue that would bring her into the belly of the town. There were no footsteps back down the short set of stairs, no starting of the car, no break in the shadow. Jenn took another step and was again aware of the sounds her feet made as she walked.

"Hello," she said to the closed door in front of her. Her voice trailed off at the end of the word and left her lungs empty and stinging. She cleared her throat and tried to speak again. "Who is it?"

No one answered. Jenn had her hand on the doorknob. She wondered how long she'd been there. The shadow was just beyond a few inches of pressed wood. She couldn't bring herself to peer through the peephole in the door. Her voice burrowed deep into her chest and refused to come out. There was a moment of silence. She held her breath. Then the knocking sounded again, the never-ending beating of the town's hungry tongue. Jenn exhaled as she opened the door.

Chapter 8

Charlotte slept through much of her first morning in Will's trailer. When she woke up, the sun was peeking over the top of the trees and showing off wooden skeleton fingers and open spaces where the leaves used to be. The thicket around the trailer had been denser, more daunting in the dark. Now, through the window, Charlotte could see right through to the empty blue sky. An unnatural calmness, perhaps it was the openness, kept her still, kept her from moving. She couldn't remember the last time she had been able to lie in bed like that. She hardly thought about meth at first. The drive away from Jim's seemed distant and dreamlike. She didn't live there anymore.

Outside, birds took up their formations and signed v-shapes like open legs as they headed south. Hardly anything else moved around her. She wanted to keep the moment in globs of paint, wanted to hold onto it forever. Only a musty smell in the bed kept her from imagining that it was her own. Then the toilet flushed, and Will came back into the bedroom without washing his hands. He was in his underwear. He found his jeans on the floor and worked them up to his waist.

"Can you drop me off in town?" Charlotte asked him. She brought the bed sheets to her chin, uncomfortable then to be in that room, though it had been so pleasant when she was alone there. She had always known rooms to become strangers in the presence of others. When she was a girl, back before she had picked up the charm that landed her among the homecoming royalty, it had only taken a visiting neighbor to turn her living room into the sort of place that couldn't live up to its name.

"I'm not going into town," Will said. His gut poked out over his waistband. He kept all the bullshit he could muster like a bowling ball under his skin. "And I doubt you want to go see Jim already."

Charlotte shuddered and wondered if the shuddering was on account of Will's half-naked body or the sobriety or Jim. She decided it was Jim. The hair that spread out over Will's chest and ran down his belly had never given her bruises. The little bulge in his jeans had only come alive and left its seed to burrow into her stomach skin. The sobriety only meant headaches and distractions and lonely hours in the dark. She could handle all that.

"I don't know why you're still going to meet with him," she said. "Are you really this goddamn stupid?"

Will pulled a t-shirt over his shoulders, and Charlotte could for a moment imagine why she'd allowed him inside of her. People weren't so bad all covered up and in the middle of things. Will had been covered up when he'd asked her to bed from the recliner the night before. He had been covered up when he'd come over to Jim's and had lunch or picked up the week's supply. Anyone worth having was covered up somehow. Charlotte had the bed sheet, after all.

"I'm getting more product, maybe having a beer, business," Will said.

"There are better ways to do business than drinking with the devil."

"He ain't the devil," Will said. "Some people'd even say he's a messiah."

"Who the hell would say that?"

"Anyone in Mayes County who's had to wait more than a day for meth."

Charlotte let the sheet fall down to her stomach. She crossed her arms over her breasts and scowled. She had gone days without meth, and still she only saw the devil in Jim. She couldn't remember being happy when she was with him. She couldn't remember being happy when she was high. She could only remember the shakes and the hopelessness, the metal end of a belt and days spent laid out in Jim's bed.

"It's all just meth and fat wallets," she said, "no matter what happens to anybody else."

Will put on a cap. His hair stuck out over the tops of his ears, and his rolling eyes set another layer of mortar for the wall that rose up between him and Charlotte.

"What about those missing people on the news?" she asked. "You know damn well they were customers of his. After what I told you about Randy and the whole thing, I'd say Jim is as suspect as anybody. Do you feel like going missing?"

His eyes seemed to linger on her exposed chest as he looked about the room, searching for a way to toss her words off into a corner somewhere, to let them lie there and rot.

"Just about everybody here is a customer of his," he said. "That don't have anything to do with it."

Charlotte hated it when he talked to her like he knew something that she didn't know. She would tear the half-smiling lips off his face if only she could stand to leave the warm spot in the bed.

"Bullshit," she said. "What about that trailer fire?"

"I know for a fact Jim ain't a part of that," Will said, "because this deputy came over here the day before yesterday on account of the fact that I'd been by to see that fellar a few weeks before he died. The dead man had wanted to buy some meth off me. I obliged him, but when that damn old deputy asked what I was doing over there, I said he wanted me to help build a fence. I chatted with that funny-talking deputy for damn near an hour and didn't say one single thing about meth. We had a beer. He didn't bring up Jim once, didn't say anything about the girl either. We had another beer and laughed about some shit he'd seen in a movie."

The blue flakes in Will's eyes were honest despite their green and wanting backdrop. Sure, he was desperate, but he wasn't lying.

"Why didn't you tell me about all that before?" Charlotte asked.

"It didn't mean nothing."

Charlotte shook her head. The room felt like it was shrinking, like the bed had been pushed into a corner, like soon it would be in every corner at once while Will just stood there looking stupid and losing property value. Charlotte's head ached. Jim was somewhere in Will's story, even if the deputy didn't say anything about it. He was a thread running through any happening on that side of Mayes County. Will would turn her safety into an argument that he could win, and Charlotte hated him for it.

Still, she knew she would stay in the trailer, would pretend that this chubby man was enough to keep Jim from trying to cast demons out of her with a creasing Bible. When she closed her eyes, she saw Jim's hands. They were covered in blood, the blood of what he called "sacrificial lambs." The tension in the back of her neck tightened like it was on a twisting key. She remembered the drive to a pig farm at two in the morning, the sounds of human grunts and pigs and Jim chuckling to himself. She kept shaking her head. She tried to knock the sounds loose from her memory. She wanted to like it there with Will. She wanted to feel that her situation was good enough to have an end. She didn't want to believe that Jim would go on forever.

"You're just plain overestimating him," Will said. "You ain't got a single reason to be afraid now. I'm gonna protect you, baby."

Charlotte loathed the stupid expression he wore when he called her "baby," the upturned lips and eyebrows that crouched with confidence. She had no reason to respond to such a face. He turned away to check the clock, though, and she found relief in the faceless body, in the tan neck and matted hair below the rim of his cap.

"I'd better get," he said, and he left the bedroom.

Charlotte was tired again as if she hadn't slept through the morning. Her bones were heavy under her skin. Will's feet were like mallets beating against the hollow area below the trailer as he walked circles in the kitchen. Maybe he was too stupid to find his way out of his own home. He was shouting.

"There's noodles in the fridge if you want them," he said. "I'll be back after a while."

The front door shut with a thump. Then the world was frozen for a moment, the sky fat and unmoving. The breeze didn't bother the tree branches. The window by Charlotte's head could have been a painting, a real painting that sold for more money than she'd ever seen in her life, not the watercolors that folks put up in the fairgrounds lobby to fund the PTA. She was alone then, and there was meth somewhere in the trailer. She tried not to think about it. She closed her eyes to make sure that she would remember the way the world looked when it was quiet. The quiet world was worth keeping. It would look fine on canvas if she could only make it stay. She took her crumpled pack of cigarettes off the nightstand and put one to her mouth. The tobacco crinkled and popped as she lit it. Then it was quiet again, and Charlotte only heard her own breathing.

Chapter 9

Jenn had expected to find a ghost or a giant mouth with a tongue on her porch, but instead there was a deputy. He told her he had some questions for her, so she stood up straight, as all reliable witnesses should. The deputy on the porch was not the same deputy she'd seen at the school a few days before. He was older. The hair on the top of his head was sparse, and it stood up in the porch light. Jenn made out freckles in the space between the hairs. His face sunk into itself at his cheeks and beneath his eyes. She wondered if he'd ever smiled before. He wore a coat over his uniform. It seemed too heavy for the weather and had a shearling collar and lining that spilled over the edge of its pockets, more hair than the deputy did.

"I'll tell you all I can," Jenn said, stepping outside and closing the door behind her. She didn't invite him in.

"When was the last time you saw Miss Springtree?" the deputy asked. His voice was strong and flat. Jenn couldn't tell if he'd been the one who had called her just minutes before, but she assumed that he'd had something to do with it. He took a notebook and pen from the bulky coat. Jenn tried to see if he was sweating. Then she told him the same things she'd told his associate at school the week before, pizza plans and all.

"We said we were gonna meet up for lunch, and that was it," she said.

The deputy mostly nodded and wrote in his notebook.

"You mean, you didn't hear back from her after you

had decided to go eat lunch together?" he asked. He looked up at her with twisted eyebrows as if he didn't believe her. "You kids weren't out doing anything else?"

"We just wanted to get some pizza. We always get pizza together."

"So, let me get this straight, what were you gonna do after you ate?"

She wondered why he had her repeat certain parts of her story as if trying to catch her in a trap. She had nothing to gain by lying to him.

"I don't know," she said. "We usually just went back to Scribbles's house and talked about life or whatever."

"Scribbles being Matthew?"

"Yes."

He put the notebook back into his pocket and just listened with his accusatory look.

"Do you know where she is?" Jenn asked. Her voice came out small and desperate.

"I can't tell you anything about that," he said. "That's for Sheriff Taylor to say. I'm just here to make sure we've got all our information straight."

Jenn's stomach sank. She realized that she'd been shivering and second-guessed her decision to stay outside and to judge the deputy's choice of outerwear. Insects buzzed about in the porch light. Jenn wondered how much longer they'd survive in the cooling weather. Questions about survival felt more personal than they had before Ava disappeared.

"Do you need anything else?" she asked the deputy.

He shook his head, his eyebrows still furrowed and suspicious.

"That's fine for now," he said.

His boots were loud on the concrete when he stepped off the porch. Jenn watched him drive away as if it were a turning point, something she'd need to remember. She could have to recall anything these days. The world didn't seem to be any good for those who just existed in it without memorizing their surroundings. They weren't worth their weight in investigators' report paper when things decided to happen.

She went back inside. She was hungry again, so hungry, she thought, that maybe she didn't have the energy to prepare any food. She lay alone in the living room. It was a cold room, an add-on that was never properly stuffed with insulation. Still, it showed signs of living, the tossed blanket of an afternoon nap and the angular shapes of VHS tapes in piles beside the TV. She left the room dark. Only the porch light crept in between the curtain split. She couldn't see the stains that had begun to show on the furniture cover her mother had draped over the couch, the remnants of sweat and dinners spilled from TV trays.

Every sound in the yard, whether it was the huffing wind or a rattling leaf, was reason to be afraid, but inside the house, there was a separation from all that. She'd found a place away from the rest of the world. Had Ava also felt safe in her home? Jenn considered turning on the television to drown out the sounds from outside and the echoes of her thoughts. She cracked her elbows and worried that she was giving herself arthritis. Lights moved again through the windows, headlights, the seeking eyes of a starving beast. She stayed still on the couch, helpless under the weight of her hunger and of the Oklahoma air that had swallowed Ava.

The new footsteps on the porch were both faster and lighter than the deputy's. No one knocked. Instead, the door opened under the authority of an unseen hand. Keys jingled from outside of a purse. Jenn's mother appeared. The dim light from the porch wrapped around her in the doorway.

"You're off early," Jenn breathed.

"It's almost nine."

Jenn tried to read the clock that hung on the wall opposite the couch, but she couldn't on account of the dark. The tension in her shoulders trickled down to her fingertips. Had she always carried tension like that? Was the weight of the world always pent up in her shoulders?

"What are you doing, laying around in the dark?" her mother asked as she turned on the overhead light. She began to take off her jacket. "It's bad for your eyes."

"The police were here."

Jenn's mother paused. Her jacket hung halfway off her shoulders like a bat's wing.

"What for? Are you in trouble? Was it that friend of yours that up and skipped town? You'd better tell me."

Jenn rattled her head from side to side. She swallowed as if there was something in her throat to swallow. Her mother's accusatory tone had been the sort of thing that she would say was a sign of her love, the insistence on a better life for Jenn. Girls who received visits from the police would not graduate or attract the kind of men who weren't ready to run off and leave them working six days a week at less than twelve dollars an hour.

"It was about Ava," Jenn said. "They asked me what I knew about Ava."

Jenn's mother draped her coat over her arm. "Did you tell them everything you knew?" she asked.

"It was weird," Jenn said. "I told him exactly what I'd told the other deputy, the one at school, but he acted like he didn't believe me."

"He's just trying to do his job. It's hard being an officer of the law, especially with a missing kid. That's hard on everyone, you know, when a young person's gone, but especially the folks that have to find her."

Jenn's mother hung her coat on an entryway hanger. She looked distracted. Her eyes bounced around the room as if she were working through a list of things she'd have to finish before bed, the piles of clothes she'd have to launder and the crumb-covered countertops that she needed to wipe down.

"Yeah, and you're not even talking about the people who actually knew her," Jenn muttered under her breath. She wished her words had been louder, but she was afraid she would anger her mother if she said them again.

"What was that?"

"I was thinking out loud," Jenn said. She could feel her cheeks turning red.

"Well, I think you did the right thing, talking to the deputy," her mother said, "but I am not too fond of having the police show up to my home. Have you eaten yet?"

And with that, the conversation was over. The deputy's coming was just another happening that was talked about and then checked off a list in her mother's mind, same as the fire, same as Ava's disappearance. Jenn looked up to respond, but her mother had already left the room.

***

The next morning, Jenn didn't speak much on the way to school. She thought that the usual car-ride small talk about upcoming tests or her lack of after-school activities would be a white flag, a concession that life would continue on as normal, Ava or no Ava, deputy interviews and all. Instead, she studied the lines in her hands and wondered if there were more of them than there had been when she was younger, a freshman, perhaps, or even an elementary school student with pigtails. Were all these lines in her palms the beginnings of wrinkles, the end of childhood? Her mom stopped the car in front of the school and turned to her.

"I love you," the older woman said in the raised pitch she'd perfected through countless mornings in front of the school. "I'll see you tonight."

The cold wrapped around Jenn's legs like it had been waiting for her as she opened the door and started toward the school. Her backpack was plump and hanging low off her back. She searched the front entrance for Ava, like she had nearly every day of high school before Ava's disappearance. The two had made a habit of meeting up and listening to music on Ava's portable CD player and sharing nail polish. Sometimes, they'd gone to the convenience store across the street for donuts and juice. Scribbles would only show up right before the opening bell.

Jenn made her way toward the building with little hope of interaction with any of the strangers she called her classmates. Her breaths were cloudy puffs outside her mouth. She watched them spread out in front of her. Then they were gone, but other breaths followed and took their place in her lungs, same as everyone else. She tried not to think about the breaths. They made her feel small, like a pin on a map that could be exchanged with any other pin.

She wondered if the deputy had gone to see Scribbles too. She looked for him in the hallway, though she did not expect to see him. She passed a bulletin board with a picture of Ava on it and an announcement about open counseling hours for "students experiencing stress as a result of recent happenings." She stopped at the bulletin board for a moment and looked at the picture. The counselor, or whoever had put it up there, had chosen a yearbook photo from two years before. In the picture, Ava's hair ran down her shoulders to the tops of her tiny breasts. She had dark makeup circling her eyes and a choker around her neck. Ava didn't wear chokers anymore. She'd cut her hair short, almost up to the bottoms of her ears. She'd certainly gained weight. Would anyone remember that Ava was nearly a woman now, or would the whole world miss her searching for a little girl with long hair and dark makeup?

Jenn walked on and put her backpack in her locker. She stood in the lapping waves of small-town students that moved through the hall. No one picked her out from her peers. She wondered if time moved as slowly for them as it did for her. She wondered if they also watched the hands of clocks move with sixty-second strokes. Then she went to class.

Jenn sat towards the back of the room during first period biology. She hardly noticed the empty seats in front of her. She was too focused on the empty seat beside her, where Scribbles usually sat. The twisted feeling from the night before returned, the internal toppling of expectation. The school day was set to begin without Scribbles. Perhaps instead of swallowing Jenn whole, the dark little town would devour everything she cared about, would create a void instead of filling its own. Or maybe Scribbles was late for class. He would lose points on the day's assignment, maybe even a letter grade, but he would hardly care. Jenn tried to clamp down on some sense of optimism, but then the bell rang. Class had begun.

Jenn did the best she could to keep to herself, to avoid interactions that would lead to questions about her absent friends. In biology, that was easier than she'd expected it to be, because the teacher handed out a worksheet and told her to use her textbook to find the answers. She kept her face down and flipped through the pages. She read short paragraphs and took from them, stole single words that completed sentences on the worksheet. Then she let the old words go and moved on to new ones. She hardly had time to look at the empty chair where Scribbles where he should have been sitting and asking her for answers.

In the next class, Spanish, the instructor didn't call on Jenn, and Jenn didn't pay any attention to his curling, foreign terms, either. She thought of missing rent checks and burnt-down trailer homes and mouthed back vocabulary words without taking hold of them. She wondered if she'd ever talk to anybody about magazines again. The class and the other students grew further away with the ticking of the twirling clock face. Loneliness became a bubble that filled her chest. She thought that she would burst and cover the distant students with whatever it was that was boiling inside her. She raised her hand.

"I need to go to the bathroom," she said.

"There are only five minutes left in my class," the teacher said. He was a tan man, a thin man with sideburns that pointed toward his mouth.

"It's an emergency," Jenn said.

"Hurry."

Jenn paced the bathroom with wobbling legs to relieve the pressure in her chest. The whole room was urine yellow, the product of bad lighting. Another student clicked his tongue as he headed down the hall. Jenn hated the sound and covered her ears as she sat on a toilet seat. Before long, the hallway outside was still, and, for a moment, she felt capable of putting cracks into foundations, of turning the world, or at least her day, on its head. So, she stood up tall and puffed out her chest as if it made a difference. She crept into the empty hall to find her way out of the building. Nothing stood between her and the exit. Teachers held lectures in closed-up classrooms with worksheets and hick-accent Spanish. She opened the door and kept going. Her legs no longer wobbled as they cut through the air around her on her way to the parking lot. Only the lifeless headlights of students' cars watched her.

She walked the five windy blocks to the pizza shop. The world had gone cold since the day before, and her skin pulled tight over her scalp. She would find Scribbles, regardless of whether he was eating pizza or decomposing on the side of the highway. The uncertainty of two missing friends was not a weight that she could bear. She frowned against the gray sky and breathed like a marching band snare through her nose. She counted out the beats as she walked. When she got to the restaurant, Shirley was cleaning the buffet with a spray bottle and a pile of napkins.

"A little early, aren't you, hon?" Shirley said. "Buffet doesn't open until 11:00."

The clock on the wall read 10:40. The place was empty except for an old man bent over a newspaper on the other side of the room. Jenn could smell tomato paste and cardboard, and that familiar scent comforted her.

"I guess I'll wait," she said. She sat in the booth where she and Scribbles usually ate together.

Shirley went back into the kitchen and returned after some time with a pizza for the buffet. The washing sounds of a flapping newspaper swarmed the empty restaurant when the old man turned its pages. Eventually, he slapped the paper down onto the table and went up to the buffet. Jenn looked at the clock again. The buffet didn't open for another 10 minutes. Still, she followed the old man's lead and took a handful of crumpled dollars to the counter. Shirley was writing something on a sheet of paper. Jenn dropped the money on the counter without speaking. Her mouth was wide open like she'd been surprised by something, as if the shop owner had leaned over and bitten her. Shirley looked up from her writing and was unamused, flat, the kind of woman who'd taken every pizza order that could be placed, even those orders without words.

"Do you want water or a soda with your buffet today?" she asked.

Jenn was surprised that Shirley had asked her that, though the shop owner habitually asked her customers, especially the high school students, if they wanted a drink when they came in during lunchtime. Jenn had forgotten that the rest of the world still turned around and around and ate pizza and sold soda at a higher price than water.

"Water, please" she said. She reached deep within herself to speak again, to reveal the wound, the missing piece that brought her early to the pizza shop. Shirley, however, had work to do, pizzas to sell. She picked up Jenn's money and straightened it in her hands. "Actually," Jenn continued, "I have a weird question. Have you seen the boy I usually come here with?"

"The one who needs a haircut?"

"Yeah, that's him."

"I sure haven't," the shop owner said. She took her cleaning bottle and a stack of napkins and stuffed them behind the counter. "You two skipping class today?"

"No," Jenn said. She ran her hands nervously over her arms. "At least, not on purpose."

"Don't worry, sweetie, I won't tell no one. I was young once too."

"Really, though, it's not like that."

"Are you sure?" Shirley laughed. "Because, oddly enough, I think I see your little boyfriend walking out of that hardware store across the street."

Jenn's empty stomach bubbled up into something like laughter. Her open mouth smiled on its own.

"That son of a bitch," she said, turning toward the entrance.

Scribbles was jaywalking to the restaurant. When he opened the door, Jenn felt the edge of laughter fade deeper into herself. There it became nauseated confusion. Her smile disappeared.

"Where have you been, kid?" she asked.

Scribbles was shaky. His eyes moved around the room as if he would need to escape at a moment's notice. Dark circles hung fat beneath them. He had loose papers in his hand.

"I've been applying for jobs," he said as he held up the papers. He turned to Shirley behind the counter. "Are you guys hiring?"

The woman shook her head.

"Can I get a buffet with a drink then?" Scribbles asked.

Jenn and Scribbles loaded their plates with pizza and sat in their booth together. Kids from school filed in and ordered lunch. Shirley took their money and brought out more pies. The room became an angular hum, the awkward spurts of noises between other noises. Scribbles took a drink.

"I've gotta figure something out for money," he said. "They'd pay me seven dollars an hour at the feed store, but I could only work so many hours there, because of school, you know?"

Jenn nodded as Scribbles spoke. She tried to keep contact with his eyes, to show him that everything was, one way or another, going to be okay, for no reason other than because it had to be.

"How much money do you have?" she asked.

Scribbles talked with his mouth full of pizza.

"Probably fifty bucks," he said.

A pair of girls in puffy coats walked into the restaurant. One of the girls, Amanda, had been in Jenn's Spanish class. Her nose and cheeks were perpetually rosy. Her grades were usually best in the class. She always wore a hair tie on her wrist, but Jenn never saw her pull her hair back.

"Where'd you go during Spanish?" Amanda asked.

She stood at the end of the table. Her friend followed close behind but didn't speak. Jenn's guts turned soft, so she forced out hard words.

"I had to go mind my own business," she said. "What about you?"

Amanda looked at Scribbles, who continued to eat. She appeared startled at first. Then she smiled at Jenn with narrowed eyes.

"Phulps was pissed that you didn't come back," Amanda said. "I know you're friends with that missing girl, and you're probably going through a lot or whatever, but things got real tense. Missing friend or not, you're probably gonna get detention."

"Oh, shut up," Jenn said.

Amanda rolled her eyes. "I was just trying to give you a heads up," she said. Her friend pulled at her elbow and then went to order lunch. Amanda frowned the way a parent frowns before telling their child that they aren't angry, just disappointed. Then she was gone, moving on with the rest of the world.

"She is such a bitch sometimes," Jenn said to Scribbles.

"She has a point, though," he said. "I'm surprised they don't have people waiting at every door to make sure the rest of us don't end up vanished."

"Can't you just nod or something?"

A scooting chair sounded like a trumpet blast in the restaurant. The old man on the other side of the room stood on his toes and poked at the TV that hung behind him. He changed the channel from a daytime drama to the local newscast. He pounded the volume button until the anchor's voice rose up over the voices of the lunching students.

"Hey," Scribbles said, tossing his empty plate aside, "they're talking about Ava."

He went over to the TV and turned it up some more. Jenn followed him. The restaurant grew quiet. Everyone danced their tiniest dances to the rhythm of the newscast voices. Their heads swayed with the unseen teleprompter. Then there was the rushing wind of a dozen pairs of lungs filling at once. The Mayes County Sheriff said that Ava's disappearance was suspicious after all. For the second time in her life, Jenn felt like she would faint.

"I am doing everything within my power to make sure we find out what happened to this young woman and to bring her home safely," the sheriff said on the television.

"But not everyone believes that law enforcement is, in fact, doing their best with the case," said a reporter.

A wind-tossed woman in a tattered fleece jacket filled up the screen, her cheeks sharp and bony. A line beneath the woman identified her as Ava's aunt, but Jenn had never seen her before.

"There's a lot they aren't telling us," the woman said, "and I want somebody to get to the bottom of it."

Scribbles's face became bright, as if someone had set him on fire. He turned to Jenn and spoke in a harsh whisper.

"A deputy came by again last night," he said.

"He came to my place too," Jenn said. She grabbed him by the hand and pulled him out of the restaurant, away from Amanda, away from the television and its bad news, away from the pizza and the styrofoam cups. Outside, the wind was still blowing. "Can you even believe this?"

They paced the parking lot gravel at the side of the restaurant. On the other side of a thin wall, people continued to eat. Jenn was sure the old man was still watching the news, but everyone else likely went back to their normal lives. Every now and again, old pickup trucks passed by with odds and ends piled up on their beds. A flag whipped against a nearby streetlight.

"Listen," Scribbles said. He was rigid up through his shoulders, but his head hung down like he had a rubber neck, his chin near his chest. "When the deputy came to my house, he pushed me around. It was like he was trying to scare me, like he thought I made Ava disappear."

"Well, you didn't, right?"

Sharp points on Scribbles's face made him look like a man. His cheeks collapsed into fierce pits. For a moment, he looked as if a stranger had been cast to play him, as if the real Scribbles had overslept and someone had to fill his shoes.

"What the hell, Jenn?" he said. "Of course I didn't."

"Chill," Jenn said. "I'm just so shocked by all this. It gets worse and worse."

Her thoughts pounded against each other like thunderclouds in the minds of children, open-ended and without grounding, misled but earnest. People had been saying plenty about Ava's disappearance, but *Jenn* had never really hypothesized about it. She had grasped at the words of others without scrutiny. Sure, Scribbles could be behind the whole thing, but so could anybody. She considered the woman on the news report. Was the sheriff trying to find Ava? Was anyone? Jenn wouldn't know any better until she strung together the words and rumors and TV reports herself.

The sun peeked out from behind the clouds and then disappeared again, leaving the day gray, same as most days that time of the year. Jenn heard the gravel crunch beneath her feet as she walked circles around Scribbles in the pizza shop parking lot. The investigation would have to be hers. Otherwise, Ava's future would be left to a loose stack of bricks without cement, the occasional statements made by human beings, which are, of course, the only creatures capable of lying.

Chapter 10

"I told you this kind of spectacle ain't gonna help either of us," Sheriff Taylor said.

Gail, the missing girl's aunt, was marching by herself on the sidewalk outside the sheriff's office with a cardboard sign that she'd covered with permanent marker, big box letters that said "No more cover-ups. Tell the truth, sheriff!" The sheriff and two deputies watched her. One of the deputies, Shriver, stood there with a dopey look on his face like he needed some coffee or a tall helping of shouted instruction. Deputy Carlson was cold and stony beside him.

Passing cars occasionally slowed in the street. Drivers poked their heads out of their windows and tried to read Gail's sign. The sheriff could feel his heartbeat in his arms, all the way down to his fingertips. Gail had outstayed her welcome, and he felt himself stray from his role as sheriff so that he could become just another angry man who got tired of people and the trouble they stirred up around him. Had he been so angry when he had stumbled onto the convenience store robbery all those years ago? Had his head been cooler then? Had the robbers been a lesser threat with their guns and their hostage? Memories were tricky that way. Everything was the same when it was happening. It was only afterward that he could make any sense of his experiences, and then it was hard to say if the memories were true to what had actually happened.

"I ain't leaving until you tell the truth, until you let the people know about Ava," Gail said.

The sheriff could feel the facade of calmness peeling from his face. A wild son of a bitch was taking his place.

"You have 30 seconds to get the hell out of here before I have you arrested," he said. "We'll throw you in a cell, and no one else will get to see your pretty sign."

"On what charge, uncovering the truth?"

Sheriff Taylor spat on the sidewalk and forced a grin.

Gail's face went soft for a second as if she had considered the weight of her defiance. That was all the sheriff needed.

"Well, we'll start with disturbing the peace," he said, "and then I'll take a look in that junker of a car you've got parked out there. I'm sure we'll find something interesting."

"Is that a threat?"

The sheriff laughed. He had scared the woman.

"My office don't make threats," he said. "We make promises, and I promise you that you'll have all sorts of hell to deal with if you don't get out of here and stop with all this conspiracy nonsense."

"Oh, fuck you," Gail said. "King piggy and his liars here ain't worth the donuts they're made of."

She didn't show her hesitation anymore. She appeared to toss her fear aside and plunge into possibility. The sheriff felt a tearing in his chest, the punctured wall that had kept demons and mushroom clouds hidden. He wondered if he'd fall right apart and if those shadowy demons would rise from the broken pieces. He started to lunge toward Gail, to take her sign and tear it into pieces, but a hand on his shoulder kept him still and frowning. He spat again on the sidewalk as a sheriff, an officer of the law. He looked Gail right in her spiteful eyes. Gone again were the pools of hell and authority, of rebellion, the empowered look of a "citizen activist with a story to tell." He called her bluff.

"Deputy Carlson," he said, feeling the brief high he felt when he moved into the irrevocable, "will you put this woman in handcuffs and book her for disturbing the peace. Shriver, I need you to go through her car. She appears to me as if she's under the influence of drugs. Wouldn't you agree?" The sheriff stepped back from the woman. "I told you it was time to get out of here."

"You wouldn't dare," Gail said.

Deputy Carlson pulled the sheriff aside.

"We don't need the trouble of keeping her around here," he said. "She's already acting up, and we haven't done nothing to her. Listen, I'll take her for a drive and talk some sense into her. We'll work everything out, and the media won't have to get suspicious."

Carlson's black hair was slicked back like a common mobster in a television show. He had half his hands in his pockets. His lower lip puffed out like he had a dip in, and he looked around as if to see if anyone had heard what he'd said. Gail continued walking circles with her sign. Her face was cloudy and sinking, but there was still fire somewhere inside her, the sort of fire that would spread too fast to be contained. Carlson would be able to take care of it, sure, but that would likely bring about a whole new set of problems. The sheriff would have to wonder what happened to her. He would again consider when compliance became contribution. There was a chance that someone would demand a press conference.

Shriver was following behind the woman and nearly begging her to leave. His shoulders slouched and his voice came more from his nose than it did his mouth. He made the woman look stronger than she was, and Sheriff Taylor worried that he made her feel stronger too. The sheriff scratched his head and considered Carlson's proposition. If Gail was gone, maybe things would quieten down again. Maybe people would forget all about this disappearance business and go back to their daily lives. Maybe he could simply wait around a few years and retire. Regardless of Gail, they'd never find that girl that she was going on about, at least, his office would never find her. Too many folks had a vested interest in making sure that would never happen, and those folks were willing to set fire to the county, were willing to kill every god to make a quick buck or to score another high. The best Sheriff Taylor could do was tell people to stay out of things they shouldn't be messing with and earn, no, *demand* the respect of his constituents. They needed him to be their hero again, to bring things back to the way they used to be before people got nosy and too big for their britches.

"This won't come back and give me any trouble, right?" he asked Carlson.

"This busybody won't be bothering us anymore, I can tell you that, and, if anyone asks, you wouldn't have a damn thing to do with it."

The sheriff sighed. His anger began to fade. He nearly pitied the woman. Even if he had been angry during the convenience store robbery, he would not have moved outside the law to relieve his stress. No, not like this.

"Just talk to her a bit," he said. "I don't need more trouble."

Carlson's lips parted, and he let out a dry puff of air, a laugh that was never shared.

"You've got it, boss," he said.

Both men watched Shriver and Gail pace the pavement. The winded deputy looked like he'd changed his colors the way he followed her, like he'd become her disciple. Carlson spat.

"Don't get yourself dirty," the sheriff said.

Carlson put the woman in handcuffs. She dropped her sign and began to shout.

"You can't do this," she said. Her face was wild and searching, but there wasn't anything to find. She jerked and swayed from side to side like she was hoping for a passerby. "You can't do this."

The dark-haired deputy didn't say much of anything back to her as he led her along to his personal car, a white Honda with rust spots that sprinkled the bottom of the fenders. Shriver stood by Gail's sign. He looked at the sheriff as if he wanted a hint at what to do next, but Sheriff Taylor looked off at the half-risen sun, the white-hot ball of morning that, like a good example, paid no mind to Gail's shouting and the slam of Carlson's car door that made things quiet again. The sheriff didn't want to think about what was next for her. He didn't want to think about her at all. Shriver stared at the sign on the ground until Sheriff Taylor took it and shoved it into a nearby trash can. Shriver did not offer so much as a word. The woman was gone, though, taken care of. Sheriff Taylor could begin to forget her. Only the night janitor would see the sign when he came to take out the garbage.

Then the world kept on waking up and getting itself into trouble. Donna from the lobby desk threw open the front door. Her face was twisted into knots.

"Sheriff," she said. "Frank Redbud says they found a body out at Pecan and 4100 Road up by Branch Creek. Fire and ambulance are already headed that way, probably highway patrol too."

"Well, shit," the sheriff said. He ran his hand over the top of his head. Something cold seemed to explode inside of him. A body would surely bring about the wrong kinds of questions. It would mean calls from Jim, calls from the press, calls for justice from the armchair lawmen. "I guess I'll go down there now. Did they say the body was a woman?"

"They didn't say."

"Let's make sure it stays that way."

He hurried to the lot behind the building where they kept the squad cars and hoped the highway patrol wouldn't show up at the scene looking to end up on the news before he could get control of the situation. He threw himself into one of the cars and left the sheriff's office behind him for the lifeless bodies that demanded more attention than their breathing counterparts. The highway lines blinked like Morse code, a message he had to heed—three dots, three dashes, three more dots. The radio in the cruiser garbled on about medical episodes and traffic violations through busy, static words. Sheriff Taylor turned the volume down until it was only a hum, something beyond his reach. The road was clear, save for the occasional semi-truck that would prompt him to turn on his lights and test the accelerator.

He turned off his emergency lights before he took the exit into Branch Creek. He did not want to draw attention to himself there. Two other cars sat at the four-way stop at the end of the exit ramp. They took their time waving back and forth to one another until one of the drivers chose to pull on through. They must not have known there was a dead body to tend to. Still, the sheriff kept his lights off. He came closer to the address Donna had given him. He was glad he'd gone out on his own, that he didn't see Shriver behind a steering wheel and sucking oxygen through his fat cheeks as if to puff himself up. The chubby deputy had no idea what kind of trouble he was really getting himself into when he signed on to work at the sheriff's office. He could have been a fireman or a gas station attendant. The kid didn't have the stomach for this line of work. Maybe he could handle blood and guts, but the rest of it would surely do him in. The rest would do them all in.

The fastest route to the body included a stretch of highway that ran the length of Branch Creek. It wound past the school, thirteen years' worth of instruction in three classroom buildings, the old county fairgrounds, and a cafeteria that went up in the eighties. The residents called the two-lane road "the old highway." Hardly anyone would have known what he meant if the sheriff had ever said "County Highway 123." That sort of change didn't exist for folks in Branch Creek. They liked things the way they used to be, and Sheriff Taylor couldn't fault them for that. He felt the same way.

On the old highway, he saw something like the ghost of the missing teenager standing in a high-necked night dress, the kind they'd worn when people were still decent. He imagined her thin and pouting with eyes that sparkled. She looked different than she had in the pictures. He hoped he would never have to see the child's face from the pictures. Each time he blinked, he saw the girl again at the side of the road. He wondered if she saw him too. Jim had been hard at work to make sure that Sheriff Taylor never said a word about the deacon's illicit activities throughout Mayes County, and the sheriff had always assumed that the old man returned the favor. There was no way to know, though. Jim may have told the missing girl about everything, about the sheriff's weak spine, about his inability to keep his wife safe and provide law and order for the poor and addicted folks who disappeared under his watch. The missing girl could know that the sheriff had done nothing to find her. Sheriff Taylor would rather face the girl's ghost for the rest of his life than live haunted by the shameful words that she could spew. He shook the thought away. It wasn't like a hero to wish harm upon the vulnerable like that.

The old highway snaked alongside the actual Branch Creek, and it crossed the railroad tracks twice. 4100 Road was almost right in the center of the two crossings. The sheriff nearly jumped out of his seat when he went over the first set of tracks. The cruiser plopped up, clip-clop, like the horse hooves of the old Texas Rangers, which no longer existed, at least, not in any real law enforcement capacity. The whole country was changing, even Texas. The sheriff had a cousin who'd moved to Austin and gone plain strange. He didn't talk to that cousin anymore. He only hoped that Oklahoma wouldn't end up like its neighbor to the south.

He turned onto 4100 Road, and the cruiser threw up so much dust off the top of the gravel that someone could have rear-ended him without seeing his bumper. The trees along the road reached up and touched each other, and it was eerily dark there. He felt that the darkness could have been a bad omen, but, then again, a body was a bad enough omen on its own. He saw a number of cars parked together in little huddles. Emergency lights broke through the browning shadow of autumn. The sheriff slowed his car to little more than a crawl. There were fire trucks and ambulance boxes and highway patrol cars and jet black vehicles without any markings on them at all. The sheriff figured the unmarked cars belonged to the state bureau of investigation, maybe the feds. He began to sweat. Men in bulletproof vests and sunglasses stood with clipboards and rubber gloves. Word of the body had grown beyond the county, and it was impossible to know what other rumors had reached the ears of the higher powers, those officials in the United States who were given reach beyond God above, beyond Mother Nature, and beyond Sheriff Douglas J. Taylor.

The sheriff parked along the side of the road behind the other cars and their flashing lights. One of the men in sunglasses waved him over toward a lump of human flesh in the grass just at the edge of the ditch.

Chapter 11

The sun had started to set, and the sky was lit up pink and gold like a treasure chest reflection. Jenn's mother dropped her off in front of the high school gymnasium and went to park the car. They were practically late. The older woman had spent forty minutes fixing her makeup as if it were prom night. Her face was thick and cakey, her eyes winged and swirling blue about the lids. She had an emergency flashlight from the kitchen drawer in her lap. Jenn did not have a flashlight of her own.

Earlier in the day, the sheriff had shown up to the Assembly of God church with his immaculate suit, clothing so stiff that it could have been armor. He'd been sweating, and Jenn had been able to make out the ribbed undershirt he wore through his wet dress shirt. He had also been quiet, had hardly raised his hands the way he did other Sundays when he visited. He had stared at Brother Freemont in the back of the sanctuary as he addressed the congregation. He had asked them to come look for Ava. Then he had sneezed. The hands and feet of Jesus Christ had fulfilled their roles by saying "bless you." After that, he'd spent most of the service staring into his lap. The pastor had come back up to the front of the church with his glasses low on his nose and said that Ava was a lost lamb who would return soon to the flock. He'd said it like her lostness was something she had chosen. Jenn imagined Ava cackling and drawing the attention of the entire room and loving every minute of it. Ava would rather not be found than to be compared to a lamb. She wasn't the type to be herded.

That evening, even Pastor Masterson showed up to the gymnasium to join the search party. He had his cane and a flashlight, a Bible verse and a scowl. A bunch of the kids from school also came, including Amanda and the others who attended the Methodist Church or maybe no church at all. Jenn wondered how they'd found out about the whole thing.

How did everyone else seem to know things that she felt had only come to her incidentally? Would she have been there if the sheriff hadn't come to her church that morning?

The search party was divided into circles of five or six people across the dirty basketball court. Jenn couldn't tell if they had divided themselves that way or if someone had told them to split into groups for the search. She wandered about the room and tried to find somewhere to belong, somewhere she could be useful. If Ava hadn't gone missing, if they had been searching for some other girl, Jenn would have sat with her in the back, away from their chatty neighbors. They would have made plans together and listened to Ava's portable CD player. They would have wondered how anyone could disappear from a place as small as Branch Creek. Ava would have said that the men in camouflaged hunter's jackets were tacky, and Jenn would have told her that her comment was inappropriate and then pointed out the flaws in Ava's own outfit, the beads around her wrist or the spots of bleach on her pant leg. Ava would have loved that Jenn noticed her subtle fashion statements.

Instead, Jenn walked among the circles of people alone. A handful of deputies stood around the sheriff near the center of the court, the hallowed ground of homecoming royalty, and laughed among themselves as if they had come together for coffee and donuts instead of for finding Ava. Jenn spied a gap in one of the circles and stood there with her head down. She tried to pass the awkward moments by eavesdropping on the people around her. Geraldine Robinson, a darling of the PTA in a hoodie and pajama pants, spoke louder than everyone else.

"I always was worried about that girl," she said, "but I didn't think she'd go missing or kill her daddy. I thought she'd get knocked up or caught smoking cigarettes."

A man with a hunting beard near Geraldine traced pictures on the court with the toe of his boot while she talked. His boots left streaks on the wood. He had, at one point, been divorced, and Jenn's mother had taken him out on a date or two at the truck stop up the highway. Jenn only knew him as Dan. Her mother had never introduced him, because he had decided to get back together with his ex-wife after he got arrested for trying to break into someone's barn. Jenn never quite understood what that was all about.

"These kids are all sorts of trouble," Dan said to Geraldine. "If I could convince Nancy, we'd pull every single one of ours out of school and teach them at home. School's where these kids learn all this shit. The other kids teach them to be little hellions, and ain't a damn leader has the guts to give them a paddling."

Jenn felt the tiny flame in her chest, the place where she carried her hope for finding Ava, flicker at the misinformed words of others. She could no longer listen to Dan and Geraldine. Once somebody found her, Ava would have no problem telling every single Branch Creek resident off for what they said about her while she was gone. She would have to right a great deal of wrongs, and none of them would be her fault. She could not help the cruelty of a small town that came alive when someone left the room.

Jenn again moved outside the circles of people, looking for a friendly face or a place where she could wait for the searching to start without being bothered. She tried her best to ignore the opinions of folks who'd never spoken to Ava before, and she hated the flippant laughter of those other folks who appeared to have no idea that a real-life child was missing, a girl with ideas and short hair, a girl who wanted to live in a city apartment with her friends and make fun of people in shopping malls if they were anything like the shoppers she saw on TV. Jenn sat by herself on a front row bleacher and waited for someone to tell her what to do. Her mother came in the double doors waving and smiling at Jeannie, her hairdresser, before she was absorbed into one of the small groups and the great roar of a town gathered together under the gymnasium lights. Maybe it was prom after all, with starry eyes and social niceties and all the makeup in the world.

"Quiet down while I explain some things real quick," Sheriff Taylor shouted from where he stood near the center of the court.

The broken rhythm of voices became a murmur, a shuffling. The sheriff was sweating even more than he had been that morning.

"We'll have about ten different groups headed up by a team of deputies and myself," he said. "We'll work our way out from here and cover a couple miles or so and then come back. Fan out best you can to make sure we don't miss anything."

The murmur grew to a hum as the sheriff continued. People began to walk toward the deputies. Jenn stood to her feet and saw Brother Fremont standing near Sheriff Taylor.

"Before we get started, though," Sheriff Taylor said, louder now, cutting into the noise of everyone else like an axe against a tree, "I'm gonna have Deacon Freemont from the Assembly of God church say a little prayer for our safety."

Brother Freemont asked everyone to bow their heads and close their eyes. He took off his cap, a mesh-backed shop cap from a welding company out of Kansas. The other men in the room followed suit. Jenn thought she saw more caps that night than she'd seen in her life. Men wore camouflage caps, caps with the Dallas Cowboys star, caps from industrial businesses she'd never heard of. At Brother Freemont's calling, they all fell from heads into the worn and wrinkled hands of folks who toiled the earth, hands that smelled like motor oil and Aqua Velva.

The room wasn't quite silent while Brother Freemont prayed. The sounds of movement that accompany a gathering of human bodies continued with their rustling and grunting. Weaving between the noises was a call for safety, thees and thous, the shaking of a holy hand at Satan. Jenn didn't close her eyes. She watched the bowed heads nod and whisper quietly to themselves. Her mother raised her hands enthusiastically when Brother Freemont told the Good Lord to keep everyone in His loving arms throughout the search. Where was God when people made such a show of asking Him for answers? Did He ignore them on account of their lack of faith? Was He deaf?

Jenn tried to put the facts of Ava's disappearance together like a puzzle, like a portrait with meaning. She looked around for Scribbles and wondered if anyone had told him about the search. Her stomach sank when she couldn't find his greasy hair or the remnants of old pimples that made up his forehead. She sat back down and rested her chin in her hands as she watched the searchers pray. She didn't have any words for God.

Brother Freemont finished his prayer, and all the hats in the room went back onto their owners' heads. Jenn soon found herself behind a group of half a dozen people heading toward the park where the Little League kids played baseball in the spring. It was almost dark out, and she had to squint to see the rows of slouching houses and their lawns all covered in sheet metal and things that used to work. The folks in front of her talked with the deputy who was leading them. He was one of the deputies who had come to the school, the man with the mustache who'd first interviewed her. She couldn't remember his name, and the nameplate he had pinned to his shirt was lost in the earth's shadow.

"This way," he said to the group.

He had trouble making the "s" sounds when he talked. It made him sound like a joke on a television show. Jenn hadn't noticed that back at the school. He was the first person to turn on his flashlight, but a middle-aged man in carpenter jeans quickly followed suit. Jenn wondered if anyone else was light-less. She avoided talking to keep from drawing attention to herself. She followed behind and watched the flashlight beams expose the workings of evening and then of nighttime, dogs on chains that barked circles behind chain-link gates, downed branches undressed by their own deaths and autumn's sweeping, dirty vinyl siding, and rusted fenders of sleeping cars that made their beds outside of driveways. Their group walked in the street, over the cracks and potholes. Jenn envisioned Ava in every yard they passed. She imagined her friend in tattered clothes in the street and hallelujahs from the deputy. The hope of discovery fell away to frustration at the regular, Ava-less world around her. It would be embarrassing if they caught her with their flashlights walking down toward the park or crouching around the side of an empty rent house behind the fairgrounds.

"I guess we have to rule out everything," Jenn said.

No one responded, not even Debbie, who asked the deputy countless questions about the investigation as if she didn't have much in the way of daily conversation, as if she needed to make up for something.

"Now, you're telling me this girl was in the custodianship of a man over on the other side of town by the trailer park, but we're spending our night looking for her over here?" Debbie eventually asked, breaking the silence.

The deputy rubbed his mustache against his nose and said, "Yep."

Debbie asked something else. Her questions were probing and detective-like. She seemed hopeful that the search would turn up answers about the missing girl. She walked up front with the deputy and pointed at everything that moved with a gasp. Most of the group seemed to treat the search for Ava like a real-life game of Clue, an exciting way to fill their evening, a chance at a prize with no real risk of loss. Still, they were eager and sticking their necks out in front of them as if the few gained inches would mean the difference between a discovery and wasted time. A man with a belly that reached out so far that Jenn doubted he could see his toes huffed and coughed as he tried to keep up with the rest of the group. He'd filled in as the bus driver for Jenn's route sometimes when she still rode the bus home from school.

"You know, it's a shame this all had to go and happen," he wheezed. "She was really a sweet kid, a quiet kid." He made a face as if he could have laughed in between his thoughts. "I think that girl could have been a nice secretary. I'd reckon she could have had the best speaking voice in the town."

Jenn waited for one of the other happy hunters to respond. Ava would have been an awful secretary, the kind of woman to swear at people at the slightest inconvenience and to take long lunches. Once, a teacher had asked her to shut the classroom door, and she'd told him to do it himself. He did it too. Jenn thought that she'd be the only person who remembered things like that, Ava's ability to push people into action. Others seemed to know an awful lot about Ava after she disappeared, but they never seemed to know the same things that Jenn did, the things that made Ava into more than a nightly headline or a passing bit of small talk. It was probably that way for most folks who went missing or died young, though. People just wanted to have a good reason to feel sorry for themselves. So, they formed opinions and forced their way into the missing girl's life, even when that meant invention.

When the search party got to the park, a group of kids took off from behind the public bathroom like phantoms. Flashlight beams followed the kids until they disappeared down the street. Jenn couldn't tell if she recognized them. The world was as dark as if it had been dropped into tar. The search party split up, unenthusiastically chasing their flashlights around the park. Jenn walked alone. She felt useless without a flashlight of her own. She sat at the edge of a water-filled ditch that bisected the park and remembered when she and Ava had once used a paper cup to catch tadpoles there. They had poured the tadpoles back into the ditch at the urging of Jenn's mother, but Ava had begged Jenn to help her find a way to bring them home. Now, Jenn wondered if the tadpoles had lived, had grown up and become the little frogs that filled the summer nights with croaking and that hopped through headlight beams in those same summer nights. She wondered if Ava would have the chance to grow up too, or if she was dead and dumped into some other ditch the way her mother had insisted they dump the tadpoles years before. She cried silently in the dark.

★★★

After the night had swallowed up every corner of the park, the infield diamond made muddy by old rain, the tops of crumpling slides and faded jungle gyms, the places where the hopeful could picture a missing teen left shivering in a t-shirt, the deputy said the search party would walk back to the gymnasium and go home for the night. They had been out for less than two hours. Despite their previous eagerness, the rest of the group had grown weary, and they seemed relieved that they could return to their homes in time to watch *20/20* or *The X-Files.* Jenn, however, was unsettled, a leaf rustled by the wind and left on the ground in such a way that it could be more easily crunched. Had anyone seriously thought that finding Ava more than a week after her disappearance would be a literal walk in the park?

Her thoughts turned to Scribbles. She wondered whether he had found a job or if the deputy had come back to bother him again. Her stomach turned sour. There was a familiar, bitter taste on her tongue. Only part of her had expected to see him at the gymnasium. She wasn't surprised when he wasn't there. Surely he had an excuse. Still, his absence was unsettling, even if he wouldn't have offered much more in the way of sharp eyes. As the rest of the search party continued back to meet with the others, Jenn split from them and started toward his house.

The light from his living room glowed against the rest of the neighborhood. The other homes on his street seemed as if they were empty, as if they were collecting dust and waiting only for the morning frost. She saw shadows inside his house, and though they couldn't have been more than a pair of arms stretching over a head, something about the shadows worried her. If he was just sitting inside his house, he could have shown up to help search for Ava. She knocked on his door, and the wood turned her knuckles red in the cold. When he opened the door, his eyes were set in dark circles as if he hadn't been sleeping well.

"Where've you been?" Jenn asked.

"Sitting here, I guess." He looked surprised.

"Didn't you hear there was a search for Ava tonight?"

"Bet you didn't find her."

He held the door for Jenn as she entered the house. He sat on the couch. She looked down at him.

"What the hell's that supposed to mean?" she asked. What had before been fear tossing in her stomach became frozen, and then it became fiery.

He didn't speak.

"Fucking answer me, dude," she said.

"Have you watched the news at all today?"

The hot feeling from her stomach slid down to the tops of her feet. Then it shrank away and left her shivering. Scribbles shook his head when he spoke. His lower teeth rose up above his lip and delivered his sentence.

"They found somebody dead outside of town yesterday," he said, "a human body, out off the old highway."

Jenn thought again of the ditch at the park and the tadpoles. The scene had become grotesque, the tiny creatures left to die in mud puddles. She felt horror at the thought of Ava's body laid out and visible along a public road that way. She could not bear to seriously consider that possibility then, not after the sheriff had everyone walking around Branch Creek with flashlights.

"There's no way," she said. "I would have heard about that."

She tried to laugh off the suggestion. She pushed Scribbles's chest as he sat on the couch. He looked up at her. His face was empty.

"I'm not playing. It was on the news."

His breath smelled like beer. Jenn looked over the room and saw a copper-colored bottle on the floor at the side of the couch. She pushed him again, harder this time.

"Have you been just sitting here, drinking? You're so full of shit. You smell like you've been drinking. If it was true, you would have come told me. You're just drunk. I would have heard something."

"Ava disappeared, and then they found a body. That sounds like a reason to drink."

Jenn wanted to ignore him. Her chest was tight, and the hot feeling from before passed over her body. She felt that when it left, it would take the life right out of her. Her eyes filled with tears.

"But we were just looking for her," she wailed, "the sheriff and the pastor and everybody. She's not dead. She can't be."

She slid to her knees at the side of the couch.

"I don't know anything about that," Scribbles said. He was off the couch now and on the floor. Slowly, his arm worked its way around her. His body was warm against her, and his voice changed. Its hard edge crumbled like clay. "I didn't think I'd be the one to tell you."

She began to sob and offered halves and thirds of sentences with her wavering voice.

"I know it doesn't seem like it," Scribbles said, sighing, tears working their way down his own face, "but we're gonna keep going still, keep living the best we can. We've got to."

He pulled her into his chest, and she cried there. Neither of them spoke. Jenn's breaths were waves that crashed out of her mouth, and then they were a stream, surging every now and again. She pulled away from Scribbles and wiped her eyes on her sleeves. The cool air outside of his arms was even cooler where the tears had been. Her makeup made black trails across her cheeks.

"You're sure it was her?" she asked.

Scribbles was still sitting on the floor next to her. He leaned back against the bottom of the couch.

"They didn't say who it was," he said. "I couldn't think of anyone else."

"Well, I mean, there are other people missing too, like from the news." Her voice became louder, her words faster. "Maybe the sheriff doesn't think so, you know, because he was the one who led the search tonight."

She looked up at him with the kind of desperate look that told him she needed his validation or she'd just as soon keel over and die. The tiniest sparkle in her eyes threatened to go the way of tears again.

"I guess so," Scribbles said.

He reached over to the side of the couch and picked up a beer. He twirled his wrist, and the beer tossed against the bottom of its bottle. He took a drink.

"How'd you even get that?" Jenn asked him.

"The guy at the gas station doesn't check ID if you go during the day."

"Pete's?"

"No, Rocket's, across the street from Pete's."

"No shit? Does Ava know?"

Scribbles opened his mouth and looked like he was about to remind her that Ava could be dead. Jenn sharpened her face, made her eyes like knives to let Scribbes know that their friend was not to be referred to in the past-tense. He closed his mouth, breathed, and then he spoke.

"She told me a while back," he said. "I guess I just never had to do it before."

Jenn went to the kitchen and saw a half-empty pack of beers on the counter. Behind it was a plastic bottle of vodka. The bottle looked like it was made for mouthwash instead of liquor.

"And where did this come from?" she called from the kitchen.

"I think my old man left it here," he said. "It was in the cabinet."

Jenn pulled out one of the beers and twisted at it until the metal cap scraped her palms. She brought it back into the living room and shook it in Scribbles's face.

"Your stupid beer won't open," she said.

Scribbles popped off the cap with a bottle opener that he kept on his key ring. Jenn took the beer from him. She remembered what he had said about the body.

"I can't believe we're just like sitting here and drinking after all this," she said. "How can you be so calm right now?"

"Because I have to be, I guess."

Jenn took a long drink. She didn't really like the taste, but she'd forgotten to complain about it after months of Ava's telling her that the flavor would grow on her. She leaned back against the couch. There was a breath or two between them in the otherwise quiet room.

"So, this is crazy," Scribbles said, "but I'm not going back to school anymore."

Jenn sat up again. She didn't understand what he was saying.

"What are you talking about?" she asked.

"I got a job. The gas station needs people during the day, and I need money. I'm not gonna have a lot of time for school."

She felt defensive, like someone was trying to take something from her, like she'd have to fight tooth and nail to keep what was hers.

"At Rocket's?" she asked.

"No, Pete's. I went by Rocket's after I found out I got the job."

Jenn was too tired to feel what she thought she should feel about Scribbles's decision, but she knew it would come later, maybe when she was in bed for the night or early in the morning, but it would come.

"Damn, kid." she said.

"I'm sorry."

Jenn drank some more. Scribbles tossed his empty beer bottle across the room. It clanged hollow against the floor. They sat there for a few minutes, and then Scribbles went into the kitchen and came back with the vodka. He took a pull from the plastic bottle and made a face like something had bit him. Then he took another pull. He offered the bottle to Jenn, but she told him she didn't want any.

"Suit yourself," he said. "It's nasty shit anyway."

"When Ava comes back, I'm gonna tell her you said that, and she's gonna make fun of you for being a pussy."

"Whatever, you wouldn't even drink it."

They both laughed, and Scribbles drank some more of the vodka. Jenn lay her head back on the couch again and closed her eyes. She could hear him glugging down the clear liquid like an oil well. She imagined a pumpjack, the kind she was told not to ride like a horse when she was little, the kind that left that boy with glasses without three of his toes, an example for the whole elementary school. Then she felt lips on her neck and a tongue between them. The ends of hair strands fluttered against her skin.

"What are you doing?" she asked.

Scribbles pulled away from her. One of his eyes was cocked slightly away from the other one. His face was red.

"It seemed right, you know, with everything that's happening."

Jenn stood up and backed away from him. His eyes were still wild. She'd never seen eyes like that before. Neither of them seemed to look at her. One looked right above one shoulder. The other wasn't too far off the other.

"I think I love you," he said.

Jenn just shook her head.

Scribbles swept Jenn's beer bottle and the vodka onto the floor with his arm. The bottle crashed and clattered, but the vodka only bounced with a shallow thud. Jenn jumped at the outburst. Her scalp seemed to grow tight on her head. She again felt the warm drip of panic along her back. Scribbles pounded away from her, through the kitchen and then out into the backyard. He had come close to Jenn and then left her alone in the living room. She heard a violent shuffling from outside and crept through the kitchen to the back door, her breath wavering with every step. Scribbles had left the door open. The outside air had grown cold in the dark. It made its way into the house through the open door.

Two downed limbs lay in the yard, one on each side of an overhead telephone wire. A shrub hung over the short ring of stones that had contained it when Scribbles's parents had lived in the house. A makeshift basketball goal that was much too small for regulation play stood above a slab of concrete that covered the bulk of the yard. Jenn fumbled to turn the porch light and began to search for the second time that night. She peeled apart the night and hoped to see another human being and to feel something like familiarity from that human being. She looked through the downed limbs, the dead tangle of branches. She found a new set of eyes, animal eyes, in the little brush pile. They reflected the light from the porch. Scribbles appeared from the side of the house and kicked at the overgrown shrub, seemingly unaware of the eyes. A mouth beneath them hissed at the sound of his kicking. Jenn couldn't think of the words for the eyes or for the hissing. Scribbles still seemed as if he were totally unaware of them. He kicked again, this time landing his foot among the branches. Jenn watched from halfway out the door as the eyes dropped down lower toward the ground. Then Scribbles turned back toward her. He was panting, manic. He had, at last, seen the eyes too.

"Get out of my way," he said.

He pushed her down onto the concrete and grabbed an aluminum baseball bat that he kept behind the door. He had become a series of explosions, a chain reaction that made dead scientists talk about the end of days. Half the county would have said that he had become a man, probably most of the church too. He had learned something of the power in his hands, and he had understood words like *realpolitik*. He would no longer need to go to school.

Jenn wanted to stand again and go inside where it was warm, but the thought was disconnected from any possible action. She knew nothing of movement. She lay on the porch and watched him stomp past her again on his way into the yard. Her palms ached. Her hip was probably bruised from where it had hit the ground.

"I told you to stay out of here," Scribbles said, trudging across the makeshift basketball court.

Jenn raised herself up and saw him standing over the glowing eyes. His body was nearly convulsing with his every breath. Then he swung the bat. Once, twice, three times. Jenn winced. The creature hissed. It tried to play dead at first. Its closed eyes left its phantom face white. Jenn worked herself to her feet and watched him swing the bat again. Blood splattered the aluminum. Red droplets covered his t-shirt. Jenn stood in the doorway without words, motionless as if he'd take the bat to her if she dared to move. She couldn't think as the bat flew into the opossum's soft body, its harmless, misunderstood body. There was nothing to think then. When Scribbles turned to face her, the blood was all over his shirt, all over the bat. There was blood clear up to his cheeks.

"I think I should leave," Jenn said, shivering. "You're fucked up, Scribbles."

"My name is Matthew. You never asked if you could call me that."

He seemed bigger than he had before, broader, like she could disappear in his shadow. His hands shook, and the light from the porch light danced along the bat. Jenn didn't know the man who stood in front of her. She turned and ran back through the house before he could say anything else or swing the bat again. She ran over the train tracks and past Main Street with its streetlights like old lamps. She ran until her breath stung in her chest, until the cold caught up to her and made its way inside her lungs. Then she stopped running. She looked at the sky. Stars twinkled in between heavy clouds that looked like black brush strokes on black construction paper. She saw her breath rise up over her head and become lost in the endless space that rested on top of the ground. She wished she had the words to pray or tears to cry, but she didn't. At that moment, she didn't have anything at all. She didn't have Ava. She didn't have Scribbles. She wondered if she'd ever really had them, if anyone was capable of doing anything more than watching the things and the people they cared about disappear like vapor in the sky. She took a deep breath and felt the cold in her chest again. Then she let the breath out and walked home.

Interlude

Charlotte woke up from the bed she shared with Jim. A hand, Jim's hand, had ahold of her shoulder and was shaking her. It was 1:30 in the morning. Jim was still wearing his blue jeans and his work shirt. He was panting out his rotting breath, telling her to get up and get in the truck. His dentures were white and shining, perfect teeth, teeth that could be bought with money made from suckers who didn't notice the livestock supplements in the meth they were smoking. Of course, the supplements didn't turn black and gooey like sugar. They burned better than salt. Maybe most of those suckers weren't so dumb, then, just unlucky. Either way, one of them had been dumb enough to steal product from Jim. So, he woke Charlotte up and told her to get in the truck.

"You're gonna drive me somewhere," he said.

He flipped a light switch. The sudden shining overhead made it hard for Charlotte to keep her eyes open. A drooping ceiling fan broke measured holes in the oppressive light, but it was not enough to keep her from squinting. Eventually, though, her eyes adjusted to the brightness, and she could see Jim grinding his false teeth, could see the muscles along his jaw clench and then go soft.

"I have some business I must attend to," he said.

Charlotte put on a sweatshirt. Her skin was already wrinkling, but it wasn't yet purpled by his belt or his fists. Things had been going much better back then. It had only been weeks, maybe months since she had heard from her son. He hadn't been arrested yet. She spent most of her mornings at that time tending to a row of tomato plants she'd planted alongside the back of the trailer where she lived with Jim. No one told her to get back inside and make breakfast or do laundry. She was high almost every afternoon for free, deep in euphoria without any notion of whether or not she'd have to swim back out of it. She felt powerful then, productive. Jim wasn't too worried about the law or about any competition either. People bought things from him at whatever prices he told them to pay. They did what they were supposed to do. That night, something changed. Someone had grown bold.

Jim drove to a trailer park where the railroad tracks passed by the creek. Though Jim's trailer was off by itself on a patch of land that he owned, Charlotte felt at home among the clusters of single-wides and the dogs that roamed among them. She had grown up in a similar trailer park. She'd made friends there, little girls with short haircuts on account of lice, little boys with holes in their t-shirts. Charlotte did not have friends in the Branch Creek trailer park though, and Jim wouldn't tell her what exactly he was up to. Instead, he turned the radio off and hummed hymns to himself as he wound through the half-lit park. His face was red and veiny. His voice was low and serious. His jaw continued to clench and then unclench. He parked outside a trailer. Charlotte sat in the passenger seat as Jim pounded on the door. She watched the house light up like Christmas morning. Then Jim disappeared inside. He reemerged a few minutes later with Brock, the bartender from the Red Fish joint off the highway. Jim told Charlotte she'd have to be the one driving now. She tried to cover up her yawning as she fought against the sting of sleep and moved to the driver's seat.

The bartender's eyes were bloodshot. He bounced his heels against the floorboard as if he were shivering, though the low air was still warm and filled with summertime. It couldn't have been any cooler than 80°F. Jim barked orders, lefts and rights in between praises to the Lord and curses for the dirty so-and-so who'd crossed him. They found their way through pastures and over low concrete bridges that flooded in the spring. Charlotte did as she was told and parked alongside a sheet metal home outside town. Jim and the bartender got out of the truck and went inside without knocking. The front door must have been unlocked.

Charlotte found it odd that her breaths were so loud when she was alone. She counted them to keep time while the two men were inside the house. Her chest rose and dropped with her breaths, and she felt like both beast and machine, like a collection of processes governed by Mother Nature herself.

Soon she lost her count, and she became consumed by the strange familiarity of breathing. Her breaths began to bore her, though, and she felt silly for spending so much time focused on them. She tried to spot constellations instead. She thought she saw a woman, maybe Andromeda or Cassiopeia, but then she realized that the woman's hip was just the splatter from a dead insect on the windshield. So, she invented her own constellations, a giant frog and a horse's head. Though she knew she was tired, she felt good as the fog of sleep cleared from her head. She resolved to get high and stay up through the morning cleaning the trailer or working on a puzzle if she could find any hint of the sun along the horizon by the time they got back. Then she heard the gunshot.

A couple minutes later, Jim and Brock came back out of the house. They carried the body of a tall Black man between them. Charlotte had never seen a dead body before, and she knew then that she had no chance of going back to sleep. The body was slack. That's how she knew it was dead. It swung back and forth as Jim and the bartender walked toward her. They tossed it into the truck bed and threw themselves into the cab. They'd become white-hot in the house. Charlotte could feel them through the already-warm air. Her head pounded with the beating in her chest, and she was aware of the various processes separating her from the body that lay just a few feet behind her.

Jim said to drive. Even back then, Charlotte knew better than to second-guess him or to ask about the body. He muttered more lefts and rights, but other than that he didn't talk. He hummed again instead. The muscles in his jaw no longer pulsated from one moment to the next. He appeared to be at peace. When Charlotte looked over at him, his eyes were straight ahead, not as if he were eyeing the road, but as if he were staring through the world in front of him at something beyond, the plane where angels and demons battled for souls. He must have been familiar with the dead to sit there like that. The bartender still shook behind them.

They'd long left the land of street lights and pavement when Jim told Charlotte to stop the pickup along a pasture of rolling hills and knee-high bermuda grass. He said to turn the lights off, and then he got out and disappeared over a rise in the road in front of them. Charlotte, unsure of what was next, felt her heart jump and stutter. The bartender's teeth chattered. The sound seemed to highlight the reality of the situation, the reason to be scared. The body in the truck bed was flesh and blood, and that blood was probably running all over the bed and seeping into the truck, where it would live forever and cry out for vengeance every time they took it for a drive, especially after Sunday services. Charlotte wondered if she'd ever want to drive again.

"Will you shut the fuck up back there?" she said to Brock.

The bartender didn't reply, but the chattering softened as if he'd covered his teeth with his lips. Charlotte lit a cigarette to keep awake, but when Jim reappeared in the street, she threw it out the window, because Jim didn't like her smoking in the pickup. He said the smell would hurt his image. She never quite understood this.

Jim waved her forward, up and over the hill. An open wire gate emerged from the dark. Charlotte pulled through the gate and over cattle guard piping. Ahead, a dirt path cut through the empty pasture. The occasional tree stood up against the night sky. Moonlight reflected off a metal building across the sea of grass. Charlotte thought that she would have, in another life, left the gleaming bits of pasture on a canvas with oil paints. She pictured herself in overalls behind a real artist's easel, the kind of validating equipment used on TV, the kind of thing they'd never had in her school growing up. Then she saw herself covering the canvas in red spatter. She saw old brushes caked with red in piles on the floor around her. Red was the only color that she could see. The world was so filled with red that it burst out of men and ran thick over her mind's eye, suffocating the possibility for anything else. Charlotte shuddered.

Jim closed the gate and got back into the pickup. He pointed to the building.

"Go ahead and pull up there," he said.

Charlotte looked up at the stars again as she drove. She wanted to forget about what it was that she was doing and to exist in those last moments before the gunshot. She couldn't continue to picture herself painting, because of the red, because of Jim, because of the chattering teeth of the bartender, and because of the dead body that she worried would leave her labeled as an "accessory to murder." Instead, she tried to imagine how it was that any group of people would ever agree that the stars made specific shapes, constellations. The scriptures said that God told Adam to name all the animals way back in Eden, but who had dominion over the stars? Someone must have had a lot of power to convince entire civilizations that the arbitrary star pictures were worth recording. Charlotte could no longer find the frog or the horse's head in the sky above her, and even if she could somehow spot them again, she would have a hard time pointing them out to anybody else. The body rolled around in the truck bed.

When they approached the metal building, Charlotte realized it was a barn. At Jim's command, she shut off the pickup, and a shuffling, grunting sound swirled from the barn like Legion. Jim got out of the car and nodded to Brock in the backseat.

"You're a good man, Brock," Jim said, "but I think you got in a little too deep with your buddy back there. You understand?"

"Yes sir," the bartender replied.

"Atta boy," Jim said, smiling. "Let's go give these pigs their supper."

Brock and Jim carried the body to the barn. The moonlight shone on the dead man's Black face, his pretty Black face with its long eyelashes. Blood still trickled red out of his abdomen onto the ground beneath him. Charlotte wanted to get out of the truck and see what shape the blood had made in the dirt. Brock had trouble walking on account of his trembling. Jim dropped his end of the body as if it were a sack of corn feed and opened the door to the barn. Then he picked the body back up and continued inside, where the grunting sounds turned to squealing. Through the noise, Charlotte thought she heard Jim laughing and calling to the pigs. She wished she could disappear, but she did not want to die, not like the man in the dark, not like the others, whose names she'd never hear. She did not want to be reduced to a count of murder.

She tried to drown out the noise with her thoughts, but the only thought that would silence the pigs' howling was the memory of the eyes that had hung lifeless between Jim and the bartender. She remembered the slack, hanging face, and she could have sworn then that it had winked at her, the long, dark eyelashes meeting and then falling back to their dead place, the place where the face would burn into her mind for the rest of her life. She wanted someone to bless that face. She imagined Saint Paul kissing its scabbed cheeks into the pearly gates. Then she saw Christ tossing the limp body into Hell. It fell next to a fire-ringed plot for herself. Jim's demonic space was nowhere to be found.

When Jim and the bartender came back out of the barn, Jim pointed to the dark spots in the dirt where the blood had spilled. He waved toward the rear of the pickup and told Brock to dig up the bloody spots in the dirt. Scrapes and scratches sounded against the aluminum bed as Jim produced a shovel. Then dirt and dried blood found their way into the bed with a series of thuds. The bartender threw up. Jim made him shovel that mess into the back of the pickup too.

They finished with their cleaning. Jim pushed Brock into the side of the truck. The bright and shining artificial teeth smiled as he opened the door. Charlotte faced forward as if she hadn't been staring at them the whole time they were getting rid of the body. Even back then, Jim hadn't been a fan of nosiness. The bartender struggled to pull himself into his seat. Jim laughed in between the notes of the hymn that he was humming.

"Charlotte, it's high time you drive us home," he said. He turned back to the bartender. "I'm about ready to go to sleep now. What do you say, friend? You've been working overtime tonight."

Brock nodded. Charlotte started the truck. Jim's humming died down to a slow whistle, and the bartender coughed every so often as if only to break up his panting. Charlotte thought again of constellations. She knew that it would have been someone like Jim who'd named them, the kind of man who was willing to feed the competition to the pigs and who truly believed that God Himself approved of his killing. Yes, she thought, Jim would have dominion over the stars if he wanted, at least in Mayes County, and he'd have no use for any painter, not when the only color left was red. His whistling continued as she drove back to town.

Chapter 12

"The medical examiner has ruled that the woman's death was due to an overdose that stemmed from drug use," Sheriff Taylor said. "Because the death has no criminal element, we will not be releasing her name at this time."

The barely-risen sun peeked into the sheriff's office lobby through an open blind. Groans and shuffling and the shutters of film cameras once again filled the makeshift conference room. Along with the early-morning tiredness, the purple bags that lay under jumping eyes and the breaths that smelled of gas station coffee, a certain eagerness plagued the reporters' faces. Sheriff Taylor didn't know why those tired faces were so anxious to hear what he had to say. Surely they had figured out that he didn't have loose lips, that he didn't want them there. Regardless, they'd made a habit of coming to see him. They challenged the sheriff. They wanted to know whether he was still the hero deputy. He was sure the reporters remembered that he had once been the hero deputy.

Sheriff Taylor had relayed to them the clinical details of the discovery. He had turned to a new list and talked about times and locations and people who had stumbled across a human body in a ditch and then hurried home to notify the proper authorities. He had decided not to mention the Oklahoma State Bureau of Investigation agents who had arrived at the scene and taken a look at the body, because they weren't of much importance then. They'd just asked their questions and decided to leave when the sheriff told them they were in his jurisdiction. No one needed to know about that.

He was careful to glance around the room when he spoke. Barbara had once told him that he looked more confident when he did that sort of thing. The reporters tried to catch his gaze when they weren't writing. They were looking for the holes in him, the places where he went to pieces. He was safer now that Gail had quit coming around. He hadn't heard from her since the day she'd protested outside his office. Though he wondered what Deputy Carlson had done to keep her out of his hair, he knew that it was best if he didn't ask those kinds of questions. The moment he knew something would be the moment that he held real accountability in the matter.

"Did the body belong to Ava Springtree?" asked the reporter with the reading glasses and the Yankee accent.

Sheriff Taylor gritted his teeth. He still wasn't sure which station had hired the nosy hotshot, but he knew that he wouldn't do well in Oklahoma, not when he talked so fast and with the kind of voice that probably rhymed "pecan" with "seek and."

"I'm not going to reveal any details that may inadvertently clue you folks in on the identity of the woman found dead here," Sheriff Taylor said. " That's the family's business. But I will tell you that the investigation into Ava Springtree's disappearance remains unchanged by this recent discovery."

The writing resumed, and the sheriff called for more questions. A reporter asked for details about the body, an age, a description of clothes. Sheriff Taylor ignored the question and asked for another one.

"I have information that suggests the OSBI may be involved in this investigation," a woman said. "Is there any truth to that?"

Sheriff Taylor was sweating again. He considered telling Barbara that he would be switching his wife-beaters to cotton t-shirts to keep the moisture from breaking through to his sheriff's uniform. Just a handful of t-shirts should last him until retirement. They only had to last him until retirement.

"Two OSBI agents in the area responded to the scene when they saw all the commotion," he said. "They left after they had a chance to look at the body and deduce that there was no clear evidence of foul play or any connection to any of their ongoing investigations. We are not currently requesting their assistance."

The sheriff wrapped up the conference before anyone could ask much more of him or accuse him of abandoning his heroism. Afterward, he sat in his office and moved sheets of paper from one stack to another. The day had turned cold. Winter would likely come early. Deputies would soon be responding to countless space heater fires at the back of the dry wind. His phone rang. He didn't answer it immediately. He stared at it instead. The caller ID screen lit up and faded dark again. This happened three times before he picked up the phone and put it to his ear. Donna at the front desk said there was someone to see him, the kind of person who shouldn't be made to wait. Then a broad man with a cowboy mustache was standing in the doorway, his hand outstretched.

"Hello, Sheriff," the man said. "My name's Tommy Richards, and I'm an investigator with the state bureau of investigation. How are you this afternoon?"

Sheriff Taylor shook hands with Tommy and sat back down behind his desk.

"How can I help you?" he asked.

"I'll cut right to the chase, here. I have a couple questions here for you about a missing persons case in your jurisdiction."

Sheriff Taylor worried that sweat would burst from his pores like little fountains.

"Whip it on me," he said.

"I hear you've still got a missing juvenile on your hands."

The sheriff tried not to move, tried not to give the investigator any reason for suspicion. He blinked when he needed to, but he didn't keep his eyes closed for long, certainly for not more than a second. He often glanced to his left and kept his hands away from his face. He knew what liars looked like, what the investigator was looking for.

"We've got a girl's been missing for a few weeks now," Sheriff Taylor said. "We don't think there was anything criminal about it, but her daddy died in an electrical fire and she took off somewhere, probably with a friend out of town. Our investigation shows that she was what some folks around here call a problem child—no job, suspected drug use, so on and so forth."

"I have some concerns about this investigation."

The room was dense around the sheriff, as if everything were stopped in a clear gelatin and hanging in-place around him with nowhere to go. Part of him wanted to sigh a breath of relief and tell the agent all about Jim and about the meth operation and the threat the old deacon was posing to the peace of Mayes County, but another part of him wondered who this investigator thought he was coming into his office and asking questions about a routine investigation. Most of him, however, thought about Barbara.

"What's wrong with it?" the sheriff asked.

"According to the fellas down at highway patrol, you haven't had much of an investigation at all. They say they're supposed to be assisting y'all with things, but her file's thinner than an origami toothpick. After they talked to me, I did some looking myself, and I don't see any communication from your office to us or the broader authorities about any of this, no alerts, nothing. Sheriff, what's going on up here? What kind of operation are you running?"

The sheriff fought hard to push his tongue across his teeth, to force the words out of his mouth the way truth-tellers forced words out of their mouths. He tried to recall the list, the gutless list of facts. He pushed away the possibility of confession, sure that Jim was the kind of man who followed through on his threats, sure that somehow the deacon would know all about the sheriff's lily liver before the agent was able to leave his office. He stuttered three or four times before he could muster up any words.

"There isn't any evidence of any criminal involvement," he said. "We think she's probably a runaway, but we've done our due-diligence, anyhow. . . ."

He wished then in his heart of hearts that he was speaking the truth, that he at least knew the truth, or maybe instead that he earnestly had no idea what had happened to that girl. He was stuck in limbo, a purgatory in which he had just enough information to know that whatever had happened to her was no good, but not so much as to have Jim's whole operation behind bars before the meth-dealing deacon could act out his vengeance.

"Due-diligence?" Tommy Richards asked, cutting off the explanation. "Sheriff, there's a missing *child* in your county, and you're sitting here in your office with me trying not to talk about it, stuttering like Porky Pig."

The state investigator's words set a fire beneath Sheriff Taylor's skin. He could feel his face turning red and his sweat glands hard at work inside of him.

"Listen," he said, "with all due respect, I think I can run my own county here. We've gone out and sent search parties all through this area. We've had contact with the girl's only known family member, and she didn't have anything to say that would warrant this sort of talk."

"Don't get defensive with me, now," Tommy said. "I think you may be a little out of your league, partner. This isn't another shoplifting case down at the dollar store." He laughed to himself. "Now, what do you say you let me and my office get involved, and we really go about finding this girl?"

Sheriff Taylor wanted to throw the son of a bitch out of his office and slam the door behind him, but instead he caught his breath and spoke slowly.

"I hope you didn't drive all the way up from Oklahoma City for this," he said. "No offense to you or your office, but I don't think that'd do much good. We're already running quite the investigation up here. Either way, she's probably down by the lake with some druggie friends. I don't need anyone else involved."

The investigator paused.

"Think it over, Sheriff," he said. "If you change your mind, give my office a call. I won't get in the way of all the cameras. I hear you're becoming quite the TV personality."

"They can all go to hell."

Tommy Richards stood up to leave.

"Well, if I hear more about this case getting passed over like a fat girl on prom night," he said, "I'll be headed right back up here, and I'm gonna make sure those taxpayer gasoline dollars are well-spent. I have a fine eye for criminal conspiracy, but surely that won't be an issue."

"Surely."

Sheriff Taylor saw Tommy Richards out. There was a handshake and a nod and unspoken hierarchies. Sheriff Taylor wanted to continue on through the front doors after the agent and head home, to call it a day and to see Barbara back at the house. He was tired. His face seemed to sag to the point of drooping. We he returned to his office, he could hardly read the paperwork on his desk. The clock on the wall, a gift from the Kiwanis members, only made him more aware of all the time he had left in the day, the time for more trouble from people he'd rather avoid. Then the phone rang again.

"Howdy there, Sheriff," Jim said on the other end of the line. His voice was thin and crackling as if he'd been recovering from a cold. "I've been trying to get ahold of you for quite some time, but that gal you've got screening your calls kept saying you were busy. Can you imagine that? I reckon you ain't too busy now, though, are you?"

Sheriff Taylor paused before he answered the question, unsure of what Jim was getting at.

"What do you need, Jim?" he asked.

"I need you to come have a talk with me here right quick before things get too far out of hand."

"What's that supposed to mean?"

"It means you'll come by the church this afternoon and listen to what I've gotta say, and you'll listen good too. It means you won't end up on my TV so much. You're making me nervous, and I'm not real pleasant when I'm nervous."

"You'd better watch what you say," Sheriff Taylor said. "You wouldn't be so stupid as to incriminate yourself over a public phone line."

"Now, Sheriff," Jim said, and Sheriff Taylor could nearly hear his gleaming teeth through the phone when he spoke, "you're right. I'm not stupid enough to incriminate myself over the phone, but I'm also not stupid enough to think you'd risk your lovely wife's well-being after, what's it been, thirty years? I don't think a smart man like you would go and do something stupid after all that time."

Sheriff Taylor didn't speak. The receiver was slick with his sweat. He wanted to break it apart, to watch the shards of plastic fly wild around the room and cut his hands wide open. He wanted to be a sacrifice, but he wasn't the sort of spotless lamb worth bleeding out for forgiveness. It would be a miracle if the phone made it through the sheriff's elected term.

"Are you there, Sheriff?" Jim's serpentine voice twisted into his ear.

"I'll be by the church at five. Don't call me here again."

Sheriff Taylor tossed the receiver. The cord kept it from hitting the ground, from breaking apart. It rocked back and forth where it hung as if to hypnotize him. The dial tone growled. He didn't have the heart to make it stop.

★★★

Sheriff Taylor had been a much younger man when he stumbled upon the convenience store robbery that turned him into a hero. Barbara had liked to run her hands through the hair that still covered the top of his head back then. They had laughed with one another, and Deputy Taylor, Doug Taylor, had filled his mind with new ways to laugh, new jokes and funny faces to make at home after his patrol shift. It seemed that he had so much mind left to fill. There wasn't yet the sort of day-to-day wear that left him with little room for those things that weren't necessary for keeping the county afloat.

He remembered later that he was thinking of some such joke when he pulled up to the convenience store. He was there to buy coffee. The robbery must have started just as he pulled up, because the couple committing it didn't have time to hop into their Ford Bronco and zip off into the sunset before he was at the door and watching them hold the old woman behind the counter at gunpoint. They had the gun pointed at him before he realized what was happening. He drew his own gun, and they stood there with their guns on one another, the deputy and the robber with the scraggly beard and loose faded jeans. The female accomplice grabbed the woman from behind the counter and forced her to the back of the store where the deputy couldn't see them. Neither of the criminals wore a mask, and that's how Deputy Taylor knew they were afraid. He could see the way their eyes darted back and forth as if they were actors waiting for their cues.

The sun was setting, leaving the whole of the county golden. It reflected off the convenience store door. The glimmering figure of Deputy Taylor held his ground before the light. He kept his gun drawn when he used his car radio to call for backup. He never took his eyes off the door.

In the end, the backup was unnecessary. The couple got tired. The man with the gun slid it across the tile floor toward the deputy, who was still standing outside with his own gun trained at the store's entrance. He had opened his car door to use as a shield in case shots rang out. It wasn't even dark yet. The man was begging for mercy and saying something about a baby and a cigarette. Deputy Taylor went slowly to the door, opened it, and picked up the gun. Within five minutes, he had both suspects cuffed and sitting in his car. The hostage was still crying. He told the poor woman that he was just doing his job, because he thought that sounded good, like the sort of thing he was supposed to say. Backup soon arrived, and there was a whole lot of talking and wiping sweat off his forehead. Then the media rolled up, and there was even more talking and sweating. Only after Deputy Taylor got home late that night did he realize that he never got any coffee.

★★★

More than fifteen years later, he was sweating again on the drive to the First Assembly of God Church in Branch Creek, looking for a distraction. The reds and oranges of fall had given way to the bare brown of an oncoming winter. It would be bleak for months. The emptied earth seemed to hide its face between the trunks of trees and under dead grass. The sheriff counted the occasional cows and read the sign out in front of metal supply company as if he'd never seen it before. As he drove on, he looked for more signs at the side of the road, and then he saw the sign for the church. "Come meet Jesus this Sunday so things aren't awkward when you see Him face to face," the sign read. He parked his pickup truck and made his way inside.

The main door to the church was left unlocked, and only the stuffy evening air filled the hallway inside. Organ pipes wheezed from the sanctuary like scores of dying birds. The space beneath the door to Pastor Masterson's office was dark, and Sheriff Taylor hoped that was because the pastor was in the sanctuary playing the organ, or, at least, listening to Jim play the organ. Surely the presence of others would ensure his safety.

As it happened, Jim wasn't alone in the sanctuary, but Sheriff Taylor didn't feel any safer for it. Deputy Carlson leaned against a pew, chewing on a toothpick. Pastor Masterson was nowhere in sight. The organ honked and whirred at the whim of Jim's fingers. Then it seemed to pull its song back out of existence as Jim stopped playing and gestured toward Sheriff Taylor with an open hand.

"Sheriff," he said, "I'm glad you came. I was just telling this young man here that I didn't think you were gonna show. That would have made the rest of my day incredibly difficult, and so, I am so very blessed to see you standing there."

"What do you want, Jim?"

"Now, that's no way to speak to a God-appointed deacon of the church," Jim said as he worked his way to the front of the stage. Deputy Carlson stayed still against his pew. "Come, let's talk."

Sheriff Taylor crept forward. The sanctuary made him uncomfortable. The cracks in the white-painted bricks seemed to smile at him with a devilish grin. He'd heard ghost stories from folks who'd been alone in churches, but he was more worried about the coming conversation than about ghosts. He sat on a pew near Carlson, who didn't speak, but instead looked the sheriff up and down as if he were trying to profile him, as if the two had never been in the same room before.

"So, tell me," Jim said, "what on earth was going on with those reporters at the sheriff's office this morning?"

Sheriff Taylor spoke with firmness in order to keep Carlson's respect, to pretend that he wouldn't fall in line for a small-town deacon.

"They came by asking about that woman we found dead here last week," he said. "I told them she'd overdosed and sent them on their way, didn't even give a name."

"I appreciate your honesty there," Jim said, "but I need to know why you keep having these folks around asking questions. It isn't too good for me, for my business."

Sheriff Taylor felt like he was too big for his uniform, as if he were puffing up like a spiny fish and the tiny holes for his arms and his head were cutting off his circulation. He unbuttoned the button nearest his throat to make more room for air.

"I don't want them around any more than you do," he said, "but you can't seriously expect me to continue to sit by and let all this disorder carry on like it's normal."

"What do you want me to do, then?" Jim laughed. "Should I open an antique shop or come and work for you like Mr. Carlson, here? No can do, friend. I have a calling. One doesn't back down from that."

Sheriff Taylor gritted his teeth. His jaw was sore. He'd been grinding his teeth in his sleep. Barbara had told him so, had asked him what was wrong as if she had no idea.

"Besides," Jim said, "you need me, sheriff. Do you know how much trouble you'd have chasing down any other fellar trafficking methamphetamines to these good people?"

Before Jim, Sheriff Taylor hadn't known many folks from the county to use methamphetamines. Before Jim, he'd worried most about ice storms and kids with graffiti paint.

"You can take that shit out of my county and leave us all alone," he said. "It was better here before I knew your name."

"Your county? It seems more like my county these days, don't you think?" Jim ambled toward Sheriff Taylor. His voice was soft, and the sheriff couldn't tell if it was from a place of sincerity or from stifled anger. He leaned close before he spoke, the same way he had when they first met. "I am doing you a service, the very Lord's work. Sure, it ain't legal, but if it weren't me, it'd be someone else. I'm running a good, moral service. I clean up after myself. I earn and hold respect. I am here at church almost every day asking forgiveness for any wrong I've done. I say to God, 'If this ain't your will, then give me a sign, make something change,' and, you know what? He has not done a damn thing to stop me. That's curious, isn't it? If God doesn't stop me, then who are you to stop me? You don't think you're better than God, do you, Sheriff? 'He that is not with me is against me; and he that gathereth not with me scattereth abroad,' says the book of Matthew. Surely you remember the book of Matthew."

Jim stepped back to catch his breath. Saliva had peppered Sheriff Taylor's cheek. Deputy Carlson broke his toothpick in half and was twirling the pieces between his fingers. He hadn't spoken since the sheriff arrived. Jim paced the stage then as if he were preparing to deliver a sermon.

"A state investigator was in my office this morning," Sheriff Taylor blurted out.

Jim looked surprised, open-mouthed. He stopped pacing. Though the sheriff hadn't planned to tell Jim about the investigator, he welcomed the strength the admission afforded him. The old deacon was feeble and adjusting on the stage, and Sheriff Taylor suddenly felt like a poker dealer with a peek at every hand at the table.

"You didn't mention this investigator, Mr. Carlson," Jim said to the deputy.

Carlson tossed the bits of toothpick onto the floor.

"I didn't see no investigator," he said.

Carlson looked at Sheriff Taylor. His dark eyes seemed black in that moment, same as his hair. The sheriff wondered if he could run out the door before Carlson caught him, or if that would really do him any good. He tried to soften Jim up again.

"I didn't tell him anything," he said, "but you've gotta understand that I can only put up with so much before something has to change."

"So, you'd rat me out and put your own wife, the supposed love of your life, at risk of harm?" Jim asked, frowning. "I was under the impression that you were supposed to be a man of character, a real moral authority."

Jim sat down on the stage. Sheriff Taylor thought of his wife, again both as the young woman she'd been when they'd first met and as his lifelong companion. He panicked.

"See, I'm not the kind of person to spare the rod and spoil my sheriff, so to speak," Jim said. "I can't have a real Judas on my hands, now, can I? Mr. Carlson, can you help me out here?"

Deputy Carlson put a hand on the sheriff's shoulder. Sheriff Taylor's thoughts became the hot and jumping flashes that he assumed deer felt before they died on the freeway, the evolutionist's fight or flight. Carlson's hand was firm. It kept him in place on the pew.

"He's right, Sheriff," Carlson said, "you've gone and fucked things up. You've fucked things up bad. We can't have that."

Sheriff Taylor pleaded with the deputy. There was a lump in his throat. He had to fight to keep it from rising up and sending him to tears.

"You know I wouldn't do anything to cause you or Jim any trouble," he said. "You know what it's like for me. Let's just take a second here and talk about this."

Jim motioned for Sheriff Taylor to stand. He did. His head had become like the endless panels of sound effects in comic books, bangs and pows in neon colors that ran one after another and then disappeared. Once the sheriff was on his feet, Carlson lunged at him and sent him backward over the tops of the pew behind him. The pew's upper ridge sent flashes of pain through his back and stopped the technicolor cycle in his mind. The seat of another pew met him at the base of his head. A tingling shot through his fingers. In his sudden confusion, he wondered if he'd lost consciousness. He was afraid then that he would die, afraid that Barbara would see him as a liar, a man with too many secrets, a sorry excuse for a sheriff, and he would not be able to defend himself. If he died there in that church, she would not remember the young deputy who was first on TV for stopping a robbery.

When Sheriff Taylor's head cleared, when he knew what was happening, Carlson was standing over him, stomping on his chest. The pounding foot sent the sheriff's insides fighting to break through his skin, to escape. He tried to roll away from the foot, but as soon as he raised his shoulder up to move, the foot knocked him flat against the floor again. He fought for breath, because that's all he could fight for, and after three or four stomps from the deputy's heavy boots, he heard Jim call out from where he was on the stage. For the first time, Sheriff Taylor was grateful to hear the old deacon's voice.

"That's enough, Mr. Carlson," Jim said. He was apparently at the organ again, because the instrument began to swell. "Sheriff," he said musically, "it appears to me that you had a nasty fall down the steps out in front of the church on your way to see Pastor Masterson about your waning faith. What do you think?"

The sheriff only grunted from the floor. A fainting darkness crept into his head. He could hardly make out what Jim had said, but he knew better than to disagree with him. He had to get home again, and he didn't know if that would be an option if he didn't do as he was told. He worried he'd be an offering left at the altar, that he'd become the dog from Jim's dream. He hadn't even had a chance yet to be surprised by the encounter. Jim was crazy, and he was powerful enough to act on that craziness. The mania that grew from the deacon made him like mold that was eaten before it was noticed. Sheriff Taylor wished that he had been the sort of man to make plans, to snuff out Jim before his gut told him it was necessary. There hadn't been much need for plans in Mayes County before. As a matter of fact, most people didn't want them. They wanted more of the same, but that was no longer an option.

"Good," Jim said. "Maybe we'll see more eye to eye now, for Barbara's sake, of course, but because you've proven to be such a selfish, greedy man, maybe for your own sake, as well."

Sheriff Taylor worked his way up into the pew. He was unable to look at Carlson. He'd long wondered if Jim's hired gun had harbored a seed of respect for him, or at least a seed of respect for his badge or his office, but now he knew that was impossible. The dirty deputy had stomped the sheriff like a worm. Sheriff Taylor tried to suppress the fire along his back and in his chest. He knew his body would be purple. He hoped he hadn't broken any ribs. He considered driving to the hospital, but he didn't want to be there alone among the old men with flu and the broken-armed children who'd fallen from trees. He didn't want to be seen with the sort of eyes that were made to hold pity. And what would happen next? He didn't know if Barbara would buy the lie that Jim had fed him. He was almost certain she wouldn't.

"Carlson, see this gentleman out, would you?" Jim asked.

The tall deputy slicked his hair back with his hand. The organ reached full volume again as Carlson took Sheriff Taylor by the arm through the dark hallway toward the front of the church. Light was shining beneath the door to the pastor's office. The sheriff figured he must have come in while

Carlson was beating him in the sanctuary. Was the pastor in with Jim? Had he grown too old to care? The outcome was the same either way.

Sheriff Taylor's chest and back seemed to burn with every step he took. He knew that Jim had won, that there would be no end to the deacon meth dealer of Mayes County without the sheriff's own portion of disgrace, that people would continue to disappear until the day when they didn't, and that Sheriff Taylor had given up control over when that day would come for cowardice's—no, for convenience's—sake. There wouldn't be any more news conferences if he could help it. He would do anything within his waning power to stay away from the state bureau of investigation. He'd cry like a child in his pickup truck over the death of the hero lawman, the death of the sheriff's office.

Chapter 13

"What did you do to your hair?" Jenn asked.

Tufts of it poked out over the tops of Scribbles's ears, which were pointier than Jenn had expected them to be. They had an elvish quality about them, long and thin like the rest of his body. He leaned against the counter at Pete's Cheap Gas and Convenience Store.

"They said I had to cut it when they offered me the job," he said.

"I've never seen you look like this. You have ears!"

Jenn was happy to see him. His short hair made it seem as if it had been someone else who had tried to kiss her, who had beat the opossum to death in the yard. She hadn't tried to contact him in more than two weeks, but she couldn't bear to spend more autumn afternoons watching the world grow dark from her living room. Aside from a work-issued polo shirt, Scribbles was dressed as he was always dressed. He was still wearing dark, baggy jeans and puffy skateboarding shoes covered in mud. A name tag on his chest read "Matt." Jenn had never heard anyone call him that before.

"What's with the name tag, *Matt*?" she asked.

"I told you," Scribbles started, lowering his voice to make sure the drunk man poking around the snacks aisle didn't overhear him, "I don't want to be called 'Scribbles' anymore. Even if I did, you can't get a job calling yourself something like that. You might as well just write 'child' on the application."

"But *Matt*?"

"I like it."

Jenn stepped aside to let the drunk man pay for a bag of chips and a candy bar. Scribbles took the man's money, dollar bills wadded up around a dime and a quarter that fell onto the floor when Scribbles tried to count them. The drunk man nearly fell over, waddling from one foot to the other as he tried to pick up the loose change. He eventually got the quarter, but he couldn't find the dime and gave up searching. By the time he stood back up, Scribbles already had his change for him. The man took a crumpled dollar back, but when Scribbles handed him the coins he was owed, they too fell to the ground with twirling, mocking laughter. The man tried again to pick up the lost money, and again he had trouble keeping himself off of the floor. Scribbles leaned on the counter and watched him struggle. Jenn found two nickels and gave them to the man.

"Thanks young lady," he grunted. He went outside, back to his business, but this time with junk food.

Jenn and Scribbles were alone in the convenience store, away from the occasional pickup truck or minivan at the pumps outside. The last time they were alone together, Scribbles had said that he loved Jenn. Now, she felt like he wanted her to be anywhere else. He hardly looked at her. Instead, he eyed the door or poked at his hands as if he were finding callouses from his days of hard work behind the register. Jenn tried again to clear the air between them.

"When do you get out of here?" she asked, an attempt to feel right with herself again.

"I'm not off until 10."

"Aren't there laws against making minors work that late?"

"I haven't been a minor for a while."

Jenn spun a Bic lighter around on the counter as she considered what he'd said.

"Try to get off early, anyway," she said. "I don't have anything to do now, not even, and God, I can't believe I'm saying this, homework. We can drink at your place if you promise to keep your hands to yourself." She paused for a laugh, but Scribbles didn't laugh. He searched the floor for any missing coins the drunk man may have left behind. "I'm sorry. I just really need things to be OK. I'm going nuts, just sitting at home, thinking about Ava and now you."

Scribbles brought his hand down on the spinning lighter.

"You should leave," he said. "If my boss comes in here and sees me talking on the job, she'll throw me out. I'll hardly be able to pay my rent as it is, working the little hours they give me."

"Are you serious?"

"Yeah, I'm make like minimum wage, and rent is—"

Jenn stopped him.

"No, I mean, are you kicking me out?" she asked.

"It's nothing personal. I need this job."

"There's no one even here," Jenn muttered. She slumped as she walked out into the sharp November wind.

★★★

She was on her way back to her house when she realized she was hungry. She didn't want Scribbles to kick her out of the convenience store a second time, so she decided against the microwavable snacks he sold there. Instead, she crossed the train tracks and passed through the field that she used as a shortcut to the Sonic Drive-In restaurant across town.

Jenn never minded the cold, just as long as it wasn't windy. It was the wind, she'd always insisted, that made her uncomfortable. If the day had been calmer, the walk to Sonic may have been bearable, but whipping gusts cut deep into her, and she shivered under her coat. She hid her hands in her pockets to keep her bony knuckles from the cold. Her finger found a hole in one of the pockets, and she pulled at the frayed edge. The simple action entertained her, filled the void of a gray, open world only broken up by privacy fences and dogs chained up and peering through the slats in those fences. The town was exceptionally quiet. Everyone must have been inside, trying to keep warm. Jenn was beginning to worry that she'd grown used to the idea of being alone, of walking through town by herself and keeping her mind busy by toying with her clothes and looking at the dogs in her neighbors' yards. She worried that one day all of that would be enough for her. Ava had begun to feel like a ghost or a memory of a dream, a shape with no outline. Scribbles was becoming something else entirely. She thought of him as a beloved actor who turned out to be the kind of person who punched women or drove drunk. Was he a good friend who'd made a mistake and then turned away from Jenn out of shame, or was he a bad friend who'd been a good actor for a long time?

There were only a couple other diners at the drive-in restaurant. They sat warm in their trucks and ate hamburgers and french fries. Jenn walked up next to one of the trucks and used it as a wind block as she ordered from the large plastic menu beside her. The truck's window was down, and the smell of cigarette smoke rolled over the smell of cooking grease as Jenn dug out the little money she had leftover from her weekly lunch allowance and paid a carhop for chicken strips. She wanted to take the strips home with her, but she worried they would grow cold in the minutes it would take to walk there. So, she took one of the strips out and ate it there at the drive-in, sliding her hand back into her pocket between bites. Two men chatted in the pickup truck behind her. She didn't look at the men, but their conversation spilled out of the truck along with the cigarette smoke.

"He's just talking," one of the men said. His voice was high-pitched and scratchy. Jenn liked the voice. It's humanness made her feel less lonely and distracted her from the cold. She tried to imagine the man behind the voice as she ate. She assumed he was probably a younger man, a wiry man, a high school dropout who worked on a farm somewhere.

"I promise you," the other man said, "there's a picture of her stripped down in his bed, and she's smiling. Hell of a body too."

The second speaker sounded like a smooth-talker, maybe a former quarterback who'd let his six-pack become a beer gut, the kind of person who probably lied frequently and was only tolerated because he'd showed promise when he was younger. Jenn wanted to see what he'd become in the years that followed what she'd assumed was high school stardom, but she only listened instead, impressed with her ability to eavesdrop so casually.

"Hell of a body?" the man with the scratchy voice said. "I ain't trying to eat with no cradle robber here."

"Well, obviously he don't mind."

The men laughed, and there was something unsettling about their laughter. It was not the typical, toothless laughter of men bragging about an illicit lay. Their laughter held a greater scandal, an abnormality. Jenn wanted to know more. Men in Branch Creek had sex with teenagers all the time, sure. Plenty of the girls at school got bored with the boyish pricks and zitty faces of the guys on the football team or in the marching band and set out for deeper waters. Even still, she wanted to see the men, to know what it was that drove them to laughing like little devils with pitchforks in a cartoon hell.

She peeked over her shoulder discreetly, as if she were merely stretching. She was still munching on a chicken strip.

"I don't believe a word you're saying right now," the man with the scratchy voice said. He was both broader and older than Jenn had pictured. He had the beginnings of a beard on his chin, but his cheeks were bald. He'd been the one smoking, and he flicked cigarette ash out of the window every so often.

The other man turned out to be a fat man with a receding hairline. The remaining wisps of his hair scattered every which way to cover the bare skin on the top of his head. Jenn turned away from the men just as soon as she could make out their faces. She hoped they wouldn't notice that she was watching them.

"Her dad owed him a butt-ton of cash," the fat man said. "That's what he says to me, anyhow."

"So he went and had relations with the fellar's daughter?"

"He killed him, you moron. I swear, you're a beach pail short of a sandbox."

Jenn stopped chewing. She couldn't remember ever hearing of murder in Branch Creek before, and now someone was talking about it in the open air of the Sonic Drive-In.

"What does that have to do with the girl, though?" asked the man with the patchy beard.

Jenn swallowed the chicken in her mouth. Maybe the men knew what had happened to Ava. Maybe they were talking about her father.

"He couldn't have her out and about and ratting on him, now, could he? Besides, she didn't have nowhere to go, seeing as her house was burned up."

Jenn dropped a remnant piece of chicken strip onto the ground. She remembered the trailer fire, the news reporter, all those fallen leaves. The fat man had seen a picture of Ava. He knew who had killed her dad. The ghost of her friend became flesh again, rose up like Lazarus in his dead clothes. Jenn turned back to look at the men a second time. She wanted to soak in their every detail, to burn their faces and their pickup truck into her memory so well that she'd recreate the scene at will, even in her dreams. She realized she was shaking again, but she knew it wasn't on account of the cold. Not even the wind could bring on that kind of trembling.

The truck was a gold-colored Chevy that seemed to be held together with little more than duct tape and morning prayers. The passenger's side door was a different color from the rest of the pickup, as if the owner had found the door at a scrapyard and thrown it on himself after a crash. The men also seemed to be patched together. Both of them were missing teeth. They had scabs on their faces. Jenn recognized the look from a video in her freshman health class. The men were probably farm workers who needed to stay up more hours than a cup of coffee would afford them, who needed the sort of illicit pick-me-up that she'd heard about but never seen. The man with the beard had a scar on his scalp that peeked out from his matted hair onto his forehead. Jenn wondered why she hadn't noticed that before. They both wore Carhartt style coats, a given for most of the area's working class. The fat man had blue eyes, which were striking in contrast to his otherwise unsightly appearance. Jenn did everything she could to keep from running up to the open window, grabbing the men by their shirt collars, and demanding answers. She balled her hands into fists and dug her nails into her palms. The brown paper sack that held her food was at her feet.

The man with the beard caught her looking at them.

"Can I help you?" he asked, tossing his cigarette out the window.

"I couldn't help but overhear—"

"You didn't hear shit," the man said. He began to roll up his window. "You better hope and pray you didn't hear one damn thing."

The fat man threw the pickup into gear and backed out of the lot. Jenn chased after the truck, but it left her further behind with every pace she took. She tried to read the license plate on the back of the truck. All she found were letters and numbers, same as any other license plate. She tried to order them in her mind, to make them into something she could remember, but then the truck was out of sight, practically nonexistent, and she could only recall that there had been a "T" on its plate. She was alone in the cold again at the side of the restaurant. Her leftover food was in the paper bag on the pavement. She couldn't imagine eating it then. It would stay on the ground until one of the carhops skated out to take care of it. Jenn had seen the outline of her friend through a glass dimly, and she was angry. She ran back to the convenience store.

***

When she got there, Scribbles was ringing out a case of beer for a couple, a tanned man with faded tattoos and a woman with chemical-kinked hair who hung on the man's arm like she had something to prove. Jenn could hardly stand patiently behind them. She danced to herself while she waited as if she had to pee. Once the couple had finally paid and left, she slammed her hands on the counter. Tears rolled down her face as she spoke.

"They have Ava," she said.

Scribbles hustled around the counter to be near Jenn as she cried. His face was soft and familiar as if nothing had ever happened between the two of them, as if there were places where she could feel safe. She couldn't remember if he'd ever done something like that before, if he'd ever really had to be the strong one in their friendship.

"What are you talking about?" He looked around the convenience store to make sure that no one else had entered.

Jenn blubbered out half-words and syllables and strings of snot and spit. She was sure she came across as a crazy person, a village idiot. Her thoughts raced around one another so fast that she couldn't grab onto them and make any sense of them. Scribbles handed her a napkin, and she wiped off her face. It immediately filled again with the gross bits of her sorrow. After what felt like quite some time, she found a gap in her stuffy breaths to speak again.

"Some old man is fucking her," she managed. "He's got her all tied up and everything."

Something like a barrier grew up between Jenn and Scribbles, and he was strange and unknowable again, outside the role, the charade. He stepped back from Jenn's still-heaving body as if she'd accused *him* of something wrong. He shook his head as if trying to rid himself of her words.

"W-where did you hear that?" he said. He handed her another napkin.

"There were these men at Sonic, and they were talking about her."

"What did they say?" Scribbles leaned back on the counter, held himself like he had no stake in the answer.

"Someone has a picture of her. Some man. He's fucking her."

Her voice broke off into a howling, the kind of raised-volume moaning that follows the deaths of movie heroes. Scribbles watched the front door to the store over her shoulder and handed her more napkins.

"You saw a picture of her?" he asked. Jenn's heart was racing.

"No, but," she made sure to make eye contact with him as she continued, "I heard them talking about it."

"How do you know it was even her?"

Scribbles looked at her in disbelief. In him, Jenn saw the same skepticism that she had seen in the doubting-Thomas deputy who had come to her house and dirtied it with his disbelief.

"Are you serious?" Jenn said. "I just know it was. They said her house burned down. Who else could it have been?"

Another customer came into the store, an old man known to most everyone around town as "Uncle Julius." He was the kind of person who sat in a booth eating donuts and talking to kids who stopped by the convenience store for breakfast, the kind of person who walked around town at all times of year, regardless of the weather, because he wasn't allowed to drive anymore. Rumor had it that he'd hit and killed a kid with his car in the eighties, but that he hadn't technically been doing anything wrong except for being too old to properly operate the vehicle. In actuality, he had probably hit a dog or light pole, because no one ever mentioned the name of the allegedly deceased, and everyone, at least in public, adored Uncle Julius. Another rumor held that he had a perfectly good car in his garage with a full tank of gas in it waiting for the day that he'd need to get somewhere in a hurry. That rumor was more believable than the other one.

Scribbles hopped back behind the counter to greet Uncle Julius. The old man in his fisherman's hat and his oversized coat from the Army surplus store, however, stopped by Jenn and put his hand on her shoulder.

"Is this boy bothering you?" he asked, nodding toward Scribbles with a warmth and a sternness that told Jenn that he meant business but that also meant that he didn't want to intrude on her personal affairs if she indicated that they were out of bounds.

"No," she sniffed, "he's fine."

"Are you sure? I think I could whoop him if you need. I know his boss, and if I can't, well, I know for a fact she could whoop him. I think I could whoop him, though."

Jenn smiled at the old man, and he took his hand from her.

"It's not that at all," she said, fighting back the urge to fall apart and melt to the floor of the convenience store, to spread out and disappear like the man's coins from before, "but thank you. I know you could whoop him. You seem like a tough nut."

Uncle Julius shuffled along to the counter and asked for a scratch-off and a 22-ounce soda from the fountain. He paid, winked at Jenn, and went to fill up a styrofoam cup and find out if he'd won the lottery.

"What do we do?" Jenn asked, turning to Scribbles. "We call 911, right? Or the news?" She felt like a puppy at the shelter, begging to be adopted. She needed someone to pick her up and to believe her. She needed that person to be Scribbles.

"What can we do? Isn't 911 just for emergencies?" Scribbles's voice was just over a hushed whisper, like he was afraid that Uncle Julius would think them crazy for their conversation. "I don't even know what makes you think that what you heard has anything to do with Ava."

"Okay," she said, filled then with the final wind that she hoped would bring her sinking ship to shore, "I'll lay it all out here. I was eating at Sonic, and I overheard these two guys talking about a picture of a girl who was tied up at this guy's house."

"What guy?"

"They didn't say, but they said the guy killed the girl's dad and burned her house down. It has to be Ava. It has to be."

"You heard all this at Sonic?" Scribbles asked. He looked over at Uncle Julius, who was seated at a booth and was working at his scratch off with a coin. Again, Scribbles lowered his voice until he was very nearly mouthing the words. "You sound like a crazy person. I know things have been rough, but there's no way you heard that. She's gone. I know that's hard to believe, but she *left*. Why do you think the cops don't even care anymore?"

"Scribbles, I heard it, all of it," Jenn said. Her mouth twitched and fought for the words.

"Listen," he said, "I don't want to be like this, but people talk, you know. I'm afraid there was probably another side of Ava, a side she didn't show us."

Jenn's stomach turned into lead.

"You don't mean it," she said. "Come on, it's all just talk."

"You know she liked to go hard every chance she got. She was always the one bringing over beer and telling us to drink with her, and, well, I guess she was probably into other stuff too."

Jenn began to sob again. She raised her voice, not because she wanted to draw more attention, but because she couldn't break through her sobbing at any lesser volume.

"You've got to be kidding me. . . ." she started. Then she fell into the silent sobs of defeat.

Uncle Julius looked up from his ticket. He tried to get up from the booth.

"It's the only thing that makes any sense," Scribbles said, shaking his head again.

Jenn gathered herself together in the space above her neck and forced what little emotional energy she had left into clear words. Again, her hands were balled into fists. Her nails dug into her palms. She could hardly feel it. She was only her words, clear words, words that burned.

"You're a bastard," she said. "I hate you, Scribbles. I swear to God, I will always hate you for this, and whenever I see Ava, I'm gonna tell her everything, and she's gonna hate you forever too. You're a goddamn coward."

Uncle Julius was hobbling toward her.

"Hey, now," he said. "What's going on?"

"You can't talk to me like that," Scribbles said, ignoring the old man. "Get out of my store. Just go. Accept what happened. Stop thinking about it. It's making you crazy."

***

Jenn turned and walked out of the store. She left Uncle Julius mid-stride and Scribbles grimacing. She slammed the glass door as hard as she could, hoping to break it into thousands of shards that would sparkle against her skin as they fell around her. Instead, it the door rattled into place. A man with a goatee and sporty sunglasses nodded to her on his way inside, apparently unaware of the wild and vibrating unapproachability that she'd taken on. Her tears were angry then. They weren't the bitter bulbs of melancholy and hopelessness and isolation that they'd been before, but instead, they'd become the marching eye sweat of a powerful young woman who would, single-handedly if she had to, make a path into the pits of hell and save her friend from the grubby hands of evil men and the useless boys who broke hearts and took shitty jobs and devolved into the scum of the earth.

She hadn't yet crossed the street in front of the convenience store, though, before her tears burned through the anger and returned to their previous, sad state. She ran through her memory to find Ava's face, but that space was blank. It had become a series of disjointed pieces from different jigsaw puzzles instead of the familiar picture of her friend. She didn't even remember what Ava's laugh sounded like, and she wanted to fall apart again and never come back together. She struggled to fight her way through the wind, to put one foot in front of the other and find her way back home, where she could see Ava's picture in old yearbooks, where she could tell her mother about what had happened and call the sheriff's office.

There was a tapping on her shoulder, something of a light hand made heavy out of necessity. She turned around, expecting to find Uncle Julius's wrinkled face behind her. Instead, there was a short, Black woman with brown eyes and hair that rose from her head in tight curls. The bits of autumn light from the sky above lit her head like a halo.

"What happened to you, honey?" the woman asked. "Are you hurt?"

At first, Jenn tried to pull away from the stranger, but soon she found herself sobbing on her shoulder. The hands that had tapped her to get her attention became like a weighted blanket that could bring her comfort with the warm pats that her mother had never been willing to offer.

"A man has my friend," Jenn said as she cried, "and no one will believe me."

"Oh, sweetie, what are you going on about?"

Jenn told the woman about Ava and her daddy and the men and the picture and Scribbles's doubting everything she said. She didn't know why she was speaking to the stranger, but, then again, she didn't remember the last time someone earnestly asked her anything at all.

"And you heard those men say that here in town?" the woman asked. She held Jenn by her shoulders.

"Yeah, at Sonic, just earlier," Jenn sniffed. "Do you believe me?" she asked. She wiped her nose on her sleeve.

"Of course, I believe you. I've got kin who's disappeared too, went and was gone without a trace." She dug through her purse as she spoke, and Jenn wondered what on earth she could have been looking for. "I've always said to myself, 'Angie, you need to go and find out what happened to Paul, because no one believes anything you say about a missing man here,' and I'll tell you, Jenn, I don't know anything about those men you're talking about, but I bet somebody does. Now, tell me, did your friend hang around any troublemakers?"

Jenn backed away from Angie and felt the hopeless anger rising up in her once again.

"I'm not accusing your friend," Angie said, at last pulling a picture from the purse, "because that's what just about everybody in town did when I tried getting help for my Paul. I just need to know, because sometimes people get caught up in things like that against their will, and you know there's devils in all the drugs around here."

Angie held the picture up for Jenn to see. It showed a young man in a cowboy hat who looked a lot like Angie. Jenn guessed it was the missing Paul that she kept talking about.

"I absolutely swear to God that Ava didn't do any drugs, " Jenn said. She was confident in her answer, regardless of what Scribbles or anyone else said.

"I know you wouldn't be swearing to God if you weren't serious," Angie said as she withdrew the picture. "We need as much heavenly help as we can get if we're gonna find out anything at all these days."

She looked like she was doing figures in her head. Jenn felt that Angie showed enough earnestness to be safe, so she stayed there in the cold with her empty eyes and wondered if the older woman had anything real to offer her, if she knew of anything like solace.

"Do you know any relatives of your friend who might know some information or might listen to what you have to say?" Angie asked.

"I don't know, I saw a lady who said she was Ava's aunt on TV once, but I don't think she was ever around, at least, not when I was around."

"That crazy lady from the news? I saw her outside the sheriff's office with a sign here awhile back when I was going up there to see my cousin, and, don't you know it, no one's ever seen her after that. At least, that's what my cousin says."

"What do you mean?" Jenn asked, hesitating. "Do you think something happened to her?"

Angie looked Jenn in her eyes with a seriousness that seemed to pull all the oxygen out of the air.

"We'd better go out to that sheriff's office together, that's what I mean. Come with me now. I'll drive."

Jenn did as she was told.

Chapter 14

Sheriff Taylor had taken to hiding behind his desk for most of the workday by the time the girl and the woman showed up to his office to raise hell about their missing loved ones. He was miserable and nursing his wounds. When he heard the excited voices from the lobby, he made sure his door was locked. The woman was making a scene at the front desk. He could hear her voice, rough at its edges like she was going hoarse.

"I said, 'We need to speak to the sheriff about some crimes,'" she said. "We've got information that could help him find that missing girl, maybe my brother too."

Sheriff Taylor heard tiny Donna shout as she came out from behind the front desk and tried to keep the girl and the woman out of his hair, but the woman wasn't having any of it. She must have pushed Donna aside and walked right on past her into the belly of the sheriff's office. She yelled and carried on. There were footsteps and male voices now too. The sheriff would have to go out and stop the commotion. His body ached when he tried to stand. He grimaced, but he kept his back straight. He knew that no respectable sheriff in this part of the country walked without a proud chest unless he had something worth hiding. He didn't want to admit to hiding anything, not yet.

Outside, he shooed away his own people and asked the pair of intruders to follow him back to his office, made them promise to keep their voices down. He remembered then what it meant to be a keeper of the peace. He wanted to keep the county as his own. He'd made his name on his own, and he knew he'd lose it if he shared his burden.

There had been no more crimes in the six days that followed the meeting with Jim, but Sheriff Taylor had heard somewhere that the Lord tended to rest on the seventh day, and that seemed to ring true. The seventh day was left to the charge of people, to the charge of hungry Satans all wrapped in flesh. On the seventh day, God may as well have been dead. The world was free to take care of itself, and it would surely run wild and remind the survivors why they'd needed gods in the first place. They would again depend on people with badges and guns and oaths in those places where good lawmen were still offering their services. One could only hope that they'd seek out such a man in Mayes County.

Once the sheriff and his intruders were all in his office, he felt he could breathe a little bit, as if neither the skinny girl nor the short, dark woman were capable of sharing with anyone how small he'd become since he'd been hurt by Jim. He was glad Carlson had taken the day off, had gone back to Joplin for some unnamed relative's birthday celebration, because he knew that the deputy would have been standing in the office corner listening to every word and offering—no, ordering—illicit action against the woman and the girl if they'd barked up any kind of tree worth barking up.

"Now, you're gonna listen to us," the woman said. Her hair hung around her face in tight curls that bounced when she talked. "You're gonna listen to this young lady. I've been trying to tell y'all about this for too long. This girl knows something."

He recognized her voice. She had called the office before, had gone on and on about her missing brother. Some of the things she'd told him were likely worth a second look, but all of them were denied that look by Jim. She had left him voicemails, but she had never before shown up and caused trouble the way the missing girl's aunt had. She likely had no idea how much safer things were for her that way.

Sheriff Taylor did not, on the other hand, know anything about the girl, who stood quietly behind the woman and seemed to peek out from around her. If the sheriff had met her before, it had not been in a capacity that would have warranted his remembering her. She didn't look like the type of kid to make headlines or end up in the paper or on television, but she also didn't look like the type of kid to run around committing crimes and raising hell. The teen made him uneasy, though. Was it only her involvement with the loud, unmovable woman? The sheriff thought that woman had too much time on her hands and too much curiosity to stay on the safe side of the simple good he'd come to expect for the residents of Mayes County who weren't caught up with Jim.

"I think I know where Ava Springtree is," the girl said. "Do you know who I'm talking about?"

"Yes," Sheriff Taylor said. He began to sweat.

The girl cleared her throat and spoke as if she'd rehearsed her words aloud.

"I was at the Sonic Drive-In in Branch Creek, Oklahoma, when I overheard two men talking about a girl who sounds an awful lot like my friend. They said someone has her captive and is having sex with her, a full-on adult. I'm not making this up."

She started to cry. Sheriff Taylor didn't like to see her cry, but he had a duty to uphold, at least in a performative sense, and he made eye contact with the girl as the tears spilled over her face. He drew little circles in a notebook on his desk while she talked.

"Do you know the men that you're talking about?" he asked.

"There was this older guy with a reddish beard on his chin, and the other one was balding, but not so much that I'd call him bald. They were farmers. At least, they looked like farmers. They had on Carhartts."

"There's a lot of farmers around here, you know."

The girl scowled.

"They drove this old pickup. . . ."

"As most farmers do," Sheriff Taylor said.

He hardly listened to the rest. He was too well aware of the pain that pulsed through his body, that kept him from sleep. The teenage girl did not know the men in any way that would give the sheriff a real lead, and that was probably for the best. The woman held her like she was a much younger child and let her cry into her clothes, and the sheriff realized that she was likely done speaking. There were times he wished that someone like that woman could hold him that way, like *he* was a child. He regretted the space he'd made between himself and Barbara. He knew his wife was the kind of woman to hold someone close. He knew she *wanted* to hold him close. He buried that thought deep inside himself. It would work its way to the very bottom of the sheriff and into a space that was nearly running over, a space where secrets went to be forgotten.

"So," he said, puffing out his chest as he adjusted in his rolling chair, "you say you've learned something about the girl's disappearance, but you haven't told me a whole lot that I can use."

"I told you about the men and their truck," the girl started.

Sheriff Taylor shook his head. He worked his face into a mask and reverted to the script.

"I know you're young," he said, "but listen, nearly everyone living in this county drives a pickup truck from time to time, and I'd wager that most of them probably enjoy eating at Sonic. Without a license plate, I'm just not gonna be able to do a whole lot with what you told me. I'll add it to the file, but I can't promise any results."

He thought about that last line and knew deep down that he'd do his best to bring about no result at all. He felt sorry for them both. His guests would never know that, though. The woman still held the girl, who was crying harder than she had been before, a scrunched nose and red skin and runny snot and spit. He wouldn't bring any comfort to either the crier or to himself, a watcher. He wanted her to leave, but he didn't want to have to throw her out. His body was weak.

"Are you just gonna sit here and watch this child and not do a thing about it?" the woman asked.

The words had washed over Sheriff Taylor before he found himself and realized what they'd meant.

"I don't need you people coming in here and throwing a fit. I've heard what you have to say—"

"We have every right to be up here."

The girl just cried. Sheriff Taylor had to watch her.

"I'll add this to the file, but I don't think this information calls for immediate attention," he said.

"You hear that, baby," the woman said, "he doesn't think he's gonna do anything. Let's get out of here. We'll find someone who cares about missing kids and Black people too."

And just like that, they were gone. They'd even shut the door. They hadn't given their names. Now, there was nothing but the bare wall across from him in the sheriff's office, the bare wall and the now-closed door and the phone in its cradle on the desk. He wondered if he'd hear from the state bureau of investigation again. Maybe there would be charges of corruption, of "criminal conspiracy." Maybe those charges would set him free, the truth, indeed.

He'd been sheriff for a long time. What had it meant to hold an office for so long, to lord over the gone, quiet years that blended together in the pre-Jim era of Mayes County? Outside, the world was changing. It would soon be a new millennium, and perhaps that millennium would not be so kind to the people who found themselves in situations like those that surrounded Sheriff Taylor. Perhaps the new people would be stronger, better suited. He only hoped they would be more aware of the hooks poking at their jaws. His body hurt all over. He had once only wanted to retire in peace, to see the fruit of the years gone by. That wouldn't happen if those high-dollar city boys came in and tried their hands at grabbing reins that weren't theirs to grab. It wouldn't happen if he didn't end up the hero. How, though, would he go about maintaining his heroism? Would it involve much more than pointing a gun at the glare on a convenience store door?

***

That night, Barbara was further away from him than she had been before, as if someone had dug a moat between them in the time he'd spent at the sheriff's office or as if that moat had been sinking down on its own throughout the months prior and then had finally filled with water. She hardly noticed his coming home. He wondered how long it had been that way, how long they'd merely coexisted. He'd wanted to tell her the distance was for her own well-being, but there weren't good words for that, so he kept quiet most of the time he was home. She kept up with her cleaning and gardening during the day. He noticed the weeded rows of thinning bushes she'd prepared for the coming frost. It was only a matter of time before she took out a black plastic bag and filled it with the first wave of winter dead. Some plants just went that way, unable to handle changes.

Still, Barbara set out his dinner. He ate green beans and pork roast fresh out of the microwave while she watched Wheel of Fortune. The nighttime news came on, images of a flooded Texas and a gay kid who was beaten to death out west somewhere for no good reason. Barbara looked up, yawned, and went to their bedroom to sleep. Sheriff Taylor turned off the television and lay back in his recliner. On the wall was a picture of him and Barbara on their wedding day. Her dress looked tan under the dust that had gathered on the picture. He had been Doug then, without the khaki uniform and the spare tire body fat that rendered clothes from his twenties unwearable. He'd said Mayes County would be like Mayberry, that he could be a real Sheriff Taylor, just like Andy Griffith. They would live comfortably. Barbara would have a proper garden outside town.

"I do," she'd said.

Sheriff Taylor knew that Doug, or even Deputy Taylor, would have kept those promises. He pulled a fleece blanket up over his legs and dozed in the recliner. The night faded black without apology and then found its footing for the upcoming day. The first frost of the season came early and covered the brown grass and the weary plants in Barbara's garden. The sheriff and his wife slept in separate rooms, and neither of them spoke of the frost when they woke up the next morning.

Chapter 15

Will told Charlotte he'd hired some kid to help him fill his orders. He said it wouldn't be too long before he was making enough money to steal Jim's buyers and run him out of town. He said she wouldn't have to worry anymore. Charlotte didn't know what it would mean for her to believe him. She doubted that Jim's absence alone would bring about the end of her worrying. She had been staying with Will for more than a few weeks the night the kid first came over. She'd kept the place clean without getting high. Will didn't ask much else from her, because he was gone for most of the day and was himself either high or drunk within an hour of coming home.

The day he had the kid over, though, he told Charlotte she should set out some plates and make something nice. Then he went outside and brought in the boy, introduced him as Mike before the boy corrected him and pointed to a name tag that read "Matt." Charlotte warmed up a stroganoff Hamburger Helper on the stovetop. She wiped off a pair of mismatched ceramic plates with a wet rag and dished out a healthy portion of food onto them. She ate the remaining stroganoff out of the pan with a fork. There had only been a few bites left, but she wasn't terribly hungry. She took the plates into the living room. Will and the kid had been talking while she cooked. She sat beside the boy on the couch.

"Thank you," he said. He shoveled the food into his mouth.

He was a skinny kid. In feeding him, Charlotte felt a semblance of the motherhood she could have had if she had not met Jim and given away her best years, the years in which her own son had lived with her, to methamphetamine. She told herself it was Jim, not the drugs, who had stolen her chance at being a mom. Without Jim, the drugs wouldn't have been there at all, or at least, they wouldn't have been around for so long. But she didn't want to think of Jim. She listened to Will and the boy instead. Will was still talking from his chair as if she hadn't entered the room, except now, he had a plate of stroganoff on his lap.

"See, Matt," he was saying, "I'm gonna need you to deliver the product. It's that easy. When I'm busy, you go and meet someone, and you take their money, and then you show them the product. You don't show them shit until that money is in your hands."

"What if they don't believe me?" Matt asked.

"We'll decide on a code word or something. Wanna beer? Charlotte, sweetie, go get us some beer."

Charlotte did as Will said out of habit. He didn't really have any way of making her follow his commands. He didn't have the sense of control that Jim did, the real conviction and tendency for violence. Will just wanted a beer from the fridge. That was fine. Charlotte even told herself that she was practicing freedom when she brought beer to Will in the evenings, because she could choose not to do so, could choose to leave him sitting thirsty in the living room.

When she brought back the beer, she wanted to grab the boy by his cheeks and tell him that everything would be alright, that he didn't need to listen to people like Will, that he too could stand up and leave. Sure, Will would yell and throw a fit, but then life would go on. Matt wouldn't have to meet Jim.

"Your cover will work great for this kind of work too," Will was saying. He'd taken to the occasional bite of the stroganoff, but his excitement seemed to keep him close to the beer and out of the food. The boy's plate was already clean as if he'd just wiped it down.

"Will, eat your food," Charlotte said, cutting him off. "It's gonna go cold."

He groaned and took another bite. Charlotte turned to the boy beside her.

"What do you do normally for work?" she asked him.

"I just got hired on at Pete's."

Charlotte didn't like the gravel he put into his voice. He sounded disingenuous. He looked scared up close, though his features were just dark enough to cover up the fear from afar. Again, she wanted his full attention, to shake him and to tell him to stay scared and to get the hell out of there. She wasn't sure where she would go if that sort of thing caused Will to kick her out, though, and she wouldn't leave the trailer until it was on her own terms. Jim was out there somewhere, and she didn't want to risk him seeing her on the street again. If he didn't beat her, he would get her high. She would never be able to create, or maybe to remember, a sense of purpose out in a world where she could be hunted by Jim.

"Pete's is good work," she said to the boy. "Why would you leave a job like that for this?"

"I need more money."

"What on earth for?"

The kid could not have been old enough to need much.

"Sweetie, would you kindly shut the fuck up," Will said through a mouth full of food. "You don't know a damn thing about making a living. This boy says he wants more work." He turned to Matt. "It's a good deal, son. She doesn't understand it, but you and I are gonna make us some cash."

Charlotte sat with her hands folded in her lap and her fingers pointing upward like a church with its steeple. She moved her hands, put them beneath her thighs. She never wanted to see a church again.

"Do your folks know about all this?" she blurted out. Will gave her a look that suggested she stop speaking, but she persisted. "Do they think you can handle being part of this world?"

Matt, now fidgeting and pulling on his earlobes, didn't look at her as he responded.

"They don't know," he said. "They don't live here. They moved off and left me. They knew what it took to make money. They'd be happy I was doing the same."

He slurped his beer and set it on the floor between his feet. Charlotte loved the innocence in the gesture, the childishness of holding the beer between his puffy shoes. He wouldn't go on holding it that way for long, not if he was choosing to get in the business like a grown-up. He couldn't have been more than eighteen. He still needed parents who would admonish the can-holding method and insist he use a coaster or simply hold the can in his hands. Charlotte had already been holding beers in her hands at that age, best she could remember.

Will had finished his stroganoff, save the sauce caught up in his beard. Charlotte knew she'd already said too much for his liking and chose to let the pale droplets stay nestled in the hairs. He carried on about how they were gonna undercut Jim and push so much product that the whole county would be paying them hand over fist to get it. Charlotte rolled her eyes. If she were a prophet, she would describe police sirens like last days' trumpets and frosty creek beds covered in the teenager's blood. Instead, she was a runaway woman with nowhere else to go and only a few weeks off her husband's, no, *ex*-husband's, supply. So, she said nothing at all. Will asked the boy if he had any money.

"Not currently," he replied.

"We're going to need some of that to really get started. Of course, we'll make it all back before you miss it, but you know, you gotta give some to get some, ain't that right?"

The boy fidgeted with his earlobes again.

"I get paid every other Friday at Pete's," he said, "but I've gotta pay my rent. I don't know when I'll have anything to give. I'm broke. That's why I'm here."

Will crushed the empty can in his hand and tossed it onto the floor. Beer dripped out of the can and left dark spots the size of dimes on the carpet.

"Honey, be a doll and get us a couple more of these," he said, kicking at the empty can from where he sat. Matt picked up his own beer and began slurping it again.

When Charlotte returned, she found a second can on the floor. Matt was looking up at her with expectant eyes. She gave him another beer and went outside to smoke. The wind pawed at the heavy skin on her arms. She had trouble lighting her cigarette. The sinking sun above her was misleading in the chill, and she wondered if someone back in school had ever told her how great the distance between herself and the sun must be to keep such a roaring, bright light from warming her. How could the whole world be so cold, even colder? Damn, it was beautiful, though.

She walked laps around the trailer and smoked a pair of cigarettes, feeling like a little girl with an imagination, the way she'd felt growing up in the trailer park with her friends. When her shaking hands refused to light a third cigarette, she went inside. Will and the boy were still seated roughly where they had been before she left. The pile of beer cans on the floor had grown. Matt was leaning back against the couch like he'd been there a million times before, like Charlotte and Will were his favorite aunt and uncle that he stayed with on weekends to keep out of trouble. Charlotte could have laughed at that.

"You know, we have a trash can just in the kitchen," she said. "It ain't even far from the fridge. You can just toss these cans in there and save us all some trouble."

"Quit your bitching," Will said, "and listen to this guy over here. He's got some *quality* information. You'll never believe what people in town are saying."

"Not everybody's saying it," Matt said, "just my friend. It's probably bullshit."

Charlotte was on her knees picking up the half-crushed cans. Beer soaked through her jeans.

"Well, what is it?" she asked.

"I don't know," Matt said. "It's just something I heard when I was at work the other day. See, my friend was over at Sonic—"

"You're killing me, kid," Will said. "Honey, he heard some old bastard's got that missing girl tied up like some kind of sex slave. Ain't that something?"

He almost seemed excited as he spoke, not in the way that someone speaks about juicy gossip, but in the way that someone speaks when they find before them an opportunity. Charlotte shuddered and took the empty beer cans to the trash. At the very least, Jim would know about something like that. Maybe he had needed to replace Charlotte after she left him. Maybe that's why he hadn't been by yet to pick her up and to punish her for her sins. She felt guilty then. The boy was speaking.

"I don't believe it, though," the boy said. "The girl I heard it from went crazy when Ava disappeared."

The more the boy talked, the more Charlotte thought that he was probably cut from the same cloth as Will, that he was only looking for an excuse to get into trouble and to take a risk for a distorted image of himself that would cancel out the things that kept him from sleeping. She wondered if all men were cut from that cloth, if all women were cut from that cloth. She couldn't help but wonder what she'd be willing to do if Will turned her out into the street.

"Did someone tell the police?" she asked Matt.

"Hell if I know," he said, crushing beer can. "I've got other things to deal with now."

"You sure do," Will said. "We're gonna make money, and it's gonna seem real silly worrying about other people's shit."

"Did you know about her, though?" Matt asked. Charlotte saw something like a softness in his eye. Then the forced, hard look returned. "I think she was using before she ran off."

"I don't sell to no kids," Will said.

Charlotte wondered why he didn't mention the visit to see the girl's daddy and the talk with the deputy.

"Figures," Matt said. "It's not my problem, anyway."

★★★

It was dark before the boy was gone and Will returned alone to Charlotte. While he sat drinking in the trailer, she had another cigarette and thought about what she'd say to him. She watched the smoke from her breath spread out over her head. Somewhere, someone was hurting a little girl, and it would probably go on that way until the girl died. She couldn't shake that thought, despite how hard she tried to take in the late autumn starlight and paint it over and again in her mind. She would, one way or another, have to rid herself of Will, to get away from this bitter line of work, or else these horrors would stain her imagination for the rest of her life.

He was on the phone when she got back inside the trailer. She reminded herself that she wasn't even living there, insisted that she was just staying *temporarily* until something better came along. The days had piled up on each other with a flutter like shuffled playing cards, and she couldn't see around to the other side of those days anymore. Will was loud, nearly yelling, on the phone. When he was done, he tossed the phone, a cordless plastic thing with buttons that lit up green, onto the couch.

"You won't believe how much money we're gonna have," he said. "That boy is gonna be good help. He doesn't have a dishonest bone in him. He won't turn into no rat."

"He looked scared to me."

She wanted Will to be scared too, to follow a more sensible line of thinking to its end, and then she wanted him to disappear.

"Scared shitless," Will laughed.

"I don't like it," Charlotte said. She too had been scared shitless while men laughed. She crossed her arms to let Will know that she was serious. She felt like crossed arms could do a bit more than most words.

"Some of us gotta survive," Will said.

He slapped a beer can from the little table beside his chair. The can hadn't been empty. Charlotte hardly glanced at it as the beer darkened the dirty carpet.

"What about what he was saying about that girl?" she asked.

"You ain't gonna like this, but I should probably mention it to Jim," he said. He was already looking for where he'd tossed the phone. Charlotte hoped he'd never find it. She stepped between him and the couch and felt like a giant who could, with her feet, make him crumble.

"Did you ever think that maybe it was Jim he was talking about?" she asked.

He shoved her aside and laughed as he found the phone. She felt small then, a student before a teacher after class or an athlete told to run another lap.

"Jim ain't a pervert," he said. "He's a man of conviction. He has his dark side, but he doesn't diddle little girls."

She pushed her smallness deep into herself and smiled, took control of her face.

"He's fucking somebody," she said.

Her own words stung her as they moved off her tongue. She hadn't loved Jim, not in any real sense, but she thought sometimes that he'd probably loved her, at least when they were both using. She had meant something to him when she thought she hadn't meant anything to anybody. Now, he was off loving someone else. She was supposed to be OK with that, but she wasn't. She worried she was jealous. But why should she be? He'd just been a convenient way to keep up a bad habit, bruises, and the fear of more bruises.

Will was dialing the phone. He knew the number by heart. So did Charlotte. She figured she always would. He had the phone at his ear and went to the fridge for another beer, went to practice his freedom.

Charlotte was back outside with a cigarette. No, it wasn't that she was jealous of the idea of Jim with another woman. She was only aware of the fact that he'd probably hurt that woman too. The consideration at first brought her relief. She was glad that she hadn't really missed Jim. Then her heart dropped. She thought of what it had felt like to cry as she imagined him beating that girl from the news. She thought of how it had felt to be beaten.

Chapter 16

Jenn did her best to keep the saline tear-snot from running down her face as Angie drove her from Pryor back to Branch Creek. The car wound through gaps in the trees and over tiny hills. Angie said things like, "This ain't finished honey," and, "We're gonna find your friend, I know it," over and over again. She crossed the centerline more than once, but she went on talking as if there were nothing wrong with that. Jenn only sniffled. The highway was mostly empty, and though it did not take long to drive from Pryor to Branch Creek, the days had grown short, and it was hard to make out the road by the time they made it to Jenn's house.

Jenn got out of the car with puffy eyes and enough loose phlegm to bring about suffocation, and Angie said to meet her in the parking lot at the high school on Friday after class let out. She said they'd call every emergency number in the phone book until someone listened to her story. She said they needed *visibility*. She spoke the word as if it were a line from a song. Jenn had never been one for visibility before. She'd taken care to disappear at the back of every classroom and to stay away from anything resembling a spotlight. There were other girls who seemed to enjoy the center stage, but Jenn was never comfortable with all those faces staring at her and waiting to pick her apart. Now, this strange woman said Jenn would have to actively seize the spotlight, and it hardly scared her when she considered what she'd heard the men say about Ava.

"Why don't we just call them now?" Jenn asked. "What if we don't have until Friday?"

Angie was shaking her head.

"Do you want them to give you a cold shoulder like that sheriff did?" she asked. "It's a lot easier to hang up a telephone, and they'll do it. I've talked to all of them—news stations, agents, deputies, investigators, beat cops—probably every badge, gun, and microphone this side of the Kansas state line, and trust me, we're gonna need to go about this with a plan."

Jenn didn't understand. They had simply driven to the sheriff's office within 10 minutes of meeting one another. Now, when things seemed their most urgent, they had to step back and make plans?

"I know they don't tell you this when you go to school, and you probably only see the policeman smiling in the Christmas parade or solving crimes on TV," Angie said, "but they don't care much what happens to the little people, poor people, people like your friend, like my brother. I've known it my whole life. I know the history. That's not to say we won't try, but you've already seen how much they care."

At first, Jenn wasn't sure why she should listen to Angie, why she shouldn't take the investigation further into her own hands. Then she remembered that she had only spoken to the authorities three times, all within the last few weeks, and never under her own prompting. The only time she'd even initiated the conversation had been when Angie marched her into the sheriff's office and demanded that somebody listen to her. She remembered her speechlessness during the phone call the night the deputy showed up to her house. The fire in Angie's eyes, however, was tinged with promise, the first promise that Jenn could remember in the weeks since Ava disappeared. So, she agreed to meet with Angie on Friday and didn't start crying again until she was inside her house and listening to the car tear out of the driveway like it had somewhere to be. She was empty and fast asleep by the time her mother got home from work.

***

In the days that followed, Jenn continued her normal routine without telling her mother about the visit to the sheriff's office or about what she'd heard from the men outside the drive-in restaurant. She feared that maternal dismissal would be even more unnerving than Scribbles's cold shoulder or the sheriff's rejection. She didn't know if she'd be able to keep up any hope at all for finding Ava if another person rolled their eyes at her in disbelief. So, she woke up and dipped into awkward silence as her mother drove her to school. She hardly thought of the conversations that could have been. In her classes, she ignored the empty desks where Scribbles and Ava used to sit and did her best to focus on her work. After school, she went home, warmed up something to eat, and watched television until her mother came home. She thought it best to give Scribbles some distance after the way he'd treated her at the convenience store, but still, she couldn't help but think of him and the way he slept in a sleeping bag in the dirty house his parents had rented and then left empty.

The only person Jenn was willing to talk to during those days was a person whose face she'd never see, the sort of person who evaded her every question as she cried out on her knees beneath her folded hands. It was safe talking to Jesus like that, because that's what He was good for, and after more than a decade of unanswered prayer, Jenn was due a miracle. After nearly 2,000 years, perhaps the rest of the world was due a miracle too. Jenn couldn't remember ever seeing miracles, but she'd seen a lot of people asking for them, people from church, people on the Christian TV channel, all of them in tears and with upturned hands. Ava had said that she didn't believe in miracles, but she believed in God, or something like God. She had never spelled out the details. Once, when they were thirteen, Jenn had asked her why she didn't stay over on Saturday nights anymore.

"I don't like that your mom makes us go to church," Ava had said.

"Don't you believe in God?"

Ava had narrowed her eyes and taken on her mischievous look.

"The God I believe in would rather I get to sleep in on Sunday," she'd said.

And that's all she ever said about it. Jenn could not tell if she was serious. Ava had a way of joking about the serious things and of sounding totally serious about things she didn't care about. The world was like a game to her that way.

***

The day before Jenn was supposed to meet up with Angie, she passed by the bulletin board with its sign about counseling, and it occurred to her that someone could be forced to listen to her while she skipped class and talked about Ava and about her conversation with the sheriff. All through Spanish class she found it hard to mouth the present perfect conjugations. She thought of her story, of all the details she'd have to include as she told it. She felt brave then. She felt as if everything that had happened to Ava, to Scribbles, to herself could be contained and molded and given its due, and someone would *have* to listen to her. After class ended and the electronic bell rang through its speaker, she stood up and found a tingling in her fingertips, the buzz of risk, of something to be accomplished or even conquered. Every heavy step toward the counselor's office snuffed out her chances of going to her locker, picking out the next class's textbook, and moving on with her day.

Her body played at coldness, though the school's interior was warm and moist with the air of pubescent human bodies and their runny noses and non-deodorized armpits. She was tired maybe, but she could not be cold. She flexed the muscles in her calves and then in her forearms to try to calm her jumping nerves, but she was nearly trembling by the time she turned down the hallway where the counselor kept office hours.

Had she felt this way before speaking with the sheriff? Everything had been so fast then, and she'd done what she could just to keep up with Angie. Her memory of that conversation had become a blur in the days that followed, an image dulled by the human brain's attempt at intoxication, a tactic made specifically by God to soothe the nerves of the martyrs, at least according to Pastor Masterson. The closer Jenn got to the counselor's office, though, the clearer her memories became. Where, then, were God and His processes in the halls of the high school?

The door to the counselor's office was closed, locked. Jenn peered through the window and found that the room was empty. The lights were out. She could only see inside on account of a half-open window blind where the sun peeked in with its fickle curiosity between moving clouds. She'd never looked into the office before, and she was surprised when she didn't see a long couch or framed Rorschach tests inside. Instead, there were potted plants and inspirational posters, a cat on a rocket ship telling readers to shoot for the stars.

"Hey, Jennifer," a voice called from behind her. It hung on to the last syllable in her name a moment longer than it was supposed to like her name was a punchline or something to be announced.

Jenn was embarrassed to be found peering into the counselor's office and fogging up the window with her breath. Behind her, Amanda from Spanish class was standing alone in the hallway with her hair pulled back in a ponytail. Jenn had never seen Amanda with her hair like that before, despite the ever-present hair tie on her wrist. Amanda toyed with the bare skin behind her ear as she spoke, as if she were trying to feign a bashfulness and add a sense of seriousness to whatever it was she had to say, which, it turned out, wasn't serious at all.

"Counselor's out of the office today," Amanda said. "I was supposed to talk to her about college stuff before third hour."

Jenn realized she was still shaking and draped one arm over the other to hold herself in place. She found that all the emotions she'd expected to spill out to the counselor were now bubbling about the top of her chest, ready to spill regardless of the audience. Her eyes filled with tears. She didn't speak for fear of crying. There had been so much crying since Ava left, and Jenn didn't remember seeing this many tears from anyone else.

"I mean, that's not why I'm here though," Amanda said, moving her hips so that she stood more comfortably, cocked and clearly in control of what was, at that point, a one-sided conversation. "I guess I haven't really seen you talking to anyone since that boy of yours dropped out. I don't know." She paused. "I'm having some people over tonight at six. I guess it wouldn't be a big deal if you came too, you know, to hang out or whatever."

She uncocked her hip and was looking at the tile floor in front of Jenn, avoiding eye contact. For the first time, Jenn wondered if someone like Amanda often felt the same ways that she did, if she'd been more than a monster made in middle school, the kind of gnashing teeth and bubblegum perfume set on classifying her peers by their cup sizes and sucking up to teachers and writing cute little notes on the chalkboard before school started. Could someone like Amanda ever feel the same ways that someone like Jennifer Armstrong felt?

Jenn noticed she was crying in the same way that one feels the rain more than makes it fall, like it was something that happened to her, something out of her control.

"Sure," she said, "but I might be late." She was choking on her tears and afraid of drowning. She wanted to avoid whatever rumors she feared Amanda would spread about her, the alleged pregnancy scare or suicide attempt bound to find its way into every teenage ear. Even still, the tearful possibility of responding to those rumors was less harmful than the possibility of spending another night without anyone to talk to. "Where do you live?"

"The big house off the two-mile road," Amanda said, "the one with the columns."

Jenn broke off down the hall toward the bathroom without responding. She was spacing out her breaths to keep them as quiet as possible. She didn't hear Amanda's dainty footsteps behind her, but she didn't dare turn around and reveal her ugly crying face to the possibility of Amanda's pursuit. In the bathroom, both of the stalls were taken. A freshman softball player was washing her hands. Jenn worried the softball player had seen her crying and would say something about it. She turned and left without stopping.

The second nearest bathroom was all the way down the hallway and across from the principal's office. Jenn didn't think she could make it there and back to geography without being late, and with no written excuse from the counselor, she would disrupt the classroom normalcy she'd created for herself over the past few days. Surely, everyone would turn around and gawk at her red eyes and runny nose and ask questions of her, or worse, of themselves. Too many people had seen her in her broken state already. It was all damage control now.

She was standing in the doorway to the classroom with her face down. Other students took out their books and hung their backpacks on their chairs. They hardly seemed to notice her when she sat, but still, every glance they took around the room seemed to stick on her for a second before returning to the normal business of pre-class desk prep. Then the bell rang, and all eyes seemed to gather at the front of the room, where the hunched old man of a teacher was putting a sheet of transparency paper on the projector. Jenn's eyes, however, were still wet and staring down at the empty desk in front of her. She sat through the entire class period that way. No one turned back to take notice.

***

Jenn walked home alone after school, the same way she had grown accustomed to since Scribbles dropped out, but with an occasional skip and self-conscious scan for any people who may have seen the skip. In the days after she met with Sheriff Taylor, she spent most of her walk home from school recreating the scene from the sheriff's office in her head and inserting the things she wished she'd said and the ways that the sheriff would have responded differently to those things. She imagined a world in which her own words had led to arrests, to Ava's return, to the end of loneliness, and she felt guilty. When she walked home, she knew the exact words that would have saved her friend, and she wondered why she hadn't known them earlier. She often thought about phoning law enforcement before inevitably remembering what Angie had said about the need for a plan. Now, however, Jenn didn't think of those words she hadn't yet said and their potential for redemptive power. She instead thought of how she'd spend the evening with other people, of how she could be loved by her peers for merely being a peer. She tried to wall away her doubts, her fears of rejection and hazing. She wanted to feel her bones tickle with the excitement of her coming acceptance.

In spite of the early glow of opportunity within Jenn, the grass stayed brown and stiff with the changing season. No one went outside. The townspeople were warm in their homes. When Jenn crossed the railroad tracks, she looked through the opening between the trees where the train would run, but there was nothing there either. The houses on either side of the roadway were sagging. They looked like pouting faces. Jenn's house was no exception. The gray sky weighed on the roof. Even inside, things had taken on a sad state. The clock frowned with its indication of the late afternoon hour. The couch sunk down at its ends.

Jenn sat and turned on the television. Alex Trebek gave answers to Jeopardy contestants who worked to come up with questions. Jenn wished the people in real life would ask more questions. Her answers seemed to be outlined in ink and waiting for color. She changed the channel. PBS offered cartoons for children. Oprah Winfrey was giving things away to her live studio audience. Jenn turned the television off. These shows were for those who were perpetually bored and in need of distraction. Jenn wanted to be distracted, no doubt, but there was something cheap about the afternoon programming on antenna television that only made her more aware of its intentions. At five there would be the news. Then there would be Amanda and her friends. That would be the real deal, something more than a distraction.

Ava certainly would have encouraged the evening with Amanda, despite the fact that the two did not get along. That is not to say that they had ongoing issues with one another, open feuds or loud, catty arguments. Ava hadn't even been affected by the juvenile teasing from other girls the way Jenn had. Ava just didn't like people who cared, or rather, she didn't like people who showed that they cared. Amanda and her friends, on the other hand, treated disaffection like poison, and Ava, in turn, seemed to act more disaffected around them. It was like she was trying to prove something, to show that her way of life was better, that they took things too seriously. When they became annoyed, she was laughing to herself or to Jenn. No, Ava did not care for Amanda, and Amanda would never have been so kind as to invite Ava over to her house, which is perhaps why Ava would have encouraged Jenn to take up the invitation.

"Go," Ava would have commanded. "See what it's like to have things."

***

The afternoon was dark enough to bring about drowsiness, but it wasn't so dark that Jenn felt it necessary to turn on the overhead light. The house was hollow without the sound of the television, and Jenn wondered if her voice would echo back to her if she spoke. She was scared to find out. Her loneliness had faded into the back of her mind that afternoon, and she didn't want to bring it back out in front. Was she scared of the evening with Amanda? Did the taste of friendship, no matter how patronizing, act like crumbs to a stomach that had been hungry so long that it had forgotten its emptiness?

She lay on the couch and looked at the brown spots on the ceiling where water found its way through the roof. The ceiling dipped and wrinkled like a deflated balloon here and there, but never enough to warrant the expensive call to a repairman. Jenn saw something like an upside down Cheshire smile and other patterns in the ceiling stains. She saw antlers and an archer, transformed the incidental into the familiar. Her thoughts returned to Amanda. There had been teasing in the past, whispered laughing over jeans that hardly reached down to Jenn's ankles and bathroom rumors based on unclaimed farts and unsanctioned time spent in the stalls, but that had been so long ago, and Amanda could hardly help that she'd been assigned that role, lest she become the object of the laughter herself. But, then again, maybe Amanda and her friends were still sitting in circles with brightly colored pillows in a house with a staircase and laughing about which girls really were sluts and which were prudes. Maybe, they were holding Bible study or speaking in tongues. It was anybody's guess. Either way, though, the night ahead would certainly beat lying on the couch and finding shapes in the mildew on the ceiling.

Engine sounds broke the silence outside and then became quiet. There was the clop of one closing door and then another. The neighbors down the street must have had company. Jenn tried to spy on the visitors. She pulled the blinds behind the couch to the side and saw a pickup truck parked on the street midway between two houses, a house with a basketball hoop and a carport and a house that had once been baby blue with an empty dog kennel alongside it. There were no people nearby, best she could tell. She found it odd that the driver had chosen to park on the street instead of in the driveway of the home they were visiting. People didn't often park like that in Branch Creek except in the neighborhoods near the park, where cars would fill all the available gaps on summer weekends when the Little League kids were playing baseball. Maybe the neighbors had invited someone in from out of town, some folks from the city. She lay back down on the couch and wondered further about the kinds of people who came to places like Branch Creek. It was more the kind of town people left from. It *had* to be somebody's destination, though. Otherwise, how had anyone come to live there in the first place?

A knocking sounded against the back door, a thin slab of pressed wood that led into the kitchen. Jenn didn't move. The hairs on her arms stood on their ends. Despite her loneliness, there was no safety in visitors. She'd spent most of her life without more than a dozen guests in her home, and now, everyone was coming by at once. The knocking sounded again. She crept toward the door to see who was behind it. Through the window at the top of the door, she saw a man with sideburns and a hunter's cap. He held a rag in his hands and twisted it over and over again. The rag was a pink washcloth covered in dark spots, likely engine oil. He looked as if he were worried about something. Jenn cracked the door open.

"What are you doing behind my house?" she asked.

"My car won't start," the man said. "I was hoping you had some jumper cables."

"But why did you knock on the *back* door?"

The man shrugged. Jenn looked around the yard and found no suggestion of danger, so she opened the door a bit wider to look at the man. He was still wringing the rag around his hands.

"I might have something in the garage," Jenn said.

The man swung his arm through the crack in the door, barged into the house. Before Jenn could make out what he was doing, he had the rag in her mouth and was forcing her to the floor. She tried to scream, to bite his hand, but the rag filled her mouth and made it hard to breathe. He was strong and could stop her from flailing her arms. She wished then she had to pee. A lady at school had said that peeing on an attacker could save her life. She couldn't force anything from her body.

"Don't make no trouble," the man said.

She had no way to answer. Her body felt like it had caught fire. The more she panicked, the harder it was to catch her breath. The man put his knee against her back. She was certain she would die there, or, at least, she would faint. Her muscles tired from trying to escape. Her arms and legs went limp. The man picked her up by the shoulders. His fingers dug into her flesh. He started to pull her through the doorway. His hands were big like the paws of a predator, a non-human animal. No one with such big hands had ever touched her before.

She had no fight in her then, and she was soon in the pickup on the side of the road, the pickup between the houses. She was in the middle seat behind the gear shift. The rag was still stuffed in her mouth. A skinny man with long, stringy hair sat beside her. The man with sideburns said it was best if she didn't talk, and she was too tired to talk anyhow. He held her while the skinny man put tape over the rag so it would stay in her mouth. They put tape around her wrists. She couldn't remember ever being so tired. She wasn't sure if the men were discussing their plans or if they simply knew what they were doing, like trained professionals in the art of abduction. They settled into their seats. The pickup roared to life and took them off to wherever it was they were going. Jenn thought of a big house with columns, of gossip and pillow fights.

Chapter 17

Charlotte was barefoot on the floor, twirling a puzzle piece between her finger and her thumb. She put the piece into the puzzle's last remaining empty space and reveled in secular art for the first time in years, the Looney Tunes all drawn up and bunched together on the carpet. Then the door to the trailer swung open and Will was there with her. She didn't look away from the finished puzzle.

"Turns out the kid was telling the truth about that missing girl," Will said.

He wore the evening cold like a robe. He'd been out on business all day, but his face was flushed. Charlotte wondered if he'd been drinking the afternoon away. He stood over her gasping, excited. He stepped on the puzzle, and she looked up at him without veiling her frustration at the now-scattered jigsaw pieces. She gathered them up to put them back into place. Will's breath smelled like rotting compost and chewing tobacco, not a hint of alcohol. Still, he seemed dizzied and out of sorts.

"Did you hear me?" he asked. Spit flew from his mouth with each hard consonant. He was wagging his finger all over the room, from crusted carpet to plain white ceiling, and Charlotte thought the greasy digit might break off his hand and crawl the earth like a worm. "That girl *is* staying with Jim, just like Matt said." Charlotte dropped the puzzle piece she'd been holding. "The old boy loading feed at the granary said another girl is gonna live with him too."

Though Charlotte had never known the girl, she felt a sinking in her body, the same way a child feels when their favorite uncle dies and they at last understand the weight of it, the empty chair at the dinner table on Thanksgiving and the missing interest in the child's stories at Christmas. It had been easy for Charlotte to blame Jim for the loss of her own innocence, though she had been using, fucking, and stealing before she'd even met the man, and this news of his involvement with the missing teenager made her sure that she had rightly placed her blame. At least Charlotte had been an adult in the eyes of the law, a self-declared burnout at nineteen. Her voice trembled when she spoke, not with fear, but with anger.

"Why would two girls in the prime of their lives go live with that son of a bitch?" she asked.

"You should ask yourself that question," Will said, "seeing as how that's exactly what you did."

Charlotte wished she had a pencil, something sharp to dig deep into his eyes, to make him pay for what he was telling her. She pictured herself standing over his body with fistfuls of his shaggy hair, but the thought of flashing lights and handcuffs chased off the racing promise of violence. There were institutions set on keeping things contained and orderly, even in Branch Creek, especially in Branch Creek.

"How did the guy at the granary know about any of this?" she asked. "With talk flying all over town like that, you know somebody or other is gonna be looking into it, young girls living with an old man and all. It's outside the law."

Will laughed at her. His body jiggled from his waist up to his neck. Charlotte wanted that body to be lifeless and for her foot to be on top of it like a conquering knight. She wanted to wobble on the waves of fat that grew from his belly and made his arms and legs look like they'd been stuck onto the wrong torso.

"Jim really didn't tell you much, did he?" he asked, still laughing and seeming to grow wider.

"He told me a lot more than he'd tell some henchman like you," Charlotte said.

"Apparently not."

His laughing turned to howling. Then all at once, his face was dark and serious and sober like an executioner's face, like Jim's face. He spoke his words like he'd heard someone much stronger say them before.

"He just about runs the sheriff's office," he said.

Maybe he was right. When Charlotte searched her gut, she knew that there was likely more unspoken than said outright during those years with Jim. She thought of countless suppers when there were only smacking mouths and glances across the dinner table. What aborted words would have filled that space? Was it possible that even someone like Will could know things that she didn't?

"How the hell would he run the sheriff's office?" she asked. "They've got a sheriff for all that." Her words fell out of her like a pacifier from a waddling toddler. She would have gone to smoke a cigarette if the little peace of mind still allotted her wasn't so dependent on what Will was about to tell her.

"Shit, even I know he'd try to kill me if I talked about it, and, like I'm saying, he'd probably get away with it." He was laughing again. "Now, that right there's funny."

She should have bought a gun. She could hold it to his head and make him say whatever she wanted. He'd piss his pants and no one would clean it up. If the living room were any smaller, she could send his head through the television screen with one strong movement up through her palms. She could leave his chubby head inside the television with whatever it was they put inside televisions.

"Will," she said, gritting her teeth, "you have to tell me what's going on. These are little girls we're talking about."

"Take it easy there." He seemed to soften as if he knew how many ways she wanted to kill him. Either that or he wanted her pliable and willing to fold right into bed once he'd had a couple beers. "No reason to shoot the messenger. He's just got some boys of his own working at the sheriff's office is all, some deal with the sheriff. How do you think he's able to keep from getting run off?"

Will went into the bathroom. He kept the door open and kept right on talking while he pissed, which made Charlotte's belly turn sour, just like every other time he did it. He was vulnerable then, though, surrounded by wet porcelain, where people die by accident all the time. That thought comforted her. "Far as I know," Will continued, "those girls want to be there with him. That one from the news didn't have anywhere else to go, her old man being dead and all. All I know about the other is Howard Jenkins drove her to Jim's place and expects her to stay there."

He finished. The dirty toilet gargled down his waste. Charlotte stood to leave the room as Will plopped himself down onto the recliner and turned on the TV.

"Wait, I thought you heard about all this from someone at the granary?" she asked, pausing for a moment in front of the recliner.

"I did, and he heard it straight from Howard Jenkins." Will spoke slowly, hypnotized by curated videos of kids falling off trampolines and laugh tracks. "How about supper?"

Charlotte took a pound of hamburger meat out of the freezer and began to fill the kitchen sink with warm water so she could thaw it. Frozen, the meat was as hard as a rock. She could bash it against his head and never make another Hamburger Helper stroganoff again. She'd live in the trailer alone and use his truck to drive wherever she pleased. She'd go after Jim next and rescue those girls, and they'd all paint together and forget the very meaning of methamphetamine. She felt the weight of the meat in her hands. And Will wouldn't even know what hit him, because he'd be so sucked into that boob tube. The sink was full, and she dropped the meat into the water. Soon, it would be soft and nourishing. She went back into the living room and found her pack of cigarettes.

"What about this new girl's parents?" she asked, stepping between Will and the television to keep his attention. The unlit cigarette in her mouth made her tough, ready for business. "It doesn't occur to you that her parents are gonna go looking for her? Even a sheriff knee deep in whatever it is Jim's got laid for him couldn't keep a little girl's momma and daddy from getting concerned."

Will shrugged and tried to crane his neck to see the screen behind her.

"That's about all I know," he said. "I don't have a thing to do with her parents."

Charlotte went outside and smoked her cigarette, put distance between herself and the stupid mass of meth-dealer in the living room. She couldn't wait for spring to return. She liked smoking, but she hated the way her fingers began to ache and then go numb as the cigarette burned between them in the late fall or wintertime. There would be at least four more months of this discomfort, but even though it was cold, she was grateful that she could be calm and separated from Will by walls, even though they were only the thin walls of the trailer.

Why did she feel the need to return to the sweaty young man in the trailer when she so often yearned for his absence? Surely the already-elapsed time would more than pay for her freedom. Surely Jim, with his new, young lovers, would find her outdated and useless by now. But, then again, it was more than sex for Jim. "And unto the married I command, yet not I, but the Lord, Let not the wife depart from her husband," the Good Book said. At least Will didn't believe in the Good Book the way Jim did.

The meat was thawed and floating in the plastic wrapper in the sink by the time she finished smoking. Leaked animal blood had turned the water pink. Charlotte imagined an entire bathtub of pink water like that, pink from blood, pink from Will's blood. She shuffled through a kitchen drawer for a knife to cut open the wrapper. Her fingertip slipped over a serrated edge. She jerked her hand back, afraid she'd sliced herself open, but there was only a pale line of dead skin on her finger, no blood other than the watery cow's blood. She put her finger into her mouth, chewed off the dead skin, and spit it into the sink along with the bloody water. Then she pulled the plug and watched the skin and the water spin its way down the drain.

The knife she'd touched in the drawer was a steak knife. It wasn't much larger than a butter knife, but still it was the most intimidating knife Will owned. She held it lengthwise in her two hands as if she were bestowing it upon herself, like she were a knight taking on the charge to protect and conquer, namely to protect her dignity and conquer a space in the world where she would be allowed to exist however she saw fit. She watched her own shadow as she stabbed at the air, a horror movie villain. The shadow looked sufficient in its villainy. She was sure Will would agree and hoped he'd fetched himself a beer or two and chugged them down while she was outside smoking. She wanted to see his pants wet with piss.

"You know," she called to Will, "if all that's true about Jim having his hand up the sheriff's ass like Sesame

Street, then how the hell were you and that kid gonna run him off?"

She turned on an oven burner and put an empty pan on top of it.

"I figure we'll undercut him," Will said. "It's basic economics. He'll go somewhere else and just start fresh from there. He knows what he's doing, and it'd probably be pretty easy for him."

She toyed with the knife.

"You and that kid?" she asked.

She cut the wrapper open and dumped the meat into the pan. It sizzled. The burner turned red.

"I've got the brains to run an operation. He's young, can learn to watch his back. We'd do just fine. How's dinner coming along?"

"You'll eat when it's time to eat," Charlotte said. She still held the knife. She was sure that it would do. "That kid you hired is just a boy. He won't do anything the way you'll want it done. He'll get burned out and tired, and he still won't do what you want him to even when he knows how. Besides, who's to say he doesn't do you like you're planning to do Jim?"

"Boy's fine. I was a boy once, and I was fine. I'm still fine. I'm about to be in the prime of my life and loaded with cash."

"You won't make a damn nickel, and you will die doing this. Someone is going to *murder* you."

"I'm not worried about any of that," he said. "I keep a gun in my truck. I can shoot it better than Jim or anybody else. I'll get the kid shooting too, but not as good as I shoot. I'll tell the sheriff that I'm worse than Jim ever was, and he'll listen close. He'll be putty in my hands."

Charlotte shuddered. Her wrist went limp, and the knife looked like a prop, a toy for children. Her slouching shadow looked timid and weak. The meat was popping and screeching in the pan. Jim would never die. His spirit was in every stupid redneck willing to end another life and keep the county quiet about the whole thing. Sometimes, it was in her too.

"What does the kid think about all this?" she asked. "He said he knew that girl that disappeared."

"Who knows? It's not my business."

The meat was done cooking, and the trailer smelled tangy and sour. Parts of the sink were still pink from the blood. It was almost dinner time, just as soon as the pasta boiled. Will was still watching TV, same as probably everyone else. The news came on, and people were talking. That's all they were good for. Charlotte rinsed the knife in the sink and put it back in the drawer.

Chapter 18

Jenn didn't remember falling asleep, but she knew she'd been out for more than an hour, less than an entire night. At first, she thought it was dark out, but then she saw the blackout curtains duct-taped around the window and wasn't sure. She tried to sit up, and her wrists ached. She had been tied to the bed with rubber cables. The cables dug into her skin, and she realized she'd felt them in the dream she was having, that strange dream just outside her memory. There was a strip of something over her mouth. She figured it was duct tape. Her captors had removed the rag they'd first used to gag her. Still, there was no sound when she tried to scream, at least, there was nothing at all like a scream.

She remembered the man outside her back door and the other man in the pickup truck, but only in the way a person remembers a painting seen in passing. They were outlines and features instead of people. She did not remember getting out of the pickup truck, nor did she remember entering the room with its walls covered in a moldy sprawl and its sour smell of mothballs and liquor vomit. She wasn't sure if she'd fainted or if they had knocked her out with a lead pipe or some other apparatus made famous by television villainy. She tried to twist in the bed and felt soreness in her legs and her back, the mushroom cloud release of blood beneath the skin, bruising. She didn't realize that she was crying until her face was wet.

At first, she feared that she'd been left to die alone in the bed, so she made noise. She used her hips to bounce on the bed springs, to utter the sounds her mouth couldn't. The bed merely squeaked as her body thumped against the mattress. Before long, she was whooping breaths in and out her nose. Her lungs craved more air than she could get to them through her narrow nostrils. Her heart slammed against the back of her breastbone like a fish at the edge of its fisherman's boat. The world became darker around her.

Then she felt something else in the bed, a shuffling, maybe a roach jumping onto the floor or the rising breath of the man who had kidnapped her. She was afraid to turn and look for her companion in the dark. When the thing in the bed was a mystery, there was a chance that it would be benign. If she saw whatever nightmare had joined her, she would be subject to its terror without any chance for escape. Still, her curiosity gnawed at her. She wanted to look across the room and see a shining opportunity for liberation. Maybe a hero, maybe Angie, had fought off her kidnappers and then found her tied up like a trailer trash Sleeping Beauty before falling asleep from exhaustion. Maybe they'd be home soon.

By the time she worked up the courage to look, she only imagined the open eyes of drooling men or, worse, their hairy cocks, prickly members like Scribbles's drawing from years before waiting for her to stir and notice them and give them her attention. Her optimism drained from her and became a sharp noise, a ringing at the base of her neck. Its absence wrapped around her head like a plastic bag. She lay still as she could, though she knew that her efforts were useless, that whatever it was on the other side of the bed had likely heard the racket she'd tried to make before.

The seconds stretched themselves out in her loneliness and became impossible to count. There wasn't even the structure of a ticking clock, just binds and fear and stink from mildew and sweating bodies. She heard the shuffling again. The sound had certainly come from on top of the bed. The mattress had dipped and risen again with hardly a squeak. Perhaps it had been an animal, a cat who slept on the mattress every night, regardless of whoever else was there. The shuffler had been small. Nothing large could have created such an accidental shuffle without the sloppiness of weight. She craned her neck to see what had made the sound as if by instinct, a reaction without the process of thought, of what-ifs or could-bes. And that's when she saw Ava Springtree.

***

At least, she saw what had once been Ava Springtree. The body next to her was thin and bony with black rings for eyes, but it was breathing. It would shrink to little more than a skeleton when it exhaled. Jenn was all tears and duct tape-muffled screams. She wanted to touch her friend, to realize that there was flesh and blood beyond the television stills of Ava's old yearbook picture, to feel the still-living skin of what had once been a ghost. Ava didn't seem to realize that anyone else was in the bed with her, though. She breathed and breathed and made tiny motions of sleep on her side of the mattress. Then she breathed again. Her eyes were closed. Jenn's own eyes were wet beyond sight as she realized that Ava may very well have been dying. The binds were too tight around her wrists to find out.

After more than a dozen breaths, after enough time for Jenn to stop crying again and to hope for something like the best, not the best itself, but something that would dry her eyes, a vision of Angie or her mother, of hugs and loosened binds, the door opened. Brother Freemont was haloed by the light from outside the room. The old man was singing.

"Make me a captive, Lord," he sang, "and then I shall be free."

Jenn tried to scream again. Brother Freemont's voice made quick, jumping turns over the lines of his hymn like he was nervous or perhaps ecstatic. He undid Ava's binds as he sang and ignored Jenn's tossing. He was not as dressed up as Jenn was accustomed to seeing him on Sunday mornings. He wore blue jeans and a denim work shirt. The top two buttons of the shirt were undone. Coarse hairs and the glimmer of sweat climbed out through the gap. The bottom two buttons were also undone, but Jenn didn't look down there. She thought of him like a teacher out at the grocery store on the weekend, foreign in his humanity. She had never liked him much, but she thought for a moment that maybe he had come in to save her. Her screams turned to muffled yelps. Brother Freemont toyed with the bed where Ava was lying. Jenn couldn't tell exactly what it was he was doing from her spot in the bed, but she could tell he had done it before. He used the practiced movements of habit. Before long, the old man had Ava slung over his shoulder. She was limp, unbound, and mumbling incoherently. Then Jim turned to Jenn. He knew she was awake.

"Young lady," he said, "you ain't gonna get much sound out from behind that tape. You'd better just stop wasting your breath before you go and hyperventilate. You'll have your turn soon enough."

Jenn couldn't see the man's eyes on account of the dark. They looked more like holes punched out of his face than like the God-given organs of sight. She knew then that Jim Freemont would not save anyone. She couldn't even scream about it. He was almost back to the door and the incandescent glow beyond when the man with gray sideburns stuck his face into the room. The man was no longer wearing the hunter's cap he'd had on when he'd knocked on Jenn's back door.

"She ready, Jim?" he asked, inches from Brother Freemont and from Ava.

Surprised, Brother Freemont jumped back from the other man, nearly dropping Ava onto the floor the way an inattentive waiter drops a fancy tray of food on TV. Then he laughed, and Jenn saw his perfect teeth were missing. In their place was a witch's mouth, bone-colored gravestones stacked here and there.

"Damn it," Jim said. His breath whistled over his teeth. He pushed the other man back from the door and took Ava with him as he left. Jenn was glad she couldn't hear him finish whatever he was saying. She shivered in the quiet. Her jaw bounced up and down again, and the chatter sounded so much louder than winter shivers did. The sound had nowhere else to go but back into her head. She tried hard to crowd the sound out with her thoughts, but that didn't do much good. She only saw Ava draped over Jim Freemont's shoulder. She had looked like a doll up there. Ava had never been particularly thin, but Jenn couldn't imagine how she'd lost so much weight in the weeks since she'd disappeared. She had even seemed shorter. What if she continued to shrink? One day, Ava would be Barbie, and Jenn would give up her reluctance for dolls and build her a tiny house where they could talk about everything that had happened, fill the missing gaps between them. Jenn wouldn't ask about the place where

Brother Freemont had taken Ava, though. She had some idea of where the old bastard had carried her friend, and that was enough.

***

Though she could not move, Jenn became lost in the space where time didn't exist, the place without the sun. Her wrists hurt. Sometimes her face would itch, and she would want to scratch the itch. When she pulled against the binds and again realized her helplessness, the itch would spread like disease and have her trying to call out. Then there would be more tears and writhing on the mattress until, at last, she would grow tired again and lose herself in thoughts about Ava and about her mother. She didn't think much about Scribbles.

Jim Freemont came back into the room with Ava. He was stripped down to a tank top and his underwear. He was breathing heavily. He was covered in sweat. Half his hair stuck to his head. The other half flopped around with his every step. Jenn closed her eyes when they entered. Jim tied Ava back to the bed and then left like he was in a hurry. Jenn heard his pounding feet and the slamming door behind him. When she was certain he wouldn't return, she looked Ava over again. The skinny girl seemed as if she'd fallen deeper into sleep during the time she'd been gone. She hardly stirred. Only her breaths signaled that she was still living. Jenn's eyes had grown used to the darkness, and she could see bruises on her friend. The bruises were tiny like drops of spilled ink. Jenn could smell the alkaline trace of the men mixed with Ava's sour body. She couldn't stop crying and only wished that Ava would wake up and hear her.

Before long, Brother Freemont was back in the room. He was singing hymns again. He had his jeans back on and fumbled some shells into a revolver. Then he came close to Jenn and put his hand on her cheek. His hand smelled like cigarettes and motor oil. He was still singing when he pointed the gun at Ava. Then he stopped.

"Now, listen here, young lady," he said, "I understand you're probably hungry, and I'm here to remedy that, but if I take this tape off your face and you go on hollering, you'll leave me no choice but to shoot your friend. It would make quite a mess."

Jenn had her eyes wide as she could make them. She couldn't take them off the gun until she followed its barrel to Ava, and then she couldn't take them off the sleeping girl. She could hear the crackling points in the old man's voice. She hadn't noticed them before when he'd spoken at church. Perhaps his missing teeth were to blame. He must have kept his righteousness in those teeth.

"You've got a pretty face," he growled. "I don't wanna see it all covered in blood. So, I'm gonna pull this tape off, and you're not gonna make a peep. You understand?"

Jenn nodded her head as hard as she could. Her insides seemed to jiggle all over each other. Brother Freemont found the edge of the tape and pulled.

The tape clung to her skin. It did not peel away smoothly, or even the quick, jumpy way a Band-aid would have peeled away. Jim Freemont jerked at it again and again with his stinking hands until it was gone, and even then, sticky remnants tugged on either side of Jenn's mouth. Her flesh was hot where the tape had been. She realized she was gritting her teeth to keep from screaming. Jim, on the other hand, was smiling his gummy, alien smile while he watched her. Once he'd decided she wasn't going to shout, he put the revolver in the front of his pants.

"Now," he said, "have a bite to eat."

He pulled a smashed-up Twinkie out of his jeans pocket and tossed it onto the bed, just out of reach of Jenn's mouth. She eyed the smushed and crumbed wad of snack cake in its plastic wrapper and realized she was hungry, truly hungry, famished. Didn't this man realize she was still tied to the bed? Was he taunting her?

"Looks good, doesn't it?" Brother Freemont said.

Jenn didn't respond.

"Come on now. I know you're hungry."

When Jenn finally spoke, she was surprised by how quiet her voice was. At some point, though she didn't know when, she'd gotten the idea that she sounded mature, that she could have passed for a woman of just about any age short of sixty. Now, she heard a child. She was weak, and she was here with this man and another girl who was even weaker than she was, a voiceless skeleton bundled in butcher paper.

"I can't unwrap it," Jenn said. "I'm all tied up."

She realized that Brother Freemont had more gaps than he had teeth. His smile was the sort of smile a devil would have had. If Jenn ever made it out of this room, if someone thought to find her and set her free, she'd tell the whole world about that devil smile. She'd have a gospel all her own, and that tar-smelling son of a bitch would never again wear a set of dentures without remembering her.

"It seems we've both got something to gain from one another, then, wouldn't it, sweetheart?" the old man asked. "If you need a favor from me, just ask. I'm a fair man, a just man, a man of God. Let me bless you."

Jenn hesitated.

"Please let me eat," she said.

"I'll open that Twinkie. I'll even feed it to you. All you gotta do in return is suck on my little fingers when you're done, clean off the crumbs."

"I don't want any part of your dirty old body near me," Jenn said, trying to sound strong but emitting only a rasp. "I'd rather starve."

Brother Freemont's smile faded around his wagging tongue, and then his mouth was closed. He was stone and black magic and man-made steel over belly fat. Jenn nearly missed his tombstone smile.

"You know what happens to those who cross a prophet," he asked, "especially one who shows you grace and mercy you ain't ever deserved?"

"You're not a prophet."

He raised his hand up like he was going to slap Jenn's face. She turned away from him the best she could and braced for the palm and the stinking fingers against her cheek. He laughed at her flinching, was consumed by a foul, spitty laugh, something not at all dissimilar to a coughing fit. Jenn wished he'd just slapped her instead.

"There was a prophet named Elisha," he said, "who overheard some youngins disrespecting the Lord and His messenger. He called upon God to send a bear to maul the offenders and restore righteous order to the land." He looked at the back of his hand like he was still considering a slap. "I don't need a bear." Brother Freemont patted the place in his pants where he'd stuffed the gun. "I spare the Lord the trouble."

Jenn was crying again, but her voice was stronger than it had been before. Her words seemed to transcend her body and become something all their own. She didn't know what it would be like to never feel scared again, but she figured that moment was as close as any would ever be. She spoke harsh words, words she thought that Ava would have said.

"It must be disappointing to have to speak for God when He's already gone and died," she said. "You didn't even get a pet bear out of the deal."

Jim wasn't laughing anymore. He was red-faced and bent over her.

"I'll put your damn body in the ground. You'll fill up a gravel mine like a common junkie, and no one will ever come digging for you." He spat on her as he talked. "Worst of all, you'll know the gnashing of teeth. You'll pray to come back here. You'll beg for a drop of water, and I'll piss on you."

Brother Freemont hadn't raised his voice, even as he grew angry. He'd spoken with the raging quiet that cuts the air and lingers in the wide, intentional pauses between each word. Veins like mole paths rose up beneath his skin. Surely the Lord was not just the mole that tunneled through this old man. God would certainly rather be dead than dwell in that crooked maze. There was quiet when Jim got done talking. Then there was something breaking through the quiet. It was a quivering, sad sound, the sort of pathetic squeak of a rabbit in a hound dog's mouth. It was Ava's voice.

"There's a second death," she said. "There's a second death, and it's after the first death."

She sounded like a stranger. Jenn didn't understand what she meant. Jim was shaking his head with a sober frown.

"This young lady's learned her scriptures," he said. "Maybe you'll be so lucky."

He picked up the crushed bit of Twinkie from the mattress and ate it. Crumbs stuck to his sweaty skin. He only spoke again once he'd swallowed the bit of cake.

"At any rate, you'd better learn to pray," he said, "because it looks to me like you're gonna begin a season of fasting."

Then he was gone. Jenn had seen his leaving, but those details hadn't been important. It was only important that he was gone, that he hadn't taped her mouth, that she was alone with Ava again, that Ava had spoken real words and was only a foot or so away on the mattress. Jenn strained to turn toward her friend, but Ava was already sleeping again. At least, her eyes were closed. Her body grew and shrank silently in the dark.

"Ava," Jenn said, "he's gone." She did not think that Ava could have fallen asleep so quickly. It must have been an act, a way to get Brother Freemont out of the room. When Ava didn't respond, she tried again. "Wake up," she said. "Please, wake up."

But Ava didn't speak. If it hadn't been nighttime before, it surely was now. Jenn was sweaty. The sweat made her itch. At that moment, she was sure that she didn't believe in God, but she thought quite a bit about Hell and decided it must have been close to Branch Creek. She couldn't help but cry out loud with her hoarse voice as Ava slept. She subsisted on her tears, the only holy water she'd ever known, and thought about the future that someone like Ava would have, that she, herself, would have. She thought about the sheriff and wondered how he could let her walk out of his office like he did when things like this happened to the people he was supposed to protect. She thought about Angie Wilkerson, and she thought about her mother. Then she thought about falling asleep. She didn't know what to think. She didn't know who to pray to, either. She just hoped she'd never see that deacon again.

Chapter 19

Agent Tommy Richards came back to Mayes County after the second teen girl disappeared, the girl who had come to see Sheriff Taylor in his office. So, the sheriff did his best to keep his nose clean. He didn't talk to Jim. He started crossing off days on his calendar like they meant something, hoped they would somehow turn into quiet years. He'd put an "x" through five days following the girl's disappearance, and there had not yet been a news conference. There had not yet been any other notable crimes. Both would have to take place sooner or later, though. The girl's mama pounded on his office door the day after he'd started marking his calendar. He'd said he would search tirelessly to find the girl, but he knew that was out of the question. He just didn't have the heart to tell her that.

Still, Sheriff Taylor promised himself that he would find some way to run Jim out of town, to bring back the law and order that left him the space to retire in peace and dignity. He would not be able to save those who had gone away before, those missing outsiders and the two teenagers, at least, not without risking Barbara's life and his own reputation, but he would have a chance at keeping the crimes from continuing indefinitely. He would have a chance at keeping the remnant safe, and he would emerge again as the man who brought the people of Mayes County back from the wilderness. This would take time, though, and the presence of the investigators from out of town and the angry women outside his door cut into the few grains of sand he had left in the top of the hourglass.

Before he could figure out how to go about driving Jim from northeastern Oklahoma, Sheriff Taylor needed to make himself appear strong, resilient. The law alone could not bring down the old deacon, but the sheriff needed material power, a heroic arc. He needed to be the portrait of Christ resurrected and ascending from the beating on the sanctuary floor. During the day, Sheriff Taylor paced his office as long as he could to try to regain the strength in his back, but he feared it would be weeks or months before he was able to stand up straight for any real time at all, and even then, he couldn't imagine another officer of the law as crooked as he was puffing out his chest and walking around without a crooked spine. Folks do what they can, though. Sometimes they only do what they have to. In the afternoons, he often filled a plastic baggie with ice and wrapped it in a towel to wedge between his body and his office chair until the ice melted and began to wet his shirt. It was supposed to hurry the healing process and lessen the pain. He couldn't tell if it was helping.

Then the girl's mama was holding up signs outside the dollar store alongside the troublemaking woman who had stopped by with the girl before she went missing . They had about a dozen people, mostly teenagers, outside the convenience stores and the sheriff's office nearly every day during that first week. One of the teenagers said that Jenn was supposed to show up to her house the day she disappeared. The sheriff's office had questioned her as if they didn't already have a good idea of where the missing girl had gone, and the teenager didn't have much to say, at least, not that amounted to anything. Now, she and her friends were raising hell for the missing. The media loved that sort of thing. The Oklahoma State Bureau of Investigation did not. Words like "conspiracy" found their way into both drunk lips and case files.

Though Sheriff Taylor was sure that Jim was behind the girl's disappearance, he did not know why the old man had taken her. What reason did he have for rounding up a second teenage girl? Sure, the girl had stopped by asking questions she shouldn't have been asking, but so had the woman, and that woman was alive and well and very public with her complaints. She had more people sniffing around Mayes County than the girl would have had. No one important would have listened to that kid, but they sure as hell listened to everything that anybody had to say about her disappearance.

***

Sheriff Taylor had grown used to sleeping on the armchair in the living room. He was at the house under the orange lamp that hung from the overhead fan. The place had grown foreign. It belonged to Barbara, who spent all her time there waiting to get herself killed and without a clue. He only visited when it was time to sleep, and he rarely spoke inside the house. He could hardly call it a home anymore, not because he wasn't welcome there, but because homes were the sorts of places where people let their guards down, and he had no such place.

The empty shells of dead insects made dark splotches at the bottom of the glass lampshade in the center of the fan. He wondered if he'd ever clean it out again. Barbara hadn't asked him to do so in a long time. He shifted in the chair. The stuffing in the recliner had become thin and matted where he sat. He tried to scoot to one side or the other of the depression that he had made in the stuffing, but before long he was back in the stiff pleather hell. It likely wasn't good for his aching body, but he was paying a penance. He told himself he'd be back in bed with Barbara before too long. He would be strong again before too long.

The sheriff watched his reflection warp and wiggle like a stranger in the dark bubble of the TV screen. That was about the only TV he watched anymore. He couldn't bear the possibility of a news cut-in, of having to hear something about himself that he didn't already know, something about his county or about those missing girls or any of the other missing people. He sure as hell didn't want to hear Tommy Richards talk about getting to the bottom of the whole ordeal. So, he only watched his low-definition body move around the chair in work jeans and a t-shirt.

A door opened and then closed again somewhere in the house. A light switch called out with its accusatory snap. Barbara was up and in the bathroom. She came out in her nightgown when she was done. The nightgown was shapeless, a barricade of flannel all covered in flowers. She'd only recently taken to wearing it, and it made her look like an old woman. Anyone in a proper nightgown was probably an old woman.

"I thought I saw the light," she said.

The ceiling fan was spinning and carrying on with its mechanical tapping as the pull chain jangled against the lampshade. The repetition was almost enough to fill in the conversation gaps, the words they'd stopped saying. The unconscious sounds of objects wouldn't be enough, though, and Barbara wasn't one to pretend.

"The bed's gone cold," she said.

"It's getting to be that time of year, I reckon."

Her face was twisted up like it had been packed into a ball by an angry child. She looked as if she'd cry. "It's those girls, isn't it?" she asked.

Sheriff Taylor didn't speak at first. He didn't want to lie outright, not to Barbara. He could no longer even bring forth his list of sanitized facts when she was nearby. He'd drained the well and then fallen into it.

"It's a lot of things," he said. He turned away from his wife and looked again at his reflection in the darkened television screen. Sometimes he felt like the whole thing might just as well be in there, might just as well be prime time TV, *JAG* or *Law and Order*. Hell, most people only knew about the disappearances from the television. To them, there was hardly a difference between Mayes County and those other cities made into settings. Sheriff Taylor wanted to know that sort of distance. He wanted to turn the whole thing off the way he'd done the television. Barbara was catching on to that.

"I don't like you sleeping out here," she said. "I want things to go back to the way they were before you started with all this nonsense."

Her voice didn't waver, but Sheriff Taylor figured it would have if she had been anything short of Barbara Taylor. He looked her over like a stranger, like he wasn't sure what it was that she was supposed to be. She had her arms crossed. Her skin was still mostly tight over her face. The nightgown rippled in tiny waves as the ceiling fan sent its breeze down on her. She looked like she was warning him of coming pestilence that way, all stern and solid beneath the moving fabric.

The sheriff stood and turned off the light. His jeans were loose around his waist, and they sagged before he pulled them up. Perhaps, for the first time in years, he'd *need* to wear a belt. He kissed his wife on the cheek.

"I've been thinking too much," he said. "I'm thinking about the girls just about all the time. These are kids, here, Barbara, and I can't justify sleeping sound in my own bed when they don't have that luxury."

He felt like a real sheriff then, and he wished that someone with a camera could have seen that. It would have sent Tommy Richards back to Tulsa. It would have everyone feeling safe again and remembering the young man they'd first elected after he'd stopped that real-life robbery. He would be able to sleep in his own bed if he spent more time talking that way. He kissed Barbara on her head. Her cold hands were around his hands. She pulled on them just hard enough to make him feel the need to be near her, even if it was only because he lost his balance.

"These people don't need some kind of martyr," she said. "They need a sheriff. I, on the other hand, need a husband. I can't have that when you're out here feeling sorry for yourself every night."

Sheriff Taylor didn't want to tell her that he had good reason to feel sorry for himself, that he was also feeling sorry for her, that he could very well kill her to save the missing girls. She wouldn't understand any of that. Worse, she could up and tell someone at the neighborhood club about the situation, and before long, the whole county would see him exposed, bare. They would see him as a coward. So, he followed his wife to bed. He watched himself disappear from the TV screen as he switched off the overhead light. Then he was taking off his jeans and piling pillows beneath his head next to Barbara in the bedroom. She held onto his thumb. With him in the bed, she didn't have much else to say, save a satisfied hum she offered once they'd grown comfortable.

After that, she was quiet for a time. Then she was snoring. Sheriff Taylor tried his best to ignore the fluttering of her fleshy throat. He tried to pretty it with his mind, to imagine it as a purr or a whisper, but that was no good. Barbara had become an old woman, an old, snoring woman. What did that make the sheriff? The snoring became louder and more regular. Sheriff Taylor sneaked out of the bed, careful to keep the old mattress from telling his wife of his departure. He went back to the recliner, turned on the light, and continued to watch his featureless body in the darkened screen. The fan blades overhead made the light unsteady like an old film strip. The sheriff liked that. He watched his reflection until he fell asleep. Then he dreamed he was the star of the show.

***

The next day, he had more calls than most *real* Hollywood movie stars. Tommy Richards alone had left him three messages before 9:00 a.m. The folks from the media had left him even more. He didn't want to talk on the phone.

"Tell them I'm busy working on a case," he told Donna at the receptionist desk. "They should know we have some teenage girls missing here. I don't have a lot of time for chit chat."

"But that's what they want to talk to you about, Sheriff," Donna said. "Agent Richards said it's real important you get back to him."

The sheriff had said all he was going to say. Words had run their course. There would instead be quiet actions over time. Somehow, those actions would be mined from possibilities and made into strategies that didn't widen the proverbial net, that kept the business of safety between the man elected to bring about that safety and the man who sought to make himself holy in its destruction. The whole world would likely be better off that sealed-lip way, except for junkies and maybe a couple teenagers. Barbara would certainly be better off, as would Sheriff Taylor's reputation.

"I'm not wasting time on the damn telephone," he said.

It rang again from Donna's desk. Sheriff Taylor ignored it and went to his office. There, he gave in and flipped on the television. A weather map like a bad backdrop in a western movie filled the screen. The meteorologist said it would be cold as if anyone was expecting anything else. When he was done, a woman in a news jacket was standing outside a convenience store with a child, the high school girl who'd been in for questioning. Sheriff Taylor knew before the reporter spoke that the girl and the convenience store were in Branch Creek. He turned the volume up and listened.

"I know we weren't all fair," the girl said, "but you have to come home, Jennifer. We miss you."

Sheriff Taylor hoped the girl's talk about bullying would pull the OSBI off his back. He considered sending a deputy over to talk to all the school kids about bullying. It would help feed the narrative. It would buy him time. At that point, he couldn't ask for much more. He didn't know if he even deserved that much, decades of service or otherwise.

The sheriff's dream of bided time dissipated then as the camera panned out and returned to the reporter. The protesting woman was standing behind her with a sign that read "Dirty Sheriff Got Blood on His Hands" in permanent marker. She was angry in her coat. As if that were bad enough, she had even more folks standing there with her, mostly other poor people, mostly folks who'd been ticketed for DUI or who had their kids taken away and put into foster care, but there were others too, a couple bored twenty-somethings with unspent rebelliousness, a tan woman who worked at the feed store. Some of the protesters were high school kids with no record at all, best Sheriff Taylor could tell. He didn't know what he'd done for all those people to turn against him. They knew nothing of his interactions with Jim. Only the woman had any idea of his reluctance to find out where the girls had gone, and she didn't know much. But still, they were there with signs and theories. Perhaps gods would die too in the new millennium.

The lost hope became dread when Sheriff Taylor saw Tommy Richards. The agent was right there on the screen, just a thin glass pane away, staring back at the sheriff as he talked. He repeated that he'd work tirelessly to solve the disappearances. Sheriff Taylor believed him. He did not want to believe him, but he did, and that scared him. Still, Jim Freemont scared him more. Tommy Richards wouldn't have Sheriff Taylor beaten. Tommy Richards wouldn't kill his wife to get his way. Tommy Richards wouldn't make a theology out of any of it. Sheriff Taylor turned the television off. He remembered why he didn't like to use the TV set at home.

A pair of men's voices moved over one another in the hall outside. Someone rapped on the door. Sheriff Taylor didn't move. He thought the voices belonged to deputies, but he wasn't willing to risk opening the door and finding himself face to face with a microphone-carrying reporter or that steel-eyed Tommy Richards. Sure, the OSBI agent had just been on the TV, but maybe that had been pre-recorded. How long ago had it aired? Had enough time passed for someone to drive up from Branch Creek? Sheriff Taylor held his breath and pictured himself invisible. Then one of the voices laughed to the other, and they faded down the hall together.

A slip of paper had appeared through the crack beneath the office door, a torn sheet folded over itself. Sheriff Taylor took the sheet and slid it into his pocket. He did not feel safe unfurling it there in his office, not where any dumb old deputy could knock on the door and find him, especially when those deputies were coming in twos. Had Carlson been recruiting? Had they delivered to him a pirate's black spot?

Sheriff Taylor was sweating. The folded slip of paper seemed to tremble with power in his pocket. He called Donna and said he was going out to "do some investigating." He made her promise that's all she'd say when callers asked about his whereabouts. He said he'd keep his radio on in case anyone needed him. Then he slunk out to an unused patrol car and started out of town.

★★★

The driver's seat was closer to the steering wheel than he liked it to be, and he thought of the tiny nobodies and turncoats he'd hired on to help him keep law and order. It was almost no wonder that he'd let Jim give him so much hell. The only sturdy deputy on the force was Carlson, and damn near everyone seemed to know where that son of a bitch held his allegiances. Other than Carlson, there were only old men and cowards. The sheriff pulled the lever at the front of the seat and pushed it back so he could breathe a little bit. No matter how far back he pushed the seat, though, his chest stayed tight. He pulled at his shirt collar. His fingers left tiny puddles on the steering wheel.

Soon, he found himself on an old paved road splitting the occasional tribe of trees and brown pasture lots where cows huddled together in the cold. He huffed and panted and fiddled with the vent in the center console. The cold air bit at his hands and then turned back into the vent before it could make its way to his body or his sticky head. If he were to go outside that way, all covered in sweat, he'd risk catching something. Maybe the common cold would go ahead and kill him, would show him mercy. Maybe God wasn't much into killing people anymore, though. He'd done plenty of that back when people were still in the business of writing things down and calling it scripture. He'd had His chance to show off. Now, people like Jim Freemont did the killing. They carried the cross of the old time crusaders through unread notes slid under office doors. What a gospel that was, the sheriff thought. It was a shame that no one took the time to write it down, but then again, there was the note.

More trees grew out of the plains and bunched the earth into little hills with their roots. Occasional driveways twisted and writhed between the trees and lay inviting before the car like red carpets. Sheriff Taylor had let Mayes County come forth and swallow him up until it was done with him, and then he wasn't even in the county anymore, just somewhere else in the sinking part of the world that ran together between the coasts. He emerged outside his jurisdiction and owed nothing at all to the people around him, though there was hardly a difference between them. Perhaps it was that similarity that led him to park the patrol car in a ditch when he saw a pickup truck turned sideways ahead, halfway in the road and halfway out of it.

A buck was bleeding in the ditch. It had apparently crushed the front of the pickup. Thick green antifreeze mingled with blood spatter on the blacktop and painted the world up like watercolor. No one else had stuck around. When Sheriff Taylor looked inside the truck, he found paper bags from fast food restaurants and haphazard CD cases. He knew the crash with the deer hadn't caused the mess. It had always been there.

The sheriff went to the front of the pickup to take stock of the damage, and he nearly forgot the note in his pocket. His body buzzed and became light. Something was happening in front of him, and he could see its end. He stood near the deer. The buck had lost the better part of an antler in the crash. Its side was sliced open. The driver had been able to leave the scene, but the buck wouldn't be so lucky. Its bloated body would decorate this rural road for weeks unless somebody came and field dressed it soon to fill their freezer for the winter. It was still alive, the buck. It wasn't just a body yet. The bloody gash in its side opened a little bit as it breathed and revealed the dark wads of tissue that kept it living. The pink-stained fur rose and fell as the deer lay otherwise still. The buck's eyes were open, and it saw the sheriff standing nearby, watching. Still, it didn't, or perhaps couldn't, try to shuffle off, to live its last moments alone in the quiet. The buck didn't even appear to be upset by the sheriff. Maybe it had other things to worry about.

Sheriff Taylor went back to the patrol car to get the rifle out of the trunk. He figured the least he could do was end the deer's pain. Maybe the good deed would come back to him one day. In no time, he had the rifle at his shoulder and was peering down the sight at the deer's face, at the animal who was already slain, who may have always been slain, as far as the sheriff was concerned. The buck was born so it could hit the truck and die. It probably didn't do much else. Sheriff Taylor wondered if he, in turn, had been born to kill the buck.

The buck stared back at him, scared, soft. It hadn't meant to hit the truck. It likely didn't deserve to die at all. Sheriff Taylor looked up from the rifle sight. He wished he'd found one of the missing girls instead. He wondered if he'd end their misery too or if he'd let them squirm all over the bloody grass. He didn't have an answer for that. He hoped he'd never have to.

***

The deer was still living when he put the rifle in the trunk again and started back to the sheriff's office. The great brown eye whipped around beneath the engine noise until the sheriff and the car were gone and the sun too was finding somewhere to hide. Then both the sky and the buck's eye went black, and no one thought much of either of them.

Sheriff Taylor found himself back on the familiar side of the Mayes County line. He parked outside a convenience store and dug the note out of his pocket. It rustled as he unfolded it. The evening dark had become the quiet sort of dark that brought to life the tinnitus in his ears. There were no other sounds, just the ringing ears and the rustling paper. He read the note by the light of a two-headed lamp above the parking lot. "The fear of the Lord is wisdom," it said. "Your wife will be dead, and you will have killed her. We are ready to sing. Turn from evil to understanding." The sheriff wept over the top of the steering wheel as he read. He wished then that he had shot the buck, had done anything by his own will before he understood what little will he really had.

When he started the car again, the needle on the fuel gauge ticked beneath the half-empty line. The sheriff dried his eyes and filled the tank like a good public servant. He paid for the gas with his own cash and nodded to the clerk and his peach fuzz mustache. This clerk would not later write the sheriff letters of praise for his actions in the store. That sort of thing was of the past, just like those holy men with their scripture writing and the dying buck with its blood that covered sin.

Chapter 20

Charlotte felt like an artist when she squirted mustard onto the plate's rim. She had form. She laid out colors with texture. She'd had decades of practice, of making cheap food pretty. The mustard was all winding vibrancy and only the occasional glob. She felt somehow better than the common men sitting in the living room, waiting for her to bring them their hot dogs, or rather, the man and the boy who waited for their hot dogs. She could imagine what creativity meant. Will hadn't bought hot dog buns when Charlotte sent him to the store, so she wrapped the pan-fried weenies in regular slices of white bread. She left the mustard on the edges of the paper plates. They could spread it onto the bread themselves.

She took the plates into the living room and very nearly dropped them into the men's laps. Will smiled up at her like she'd brought him something good to eat. He asked for a can of beer. The boy, Matt, kept his head down, and Charlotte knew she had, in fact, brought him something good to eat. He didn't speak until after he finished his hot dog, but even still, he was already talking before she came back in with her own paper plate and the beer for Will. She hadn't taken any mustard for herself. She couldn't see herself smearing the color around the plate's grooves and then eating away the evidence. She was a creator, not a destroyer.

She had been far from Jim for weeks, for so long that her sobriety had become more than lonely days spent rolling around in her own sweat. Now, sobriety meant sunrise mornings and hot tea, and still, Jim hadn't come knocking, hadn't beaten down the door with his Bible and punished her for fornicating or for whatever other Levitican rules she'd broken. That night, though, Jim was coming over to talk to the boy and to Will too. That's what the boy had said. They had to talk business, probably murder and kidnapping, probably nothing that had to do with Charlotte.

The dread, or the anticipation of dread, concerning Jim's visit reminded Charlotte of the way she'd felt when, as a girl, she knew that her father was coming home from work to punish her. She remembered how she'd once sat in her room with her mute Chatty Cathy doll until the time for dinner came and went, how she was never punished for those bad marks on her report card, because there was no longer anyone to punish her. She'd blamed herself for her father's disappearance and pinched the soft skin at the back of her arms to pay for her sins, to even things out in her childhood bed.

Now, though, the fear of the coming man returned. It must have picked up right where it had left off. She tried to file the fear away as something that she had grown out of. She moved between worst case scenarios and cold, logical analyses, though she knew that the latter was well beyond a Spirit-fevered man like Jim. She was supposed to be out of sight by the time he pulled up, but surely she could afford to eat a hot dog first. She peeked out the front window between every bite, looking for headlights.

"Giles says he fucked them girls with Jim two days ago, says they were in the same room," Will was saying.

"I didn't see them," Matt said. He folded his paper plate until it was just a triangle with a rounded edge. He didn't look up from his hands.

"Reckon Jim'd know that you were friends with them?" Will asked.

"I told him so when I was up there."

When the boy talked, he sounded like he was referencing a script, like every word he said had been written down and read and re-read, like he had to prove something that was beyond himself. Still, he wore a teenager's puffy tennis shoes and baggy jeans that left too much room for his chicken legs. He was a green boy from town, no matter how bad he could make his words sound. His face was smooth. His belly hadn't yet swelled with age.

"They ain't there," he said. He kept staring at the folded plate.

Will held up his own empty plate, and Charlotte took it from him without speaking. She watched Matt as she went to the kitchen. His eyes were still big and scared, but dark bags had begun to show beneath them, the first sign of adulthood. Charlotte knew what it was like to miss out on sleep on account of Jim and Will and methamphetamine. If only she hadn't, like Matt, kept such a hole in her stomach and such thin skin running circles around her eyes, she could have grown used to houses and work and door-holding gentlemen. She pitied the boy.

"I don't want to talk about them anymore," he said about the girls. "It's best if they stay gone."

Charlotte gave Will his second hot dog. She hadn't bothered with mustard. She had to leave the trailer before Jim came by, before she gave into the urge to pick up the teenage boy and steal him away like an artifact.

"I'm gonna take a walk," she said.

Outside, the wind whipped at her face and made her lips pucker. She had her hands balled up inside her jacket sleeves to keep her fingers warm. The earth was dry and nearly frozen beneath her. It cracked and crumbled with her footsteps. The signs of an early winter had sucked the life from Mayes County.

She was glad to be out among the trees and the dens where the gray squirrels slept when she heard the diesel putt-putt of Jim's pickup truck. Though she couldn't hear his voice, she imagined his singing on his way up to the trailer, his knocking at the door and smiling through his dentures. She wondered if he asked about her, if he remembered that a woman had run from him, had escaped, had fucked one of his sellers and hidden in the woods. She didn't want Jim, but she knew that if he were any other man, she would want him to want her, if only to validate the time she'd wasted in his bed.

She distracted herself with questions, her mind made curious by her time alone. Why did the sun only look like it was moving when it was setting? It was hardly five thirty. Was everything so big that Charlotte didn't matter? Did she spin around and around on the earth while something massive like the sun sat still and watched? What did the ants do about all that bigness? And what about Jim? She wanted to cry. The sun was saying goodbye for the night. The world was only growing colder. Charlotte thought of the two men and the boy plotting with wild eyes. She thought of finding Will and the boy dead on the floor. She thought about their blood and the way it would stain the carpet. She thought about the way Will talked about profits and the promise of power. The branches of trees looked down on her like they had something to say. She turned to them with more questions. They never responded. Still, the world was spinning.

★★★

When Jim finally left, Charlotte was sitting on the ground and shivering in the dark, her back against a tree trunk. He had been at the trailer for hours, and then he was carried away by the noisy pickup truck. Charlotte held her arms against her chest and crept back up to Will and to Matt. Her knuckles burned with cold. She put her hands under her shirt every now and again to try to warm them again. No luck.

The man and the boy had limp necks and bobbing heads when she entered the trailer. Their eyes were half-open at best, or maybe half-closed. They'd left beer cans on the floor. A bit of metal flashed up on the couch next to the boy, a gun with its proud, polished shine. Charlotte could hardly choose her words before she said them.

"Who are you shooting?" she asked.

Will rolled his fat head over to her. Chunks of his hair stayed plastered to the chair when he turned. He didn't even look at the gun.

"He's a fucking imbecile," he said, "a scared son of a bitch."

"And that's your fault, I'm sure," Charlotte said. She held her hands out in front of her. They were red and still stinging. She turned on the stove and put them over the warmer. She had to look back over her shoulder to talk to the boy and the man in the living room, but still she talked. "What's he scared of?"

"He's got them girls," Will said. "He's gonna pay Matt to play guard dog outside his trailer."

"He didn't say anything about the girls," Matt said. His voice was shaky, and he swallowed nervously like something out of the Saturday morning cartoons. "I'm sure it's something else."

"He's a meth dealer," Charlotte said, "always guarding something. It's part of the job." She wanted to comfort the boy. She wanted to keep him from ever using the gun.

"Yeah, it's just part of the job," Matt said.

"You two don't know shit," Will said.

And they went on like that, Will drunk and the boy trembling. Charlotte's hands warmed up. She turned off the stove. Her skin was still red. Her face had been burned up by the wind. She tried not to think of the girls or the boy who would guard them for Jim. She tried not to think of the gun. The trailer was small though, and Will kept jabbering and slurring about everything she didn't want to hear about. She sat for a while on the closed toilet in the bathroom to get away from all the noise. She heard Matt laughing his forced laugh, that "ha ha ha" when Will said anything at all. She pitied the boy. He had to survive, just about everybody did. Sometimes survival was laughing at a drunk man who gave you money to sell his meth. Sometimes it was guarding a trailer where another man raped your friends. Sometimes it was running away. It's often hard to tell what it really takes to survive until a person's gone and made a fool of themselves trying to do it.

Charlotte flushed clean water down the toilet. The man and the boy were carrying on the way they'd carried on since she came inside, and despite her wind-whipped face and stiff fingers, part of her missed being out there, out in the cold, out where she went and turned red. The world was quieter there, and damn it if she didn't need some quiet. There had to be other places without all that noise. Hearing about Jim had somehow become as bad as living with him, and the weeks in the trailer only seemed to prolong the pain he'd caused her. Besides, it was probably about time for Christmas lights, and she couldn't remember the last time she'd seen them in person.

They hardly noticed her leaving, the slammed door to the trailer, the chapped and bleeding lips she carried with her on her way out. Sure enough, the night was quiet. The chirping things were either dead or burrowed away. The world slept, except for Will and Matt, and they were laughing about something that wasn't funny. The wind picked Charlotte up and took her away from the trailer. She couldn't hear them anymore.

Chapter 21

The second time Jenn heard Ava speak in Jim's trailer, Ava was a step, or maybe half a step, closer to how she had been before she'd disappeared.

"I never asked to be here," she said, "and I never asked for you to be here neither."

Ava closed her eyes tight after she spoke. Jenn watched her cry with her eyes scrunched closed, and then Jenn cried too.

Jenn figured she'd been in the trailer for more than a week. At least, she'd gone to sleep more than seven times. It was hard to tell in the perpetually dark room, and she was unable to discern real sleep from brief rests. She knew she was in a trailer, because she could see it end to end whenever Jim took her out to the other room, the room with the sunlight chopped up into thin lines across shuttered windows, the room with the carpet and the beer cans. Her first time in the other room, she'd bled, but not as much as she'd thought she would. She'd bled the second time too. It hurt some, but he covered her mouth with his hands when she cried. She didn't want to be anywhere near those hands. She had to forget that it hurt.

After Jim was done with her, she got to go into the bathroom and spend a few minutes there alone before he took her back to the bed. Sometimes he let her go to the bathroom without first taking her to the other room. Other times she was surprised with how quickly her urine turned cold around her in the bed.

When she was in the bathroom, the first thing she noticed was that there was a mildew rectangle above the sink, an outline where a mirror had once hung. She'd stopped eating, and she felt small and weak like a child. She wanted to see if she also looked like a child. Because Jim had removed the mirror, she was left to find her face in the shiny bits of the sink's spout. She saw formless pink flesh and a mass of hair.

The only other reflective surface she saw was a narrow mirror on the wall across from the room with the sunlight and the dirtied bed sheets. Jim carried her in so quickly, though, that she couldn't find herself in it. So, she thought herself pretty. She didn't know anymore whether or not she had zits on her face or if her eyes drooped with sleepiness. She was just the perfect symmetry of her memory, messy hair and no mole on her cheek. She tried to believe that a mirror would prove that.

She never saw any other men in the trailer after that first day, when Jim had come and taken Ava away to be with the sideburned kidnapper. Sure, she heard the other men. She knew Ava saw them when Jim brought her out to their whistling voices, their toothless howling. Jenn, however, did not see them. She just knew that their arrival meant that it was evening, that Jim had returned home from whatever he was out doing in the world, and that evil was about to fill the place. She learned to think of the other men as clocks without faces or hands, but she knew they were much worse than that to Ava, that they were the sort of faces and hands that Ava would likely never be able to wash away from her memory.

Ava hadn't been the social type. Jenn's mother had brought her along to Tulsa for Jenn's fourteenth birthday, and they'd all eaten dinner together at a Mexican restaurant with an arcade and a waterfall and a dozen adobe-colored rooms. Three older boys in jean shorts and hair gel tried to talk to Jenn and Ava while they played Skee-Ball in the arcade. Jenn blushed at the attention and told the boys they were from someplace far away, someplace imagined in Texas or Arizona. Ava stood back, away from the boys, by herself. She was speechless during the entire exchange, without her usual electricity or her sarcastic responses. When Jenn tried to nod to her and get her to come closer, Ava was looking at her feet like she was nervous. Jenn never forgot about the way her big, adventurous eyes went small and quiet when those boys came around. She wondered if Ava was always like that with other people or when she was outside her element, if her trademark sass has been something she only shared with Jenn and with Scribbles or in the confines of Branch Creek. That night, they stayed at a motel. They wore their normal clothes to the pool, and no one else was down there to tell them to change into bathing suits. They lay in the same bed with Jenn's mother, all three of them together that way, though Ava had at first offered to sleep on the little couch by the window. Jenn fell asleep last, watching Ava next to her. She liked the way that Ava looked comfortable again, familiar as she slept.

Now, when Jenn was in the bed alone, when Jim came and took Ava away, her thoughts wandered to her mom, to her aunts and a great-grandmother who had a little dog and ceramic figurines in her living room, to any woman she could remember, but she tried hard not to think of Scribbles, the sheriff, or other men. It was the fault of men that she was still in Jim's trailer, and it was man-making flesh that left her bleeding and full of tears in the sunlit room. The other men she knew had left her there, had neglected to find her. Maybe Ava somehow knew this too. Maybe that was why she had backed away from the boys at the arcade in the Mexican restaurant.

Jenn once saw a set of false teeth in a cup on the nightstand while she was pinned beneath Jim's bulging belly. She had to look away from the teeth. Jim had tricked her with his fake teeth for every Sunday as far back as she could remember. She closed her eyes and fantasized escape. She imagined the trailer in flashes as she moved from room to room. She imagined her running feet. She imagined Ava holding her hand in an open field like they were a pair of storybook heroines. She imagined laughter and Jim Freemont's dead body and how heavy it would be and how light their heads would be in the sun. Then Jim would finish and take her back to the bathroom and to her cell again.

The third time that Jenn heard Ava speak in the days they spent together on the bed, it was impossible to make sense of Ava's words, the disjointed mumbling and the rhythm where it fell. Jenn tried to reply with whispers like leaves whooshing over one another on the sidewalk, the scapegoats for trailer fires.

"Ava, it's me," she said. "What are you saying?"

Apparently Ava hadn't known what "me" meant, which was only fair after so much time in a room so dark. She had track marks above the binds on her arms. Jenn didn't know exactly what had caused the track marks, but she knew that she'd never seen them there before. They had something to do with drugs, but she never said that out loud. Jenn figured she must have developed special nocturnal vision. She could see the details of Ava's changes, but Ava saw nothing but the Lord and the heavy sort of loneliness one would expect of a girl who lay alone in a dirty bed for most of the day and whose only respite from that bed was in an even dirtier bed with an old man or in a bathroom without a mirror.

★★★

At some point, Jenn took it upon herself to weigh the objects in the bathroom in her hands. None of them were particularly heavy. There was a bar of soap beside the sink, and it may as well have been weightless. The shampoo and the lotion on the edge of the bathtub were also only heavy enough to remind Jenn of the fading strength in her arms. The detachable shower head, however, was made of hard, shiny plastic, maybe even metal. She slid it from its mount and let it sink into her palm. She didn't feel strong anymore, but she felt desperate. The next time Jim came for her, she imagined the shower head's potential to crunch bone and tear into skin.

The fourth time Jenn heard Ava speak, she had spoken first.

"I think we'll make it out of here," Jenn said.

Ava only moaned and tried to turn back and forth in the bed. The binds kept her from doing anything more than twisting slightly. Jenn spoke again.

"I'm saying I can rescue you," she said. "He's just an old man."

"No," Ava said.

She didn't say anything else, and Jenn cried as if for the first time she truly realized that Ava had disappeared. Then Jim came to untie Ava and take her out of the room. Through her tears, Jenn watched Ava's drooping face over the old deacon's shoulder, and she saw that Ava's eyes were open. They looked like dusty marbles in the living room light before the door closed and she was gone.

★★★

The sun wasn't even shining through the blinds the next time Jim had Jenn beneath his belly in the other bedroom. It was dark. Jenn had grown used to the dark. She didn't seem to know much else besides the dark by then, the dark and the sorts of hurt she was better off ignoring. She also knew the weight of the shower head.

"You've done good," Jim said, panting. "You've done real good." Then it was back to whistling hymns between his teeth.

He took her to the bathroom, and she sat on the toilet. She'd learned to push the Jim out of her body there instead of waiting for it to seep out cold onto the bed, though she didn't know what good it did, biologically. The science textbooks from back before the trailer didn't say anything about the muscles that pushed out evil from her broken open body, from what Jim called her gash. She could no longer think of another word for the folds between her legs. She couldn't remember when he'd first used the word. He may have leaned it into her on any given night, the fat old man with a hymn and genital slang on his lips. She wished there was a muscle deep in her that could push these memories from her too, but if there was, she didn't know it.

"Pinch it off," Jim said from outside the door. "It's about time to go."

Jenn tried again to make out her shape in the sink's silver spout. She preferred to hear the old man talk about the vulgarity of her body over the holiness of scripture. She could exist in a world where folks talked about human waste, she'd seen it before. She'd never seen holiness, though. She didn't think it'd do much good in the sort of place filled with all that waste. It sure hadn't since she'd been tied up in Jim Freemont's trailer.

"I said, 'Let's go,'" Jim said. He was shaking the door as if there was a lock on it. Jenn pulled up her panties. She felt the shower head in her hands. It didn't reach even halfway across the tiny room. Then the door was shaking again. She didn't speak. She stood barefoot in the tub.

Nearly two minutes passed before Jim finally opened the door to come get her. Jenn had counted out the seconds.

She'd reached 102. When Jim's wrinkled arm pushed open the shower curtain, she brought the shower head down onto his scalp with both hands and felt the crunch against his skull. He fell down, and his face hit the porcelain edge of the bathtub. His white hair had started to turn red with blood even before Jenn could high-step over him and slam the door behind her.

She saw herself running into the room. She saw her fingers untying Ava's binds. She heard Ava's breaking voice thanking her and telling her the way to the road. She felt the life reignite in her friend as they made for the front door together.

But that wasn't what happened. Instead, she ran into the room where Ava was still tied to the bed, sleeping like she hadn't been a captive, as if nobody had killed her daddy and pumped her full of drugs and split her childhood wide open between her legs. Jenn had Ava in her hands and was shaking her.

"We've gotta go," she said. "I did it. We're gonna get out of here."

Ava jerked her shoulder as if to make Jenn let go, but Jenn kept pulling at her.

"Ava, I've saved us," she said. Her voice was hoarse. She hadn't used it so much in days.

Skinny Ava opened her eyes and stared up at Jenn, all cheekbones and rib cage and cleft chin. Even in the dark, Jenn could see how wet Ava's eyes were, but still, the brightness she'd hoped for was gone from them, cut off by the sagging eyelids. Tears oozed from her like a wound when she blinked.

"There's a second death," Ava said, and that's all she said, over and over again as Jenn tried to untie her. "There's a second death. There's a second death. There's a second dea—"

Jim groaned from the bathroom. His fingers beat against the side of the tub. Ava was still speaking her lines, the lines she'd been given by methamphetamine and the gospel. Her mouth was quivering. Jenn slapped her. Then she slapped her again. Still, Ava kept on with her recitation. There was nothing else for her to do. Jim groaned again. Jenn pictured him pulling himself to his feet. She saw him upright and bleeding and mad as hell. She took off running through the trailer alone.

She found the front door before Jim could emerge from the bathroom. She passed the mirror beside the bedroom where Jim had fucked her, but she couldn't bring herself near enough to that room to look into the mirror. For a little longer, she would be flawlessly beautiful, the way she'd kept herself in her head. She opened the front door and stepped back into the world.

The outside of the trailer was lit up by a porch light that buzzed with insects. The trailer was settled in a patch of grass. The grass was surrounded by a gravel driveway, more grass, and enough trees to keep Jenn from imagining what could be beyond them. Her feet were well across the tiny lawn and into the gravel that encircled it before she really understood what it meant to be barefoot and without a coat at that time of year. The gravel stuck to her skin and then fell off with every step. She felt the dull claws of the coming winter turn sharp. Then she was in the grass and making her way to the tree line and shaking the whole way there. The light from up near the trailer faded before the endless army of bark-clad, sun-eating giants and their winding arms.

Jenn worked her way over the crinkling autumn remnant on the forest floor, the pale and forgotten leaves that only made themselves known with crunches and shouts from the ground beneath her feet. She climbed over downed limbs and tried to keep from hooping and hollering. She did what she could. That was all anyone could do. She imagined her movements like fireworks, like explosions and acrobatics and bullets in gelatin. She didn't hear Jim behind her, but still, she ran. She thought about Ava, thought about how her own skinny hand would have fit over Ava's skinnier hand and pulled them both through the trees. It would have been something like heaven when they broke through to the other side.

Jenn heard a crackling leaf from well beyond her feet. She stopped running and looked for another body in the dark. Though she'd grown used to the dark in the trailer, she couldn't see much beyond herself in the wild dark outside. Regardless, she knew she'd heard that crunching leaf. So, she kept still.

A beam of light swung through the trees, a dancing

movement that belonged only to light and not to darkness. The light danced and then shivered and then stopped. Jenn heard human voices, but she couldn't tell what they were saying. She knew that they had come from the dancing light. She knew they had not come from Jim. She did not think Jim had yet made it to the trees. There was hardly a Christian hymn in the world that could have been there with her in the dead forest. So, she sneaked up to the light and to the voices. She stepped her tired feet over more branches and leaves. She kept herself quiet and forgot that she'd ever had any reason to shiver. Mayes County was crisping wind and the promise of frost, but it was better than that trailer. Soon she was able to make out the people who were standing in the light.

Scribbles, the man-boy Matthew with his real job, was holding a flashlight and talking to a uniformed deputy with slicked-back hair in a small clearing up ahead. Jenn kept behind a tree. Her breath made clouds in front of her, and she could see Scribbles standing there with the flashlight. He wasn't all that far away. He talked to the deputy and laughed, and he looked like someone she'd never met before. Still, she wanted to be near him. She wondered if her time in the trailer had made the whole world foreign to her. She wondered if she'd ever get used to Scribbles's haircut. She wished she had the voice to shout. Instead, her teeth chattered from behind the tree. She tried to step out and tell both Scribbles and the deputy that she was someone to be saved. She was waving her arms and rasping like a mute.

Both Scribbles and the deputy seemed to jump up into the air. They yanked at their belts, but Jenn could not tell what for. She wondered if Scribbles would recognize her, if she looked strange to him the way he looked strange to her. Scribbles dropped the flashlight. The beam of light hit her eyes as it found its way to the ground, and then the rural darkness consumed the three of them. At last, the town had swallowed Jenn, and she was in the belly of Branch Creek with Scribbles and the deputy. She gasped up all the air she could trying to shout, but someone fired a gun instead. Her voice was useless compared to the sound the gun made. A deep crack like a falling branch filled the space between them. Jenn fell onto a patch of sharp, cold grass. She felt like someone had thrown a stone into her stomach, and then she felt weak. She thought she would faint again like she had during the church service. Her warm blood began to thaw the earth around her. A burning sensation spread out from deep inside of her as if she were leaking out all the hell that had been pumped into her at Jim's trailer. She saw Scribbles scrambling for his flashlight. She saw him pick it up and wave it around so that it lit up the scene in separate, momentary pieces. The deputy was frowning when the light splashed onto his face. Jenn didn't want to see the deputy's face, though. She wanted to see something familiar. As she grasped for words, she realized that she was praying, asking someone for forgiveness. Then there was a peace that passed beyond her understanding. Soon, she thought, it would be morning, and all would be light again.

Chapter 22

Sheriff Taylor didn't hear about the dead girl from Jim. A teenage boy was sitting alone at the trunk of a tree with his head between his knees when he pulled up to the woods around Jim's trailer with Deputy Shriver. The squad car lights were off. Sheriff Taylor had wanted to conduct the whole business from his truck, but Shriver had said that it just didn't seem right to go about things that way. The deputy had likely never seen a body before, at least not like this. Sheriff Taylor tried to make it easy on him. He only hoped Shriver would return the favor.

The boy at the tree took off running east toward the dawn. The sheriff turned off the car and opened the door. The boy's scattered footsteps caused bits of leaves to crunch and then whirl like tiny sirens.

"Stop," Shriver said, but the sheriff put his hand up and told the deputy to shut his mouth.

"We're here to find a body," Sheriff Taylor said. "It's too early to go on hollering like that. We don't need to make a scene."

Shriver didn't speak again for quite some time. They could see the body from the car. The girl's face seemed to glow against the balding forest floor. Even the grass had gone and died in Mayes County. Frost covered the earth like a sea of glass except where the girl's sticky blood pooled up around her. She looked like the Virgin Mary figurine Donna kept on her desk. Sheriff Taylor put his thumb on her neck and only felt the sagging throat of the dead. All her life, her 16 and some years, had gone and run out through a hole in her stomach. Sheriff Taylor didn't know how long it took for a young person's entire future to drain out of them, but he figured it hadn't been more than a few minutes, maybe an hour, depending on what parts of her had been torn open by the bullet. He thought about compressing fifty years into twelve, fifteen minutes, and he thought that those minutes must have been fuller than any he'd ever known. Her eyes were still open and curious, her long eyelashes frozen stiff.

The sheriff wondered if Carlson was nearby. He toyed with his hands as he looked over his shoulders. His wedding ring felt loose, and he hoped he wouldn't lose it. The sun lit up the ground and the teenager's body in the dirt. There was only Shriver and the body and the blood. Even the boy was long gone.

"Should we call for backup?" Shriver asked. He was nervous and lisping. "You think the killer is still around? It had to be that boy, right?"

"What killer?" Sheriff Taylor asked. "This girl's just overdosed."

Shriver's face was working its way around the scene.

"She's got blood all around her, sir," he said.

"Common consequence of drug use," the sheriff said. His eyes stung in the cold.

"Sheriff," Shriver went on, "this girl's been shot."

"Are you the medical examiner now?"

Tears rallied up along the sheriff's eyelids. The growing sunlight grabbed onto a piece of metal over where the boy had been. Sheriff Taylor made his way toward the glare, unaware of whatever Shriver was saying.

The kid had left the gun behind. It was almost smiling, all polished steel and heavy in the dirt. Sheriff Taylor picked it up and put the butt against his cheek. The metal nibbled at his skin. Perhaps it would clamp its teeth down on him, would either wake him up or put him into the deepest sleep. Shriver still stood by the girl's body, and the sheriff couldn't tell whether or not he was still speaking. The sheriff turned his back to the deputy and ran the gun barrel along his lips. It nibbled at him again. He wanted to feel his way deep into its mouth, between its jaws. He wanted the space where there was no light or darkness, no touch or anything at all. He wanted the curtain to drop on him and end the show.

He turned again. Shriver stood behind him, an arm's reach away. Sheriff Taylor hadn't heard the deputy approach. He took the gun away from his face and handed it to the deputy, who took it without speaking. Shriver's mouth hung open like the words he'd conjured up were confused and hardly appropriate for saying. Sheriff Taylor was tired then. It was early in the day.

"Go on and put that somewhere," he said, "somewhere no one will find it. Your prints are all over it now."

Shriver stared back at him.

"Go on," Sheriff Taylor said.

"But this is a murder weapon," Shriver said. "I can't do that."

"There is no weapon. She's just overdosed."

Sheriff Taylor was crying. He couldn't remember when anyone had last seen him cry like that. The tears made him feel like a clown in wet face paint.

"Somebody shot her dead, and you keep saying that like I'm a common idiot," Shriver said. He held the gun out in front of him in his cupped hands. It looked too big for him to hold. Did the deputy's issued gun looked so strange when he held it? Had the sheriff ever seen him shoot?

"I'm not gonna tell you again," Sheriff Taylor said. His voice broke, and he had to clear his throat before he could force himself to keep talking. "Drugs killed this girl. Overdose or bullet, it's all the same outcome with different paperwork. She's still gonna turn blue over there, and her mama's still gonna have to bury her, and that mama's gonna bawl like hell when she puts that girl down into the ground. No one's gonna bring her back to life. You think there's any way for a person to pay for that kinda sin, killing a girl like this? The way things stand, you or me's more likely to pay for this than anybody else. Do you understand me? This girl died of an overdose."

"Where's the justice in all that?" Shriver asked. He still hadn't done anything with the gun.

"Justice? We're all just trying to feel good, Shriver," Sheriff Taylor said. He swept his bare hand over the tears and spread them so thin they disappeared. "More people would rather feel good than would care what happened to this girl or to you or to me or to anybody. There ain't a bit of justice in the whole thing. Justice is just a word for winning votes."

The sun was up and bare in the sky, a great big spotlight. All the world could see the sheriff out there by the dead girl if they wanted to look. The only person who wanted to look was Shriver, though, and he was too stupid to take his eyes away.

"I'm not gonna lie for you," the idiot said. He went on about swearing an oath like he knew anything about becoming a hero. Still, he held the gun in his hands.

"Either this girl's gone and overdosed or a whole lot more people are gonna go and overdose on the same stuff, people like you and me and all those poor folks we call our families," Sheriff Taylor said. "I'm gonna do my damnedest to keep the people I care about living and breathing."

"Who was gonna do that for her?" Shriver gestured toward the girl's body.

Sheriff Taylor kicked the body, and more blood and fluid seemed to puddle up around it. Soon, it would drown the lot of them, the whole damned county, probably the world. "No more water," they would sing. "It's the girl's blood next time."

"I'm sure you'll find reasons of your own," the sheriff said.

He knew then what it meant to be unclean, why the old Polish men at the corner store when he was a kid had told him never to touch anything that'd died. Death comes up out of the body and eats you through and through. It makes you sick in such a way that you can't do anything about it. The sick is too deep in you. It's been there forever, but the dead are the only ones who can bring it out of its hibernation. Sheriff Taylor could hardly look at the dead girl anymore, because he only saw Barbara.

"I don't understand," Shriver said.

"You don't have to understand. You have to keep your community safe, same as you swore in that oath you were talking about. You just have to help me take care of this and then go on taking care of everything else as best you can."

"And what if this isn't how I'd keep my community safe?" Shriver asked. His voice was full of the early morning cold. No one talked like this aloud in real life.

"Then you're taking things into your own hands. I ain't gonna be able to keep you from your own overdose. That son of a bitch from the state ain't gonna be able to keep you safe from it either. You're gonna be in trouble, and no one is gonna believe that you're in trouble. If anyone does believe you're in trouble, they're gonna be too worried about themselves to help you out a lick."

Neither of the men spoke for some time. Shriver studied his own boots, and Sheriff Taylor looked at the deputy with the gun in his teeny little hands. The sun was roaring in the sky, but neither of them could hear it.

"A drug overdose?" Shriver asked. "What the hell are we even gonna do with her?"

"Same thing we do with any body. We get it to the medical examiner, who does some examining and says something about an overdose in an official report that we then make public."

"Is it always this way?"

"In the end, yes," Sheriff Taylor said.

"Who knows about it?"

The sheriff thought about Deputy Carlson and the kid who took off when they'd arrived to investigate the body. He thought about the dead girl and the people who made signs to hold up on the local news. He thought about the two voices that had delivered him the note beneath his door.

"Probably more than you'd figure," he said, "but not enough for us to go on running our mouths. Some folks want to stay alive bad enough to forge their own paths. Other people probably don't have to worry much about staying alive."

They stood around the body until they ran out of things to say about it. The frost was still proud and shining. Sheriff Taylor stood up as straight as he had in weeks. It hardly hurt. His breaths were only puffs that disappeared before he could tell how large they were. He thought about moving north, retirement be damned. He wanted to watch every breath he had left in him. That seemed better than crossing days off calendars or counting the bouncing second-hands of clocks.

"What did she overdose on?" Shriver asked.

Epilogue

The old couple who owned the thirty acres of naked land between the Neosho River and the house where Charlotte ended up had said that any of the neighbors could fish the river whenever they wanted as long as they left the cows alone and picked up when they were done. After dark, the fishermen had to stay away from the house near the front of the property, though, because the man who lived with his wife in the old worker's quarters there said that he believed that buckshot was the best deterrent for thieves.

"Shoot them all and let God sort them," the man said. "It's my life or yours."

Charlotte didn't like to fish. She'd cut her hand on a catfish fin as a child, and now she didn't have the heart to touch any living thing that came from the water. Instead, she sifted through the plastic bags of trash on the riverbed every couple weeks to see if there was anything worth saving. She didn't find much. The practice became more an exercise of passing time than making discovery, but she imagined that either the landowners or their renters would have to rid themselves of something valuable at some point. When they did, she would carry it proudly into town and leave it at the pawn shop by the highway in exchange for enough money to buy a paint set and a notebook of canvas paper. She had already brought a plastic bin back from the muddy river. It had a crack down the side of it, but she told Peggy back at the house that it would be good for kibble if the litter of kittens and the round momma cat kept coming by. Peggy's daughter, the little girl with baby-fat arms that ballooned at her elbows, said Charlotte should try to find her a doll. The closest she ever came was a plastic castle with wooden Sesame Street figurines. All four of Peggy's kids were wind-chapped and red, but they didn't complain of cold for a few days after Charlotte brought back the castle. Peggy said Charlotte didn't have to go and bring the kids anything at all. She took out a warm ten dollar bill from her bra and gave it to Charlotte for her trouble.

When it was warm, when the trees were clothed again and unashamed, when the bermuda grass was more than ankle-high in the sections of pasture where the cows hadn't been in a while, Charlotte was still out tossing lumpy sacks of garbage this way and that in the riverbed. In the afternoon, she heard a growling from the other side of the rise where the man stayed with his wife and his gun. Before long, a familiar pickup truck was rising and falling over the little hills and dents in the ground, drawing attention from the cows in the pasture that expected an early supper of hay or corn feed. The pickup rumbled as it pulled along the river. Will rolled down the window. Charlotte saw his chubby face behind the steering wheel. She hadn't seen him in the better part of four months. He'd shaved recently, and his cheeks were pink with rosacea like a child's cheeks or like the cheeks of a Coca-Cola Santa Claus.

"That woman you're staying with said I'd find you back here," he said. His words sounded rehearsed, but he had phlegm in his throat. His jawbone had outpaced his voice box.

Charlotte tossed another plastic bag away and walked closer to the river. The water was low, but still it splashed along. She heard Will's voice, but she'd already seen more of him than she wanted to see.

"I was right about Jim," he said louder, clearing his throat. "Them girls was there with him the whole time."

The truck door slammed, and he was standing in the pasture.

"I don't wanna hear about any of that anymore," Charlotte said.

Her heart jumped around within her. Her feet were dipping down to the ground without her having to tell them to do so. Usually, she kept along the periphery of the garbage. Now, she was wading in it. The sorts of rotten juices that people had no use for dripped onto her ankles as she walked. She didn't dare look back behind her.

"He's gone now," Will was saying. He was out of breath and keeping on. "He's off in Missouri, same as your boy. Not in jail, though. He's making his own town, some kinda 'fortress of Christ,' he said, some kinda compound where even the police won't bother him. The girl went with him."

"I already told you I don't give a damn about any of that," Charlotte shouted. She was near the river then, and she knew her feet had gone dirty in the garbage.

"The kid's still around," Will said. "He does good work. I take care of him."

He was standing up at the top of the trash heap, tall like an icon with his arms crossed over his chest.

"You never had any right to bring him into any of that," she said. "You're doing him like Jim did you and did me and did everyone else he ever met."

"You gave up any right to tell me what to do with my life when you went and took off."

Charlotte felt the splashing of water at her feet then, and she realized she'd gone all the way down into the river. Will hadn't followed her. He was still at the edge of the garbage. She took another step into the river. It wet the end of her pants. Though most of her body was dry and unaffected, the cold moved all through her from her wet ankles.

"I'm not going back with you," she said.

"Why not?" Will called down. "You heard me. Jim's gone."

Cool air swept down the hill of garbage and turned in loud circles as if from a trumpeter's lips. Charlotte was on her knees in the shallow river. Then she was on her back. She felt the water rising over her skin and making her clothes dark and heavy. She could only see the sky. The water filled her ears, and she couldn't hear Will. The river was halfway up the side of her face and bouncing across her skin in tiny waves. She lay there in the river like that until she was sure that the world had changed, that something real had happened and shaken up the order of things, that Christ had come to Oklahoma and chased the devils into pigs, that the pigs had run off a cliff and died, that no one else would ever have to perish again because of it.

Will was gone when she stood back up. She was alone again and left to dig through the trash. She patted herself down for her cigarettes, but they'd been soaked with river water. She tossed the soggy cardboard and tobacco into the garbage that surrounded her. Then she started up out of the riverbed. The pale green of springtime framed piles of thin white plastic. She marched through things that had been deemed useless. It was time for lunch.

When she was halfway up the riverbed, very nearly to the edge of the tree line and the mouth of the pasture, something caught her foot and sent her falling over herself into the garbage. Her elbow stung, and she was sure she was bleeding. She hoped she hadn't torn her shirt. She sighed and sunk down into something wet. Her head was on a bag of shredded paper. She felt a burning in her ankle. She was sure she was bleeding there too. Whatever it was that had tripped her had scraped against her skin. She didn't immediately have the will to stand again. She turned onto her side and felt like sleeping. Half-buried in the mess was a wooden easel with a crack along its base. Its angular legs had brought her down. With a little glue, though, the easel would work out just fine. It wouldn't be pretty, but nobody cared about whether anything was pretty anymore. Whenever Charlotte stood up, she would bring the easel back with her and show it to Peggy's kids. The whole lot of them would like that. Maybe she'd find some paints too.

She rested in the trash. The little river splashed on through Mayes County and found its way to Lake Hudson. She heard it washing the earth beneath it the whole way. There wasn't a well-kept lawn between Springfield and Tulsa, but that was fine. Short grass never did a bit of good. No decent life was made on short grass. Charlotte turned onto her back again. The winter had finally given way to spring. Sure, there would be another winter, but folks would have plenty of time to plan for that sort of thing or to forget about it entirely. Some people would even have time to rest. They'd all enjoy the sunshine for a while. Charlotte lay there against the refuse and thought about the way the new leaves stood out against the endless sky. Then she smiled, and though it was still light, she thought she heard the whir of buckshot from the house across the pasture.

THE END

SINNERS PLUNGED BENEATH THAT FLOOD

About the author

G.D. Brown has worked as a literary editor and as an award-winning news writer. His literary work has appeared in *The Woven Tale Press, COUNTERCLOCK, Abandon, Full Stop, Oyster River Pages, The Champagne Room, Jokes Review, Westview, PopMatters, Oracle Fine Arts Review, The Tulsa Voice*, and elsewhere. He is a Goddard College MFA graduate and lives in Milwaukee, Wisconsin.

Made in the USA
Columbia, SC
11 July 2022